THE TOXIC AVENGER

THE OFFICIAL MOVIE NOVELIZATION

THE TOXIC AVENGER

THE OFFICIAL MOVIE NOVELIZATION

ADAM CESARE

BASED ON THE FILM BY LEGENDARY

TITAN BOOKS

The Toxic Avenger: The Official Movie Novelization
Print edition ISBN: 9781803360324
E-book edition ISBN: 9781803360331

Published by Titan Books
A division of Titan Publishing Group Ltd
144 Southwark Street, London SE1 0UP
www.titanbooks.com

First edition: September 2025
10 9 8 7 6 5 4 3 2 1

A CIP catalogue record for this title is available from the British Library.

EU RP (for authorities only)
eucomply OÜ, Pärnu mnt. 139b-14, 11317 Tallinn, Estonia
hello@eucompliancepartner.com, +3375690241

Typeset in Dante MT Std by Richard Mason.

Printed and bound in the United States.

"If you know the enemy and know yourself,
you need not fear the results of a hundred battles."

SUN TZU

"I am, as I am; whether hideous,
or handsome, depends on who is made judge."

HERMAN MELVILLE

"If this gonna be that kind of party,
I'm gonna stick my dick in the mashed potatoes."

MANTAN MORELAND

PROLOGUE

Lightning flashed and, a half-second later, thunder cracked. The electricity in the air made Mel's fillings hum and throb, or maybe that was the booze.

His phone vibrated across a stack of papers and he snatched it up. The text was from Sneaky Cheetah:

Update?

He set down his glass and began to peck out a reply, needing both thumbs:

My agent is on route

No, autocorrect, you prick.

en route

Melvin Ferd: grizzled investigative reporter, sipping scotch—*cheap* scotch—in his shitty rented office and corresponding with a codenamed source via text.

There were a lot of cliches here, in this life of whistleblowing and wire-chasing that he led. But as long as Mel kept those cliches off the page and out of his writing...

His phone buzzed again.

OpSec? Sneaky Cheetah asked.

OpSec? He knew Sneaky Cheetah was legit, but there were times when their correspondence made Mel wonder, was his contact really a fed? Or were they playing the part a little too cleanly? Was Melvin Ferd about to be double-crossed?

There was no time for second guesses. Not now. Not with what was on its way to his office. En route.

Intact, he typed.

He *hoped* their security was intact. With all the psychos that Garbinger kept on his payroll, ex-military, mercs and—

Bzzzzztt.

Mel shoulder-rolled away his shiver, then looked to the security-camera monitor. He never kept that thing on. Never needed to because he never had visitors. He was amazed the monitor still worked. But the small CRT TV had been on for the last few days, as the shit got more real, as he felt the walls closing in...

Was that J.J. out there? It was hard to tell, the camera was so grainy and the contrast on the monitor so blown-out. But then the hooded figure on screen raised a hand and waved at the camera impatiently—not just impatient, in fact, but vibrating with excitement.

Yup. That was J.J.

OpSec intact.

God, Mel was starting to think like Sneaky Cheetah now.

Intact and nearly finished being *en route*, with his informant just downstairs.

They'd done it!

Well, nearly done it.

Mel pressed the button under his desk to unlock the magnetized outer door. On screen, J.J. pushed through and out of frame into the service stairwell.

Here it was. That dropping feeling at the bottom of Mel's stomach. Excitement and fear mixed together, with a strong indignation chaser that helped him to keep the fire burning. It was the feeling Melvin Ferd got when a story he'd spent months on—a whole year, in this case—was days from newsprint.

Newsprint and a modest paywall, of course, for all digital subscribers.

And a subpoena for Garbinger if Sneaky Cheetah held up their end of things.

Okay, BTH. Okay, you dirty, corrupt, corporate scumbags. You toxic assholes.

Mel stood up from his desk, toasted his own reflection in the framed headlines and small-fry journalism awards he kept on his walls, and finished his drink. Very Good Investigative Journalist, runner-up. Embarrassing. Why did he even hang that one? He'd have to throw those awards in the trash to make room for his Fulshinger Award and Presidential Medal of...

He opened his office door and leaned out.

There were footsteps on the stairwell, echoing up and down the hallway. The dropped ceiling had a few tiles missing and more dead fluorescent bulbs than live flickering ones. Maybe, at the end of all this, Mel would be able to afford to rent nicer office space. Maybe two offices, one with a corner view out on the good—well, less irradiated—side of town. Every time he looked out his window, it seemed like the junkyard waste of Outer Tromaville was creeping closer.

J.J. appeared at the end of the hallway and yelled, "We got these fuckers now!"

She was so happy. Melvin couldn't help it—he smiled too, wider than he had in years.

"Were you followed?" he asked, shuttling her inside his office and locking the door behind them, the knob and then the deadbolt.

"Followed? *Please.* I ran three reversals and a Kaufman field loop getting here."

As she said this, J.J. Doherty kicked away Mel's roll chair, crouched over his computer, and connected an external hard drive to one of the USB ports.

He was going to offer her a drink, but she was right. There was no time for pleasantries. No time for premature celebrations. He had to see what she'd brought him.

"Is that it?"

The hard drive spun, a soft electric whir, and J.J. unzipped her hoodie, then began to undo the buttons on her Body Talk Healthstyle work shirt. What a dumb name, Mel reflected. No wonder most people shortened it to BTH.

With her button-down shirt gone, it became clear that J.J. had been wearing three layers—the hooded sweatshirt, then her office-drone attire, then her own clothes underneath: stockings, buckles, patterns and straps. J.J. was a punk shedding her corporate skin, letting herself breathe.

"I spoofed an exec IP, dug this out of their internal network," she said and pointed at the computer.

"Risky," Mel said, nodding at the information that was beginning to flood his screen. It was a cornucopia of fishy-sounding file names. There was so much here. Maybe press-time wasn't going to be tomorrow, the next day, or even this week if he didn't have the hours to sift through it all, and then more time for Sneaky Cheetah and the rest of the feds to build an ironclad case for an arrest. Mel needed to be patient. Do this right. If he didn't have what he needed spelled out, hard proof in black and white, he might not get a second chance.

"Only other option is a physical sample from on site," J.J. said, stepping back from the computer. "I've got a collection of hardware stashed at my place, but like you said, this was risky enough. Letting my employer know I have that stuff, that *I* stole it..."

"That'd be suicide," Mel said, nodding.

Her BTH employee lanyard still pinned to her studded belt, J.J. stepped back and let Melvin take a look at the computer.

"This is..." Mel said, looking at the screen. "You've done enough, kid." And he meant it. He was grateful for everything J.J. had done, the risks that she'd taken. But it was hard to elaborate on that now. Not while he had these files opening up.

Melvin felt his eyes burning. Not wanting to see everything he was looking at, but not daring to blink, unless this prove to be a dream...

A study about the long-term effects of cranial stims, phrases like "lobe scarring" and "mostly malignant, usually fatal" and then internal documents detailing how best to seek approval for "over-the-counter use." And then there was a similar study for hemo guns, whatever the hell those were. The data made them sound just as dangerous, but they came in both pink and polka-dot designs, and there were additional memos asking about their efficacy in children.

He moved the cursor over a spreadsheet bearing the heading "Test Subject Survival Rates."

Then there were swaths of legal memos, sorted into folders for outstanding and settled cases. Even if you ignored their tendency to conduct bioweapons development under the guise of cosmetics testing, BTH's boilerplate NDAs were as strongly worded as most bomb threats.

Then he scrolled down further, opened a few more windows, and got to the *really* horrific shit. Pictures of animals, before and after shots. He tabbed through, finding it hard to watch as the cute and fluffy house pets were turned into mewling, blood-soaked abominations.

"Those bastards," Mel heard himself say.

"It's worse than we thought," J.J. said. "And they knew it all along."

"Look, I can't tell you too much," Melvin said. He didn't want her getting too involved. What she knew could hurt her. "But they've already got a case going. This is exactly the kind of evidence Sneaky Cheetah needs to blow this whole thing wide open." *And get me that Fulshinger,* he thought a little guiltily. But he was helping the city by doing this, wasn't he? Was it so wrong to want some recognition for his work?

"Sneaky Cheetah," J.J. said with an eyeroll. The name did sound silly when spoken out loud. "When do I learn his real name?"

"When it's over," Melvin said. "When this goes wide." *Goes to print.* "Until then, we're vulnerable. Keep one eye over your shoulder and help me keep this..."

"...compartmentalized, yeah, yeah, yeah," she said. She was impatient. He could be that way too sometimes, but he hoped that neither of them were impatient enough to get sloppy. If they got sloppy, they'd get dead.

"Patience, J.J.," he told her.

She was a nice kid. Brave. Hellbent on doing the right thing, or at least getting her revenge. She reminded Mel of himself a few decades younger, gender swapped and—he remembered trying to put a pocket protector on a Members Only jacket—with a *very* different fashion sense. "You did real good here. You—"

And before Mel could get mushy with it, before he could say words like *proud* and *heroic,* there was another *bzzzzzt* at the outer door.

Shit.

"How did they...? I..." J.J. began, her voice small and defeated. "I... I ran a Kaufman loop."

Even before Mel could realize what he was looking at on the

security monitor, J.J. already knew what this meant for them, and who had to be out there. And she was correct—there on the monitor, in black and white. One of those freaks. They were standing much too close to the camera, waving, the motions much more playful than what J.J. had done. And that playfulness made them even scarier.

"Let's go!" Mel heard himself yell, already pulling wires, gathering up the hard drive and his phone, then running to the office door and unlocking it.

The freaks were still downstairs and needed to bust their way in. By taking time to frighten Mel and J.J., the dumb assholes had given them a headstart. They still had a few seconds. There was *still* a way they could escape.

Mel opened the door, turned down the hallway, and stepped into a nightmare.

The figure was huge, a hulking monstrosity that cut a much different silhouette from the one on the monitor. The figure lumbered forward, the top of its head nearly scraping the ceiling. But the head towering over them wasn't the top of a human head... It was a red, fleshy rooster's comb.

Shit. Melvin felt his legs buckle, kneecaps turning to jelly. As a younger man, he'd been in war zones. He'd reported on terrorist fire-bombings of embassies. But nothing he'd experienced in-country had prepared him for the dread he felt now.

Now that it was too late to escape.

Mel looked down. His phone was in one hand, the hard drive in the other. Both felt hot in his palms. So close! They'd been so close, and now they were going to die.

No, wait! There was still a way out. He could still win. *They* could still win.

He whirled, hands out, pushing against J.J., trying to get her to run the other way. "Go!" he yelled.

"What?"

Mel shook his phone and the hard drive, then mouthed "Take them!" She didn't, so he pushed them into her palms and let go, leaving her no choice but to hold them or let them drop. And she was too good a kid, a natural at this. She knew she couldn't let all that evidence drop to the floor.

"Go!" Melvin yelled. "Run!"

And this time, she did.

J.J. didn't look back. She just ran, head down, shoes padding tile until she was across the hall, disappearing around the archway to the building's main atrium.

Mel remembered when this building used to have a functioning elevator, when reputable businesses kept their offices here. There'd even been a small deli counter here in better days, back when this was a nice place to work, back when this town was any kind of place to live. Back before BTH.

"Okay, you big bastard," Mel said, turning to the chicken freak. "I've got what you came for! Come on and take it from me, if you can."

But the massive figure took its time, marching down the hallway. And despite the fight in his words, Mel was deeply afraid.

Fuck.

Codenames.

Fuck.

Spoofed external hard drives.

Fuck.

Spy shit.

What had J.J. been thinking?

She reached the railing and started to make her descent down the left side of the atrium's twin staircases. Then she looked down at the vestibule and the first floor beyond—and the two shapes moving up to meet her, one on each stairwell.

Spindly elbows, the click of heels, and the glint of flamboyant attire. They weren't exactly ninjas or paramilitary, but still there was something frightening about these goons, and something very familiar.

"Koo-koo-koo!"

Fuck. What even *was* that sound he was making? Was it some kind of song?

She looked behind her, could hear wood splintering, jeers and taunts, and Mel Ferd yelling at someone to stay away.

Melvin was buying her time. He'd put his faith in her, and J.J. couldn't let him down.

And that was when her eyes fell on the window. Three of the four window panes had already been broken out—kids playing with rocks, probably, telling each other they couldn't hit the second floor from the street. It would be a single-story fall, maybe a story and a half, since the atrium had high ceilings. Most likely she'd be landing on asphalt or gravel.

She would probably survive that, right? Probably wouldn't hit the ground and incapacitate herself with a compound fracture… right?

"Koo-koo-koo!"

The singsong sound was closer now, almost at the top step.

They'll hurt you a lot worse than any fall could. Because you know who they are now, don't you?

J.J. Doherty took a running jump and smashed through what remained of the broken window. She felt weightless for a second, before the fall began and gravity took hold.

Before she realized she'd lost hold of the hard drive.

She heard the plastic shatter as they both smacked into the ground.

Fuck.

There went the evidence.

Melvin Ferd put up both fists and prepared for what came next. He was a pugilist on the page but no boxer in real life. He'd never once been in a fight, unless you counted being pushed into a few lockers as a kid.

The door to his office exploded inward. The huge freak with the comb, feathers, and wattle pulverized the wood in one kick. And the big guy wasn't alone. There were more freaks with him. Smaller freaks, with shadows over their faces—a whole gang of them. *A band of freaks*, Mel thought.

He figured it'd be them. He'd dreamt it'd be them, actually, but in his nightmares it had never been this, well, cinematic. Maybe he wasn't as imaginative a writer as he thought.

There were four of them in all, and more in the hallway from the sound of it. That added up. The missing two were probably chasing after J.J.

Please, kid. Get away. I need you to get away.

"You—" Mel started, but the word caught in his throat. He looked over at his cork board. All those pushpins and twine, all that wasted printer toner. All the pieces he'd put together through months of research. If J.J. made it out of here, the twisted bastard who employed these goons was going to pay for what he'd done.

One of the figures approached, knocking over the desk lamp. He thought it was the one in the ski mask, the one with the number in his name, but Melvin couldn't be sure. He could never keep the six of them straight.

Another figure moved in, and now the office felt a lot smaller. The lamp's bulb popped under a boot heel, sending the room into shadow.

"No," Melvin said, trying to stay strong. These freaks didn't scare him. He wouldn't be intimidated like this. "You assholes are too late! I've already sent what I know out wide. There's nothing at all you can do to me—"

Bang.

The gunshot took Melvin's words, the bullet entering just above his belly button. The sudden bloom of pain was excruciating, but something about the clarity that came with pain… the resolve. It made him stand up from where he'd doubled over.

These fuckers weren't going to silence him.

"There's nothing *at all* you can—"

Bang. Bang.

Melvin Ferd felt parts of himself blown off. Chunks of him, *critical* chunks, painted the drab white walls of his office.

He fell backward. The crown of his head hit the cork board. Its spongy, thumbtacked surface felt like a pillow. He was so tired, with the blood rushing out of him, but still he had to speak. He had to try and stay defiant.

"Nuh… nothing you can…"

And then another figure moved forward, and this one wasn't holding a pistol but a shotgun.

Oh, come on! He had a chance to think, admire the absurdity of it all.

The blast was the loudest thing Melvin Ferd had ever heard.

By the second gunshot, J.J. had found her breath, and by the third she'd found her feet but had lost all hope that she'd see her mentor alive again.

"Koo-koo!" a voice yelled from above her.

Neck craning, jewels of glass in her forearms and knees, J.J.

looked up to see a figure waving down at her from the broken window. Was his face covered in... greasepaint?

She started to run, the silicone and metal of the hard drive crunching under her feet. The piece of tech was obliterated. There was no use even trying to salvage it.

But you still have Mel's phone, which'll have his contacts, she thought. *And that stuff under the floorboards. Remember Sneaky Cheetah!*

She could carry on the investigation, make them pay. But not if her pursuers caught up with her.

She looked around, frantic, on the verge of hyperventilating.

There! A dumpster. She could use that.

J.J. dropped her shoulder and threw her weight behind it. It didn't move at first, just rocked on grungy, trash-encrusted wheels. She could hear them now in the building, soft footfalls descending stairs and louder *koo-koo-koo*s.

Come on!

She rocked the dumpster on its wheels, tapping into the kind of adrenaline spike that allowed mothers to lift cars off their trapped children... or allowed punk girls to wheel large dumpsters in front of service doors.

BOOM!

Another gunshot echoed down from Ferd's office. It was a louder sound, from a bigger gun.

There were two different guns.

Wait. Was Ferd returning fire? It didn't seem likely, but she allowed herself to hope.

With the door barricaded, she had to get out of here. She had to—

Cutting off that thought, there was a pressurized *whoomp* followed by the sound of breaking glass.

Before J.J. could track what had happened or get out from

under it, a large, steaming pile of meat was dropped onto the asphalt in front of her.

SPLAT!

Warm wetness splashed up, spattering her face and hands.

"Nothing," the meat pile said in a raspy whisper, "at all..."

Melvin Ferd, her friend and mentor, stared up at her from the asphalt through mangled, lidded eyes. The metallic glint of a harpoon impaled him through his pulped torso moved slightly, and there was a metallic glint as he shuddered, trying to suck air into collapsed lungs.

They'd shot him with... a harpoon gun?

Behind her, fists began banging on the service door. Soon they'd get the dumpster moved, or come out from around the side stairs and have her surrounded, which meant she didn't have time to stay with Mel while the light left his eyes.

She ran off into the night.

Those bastards were going to pay.

GREETINGS FROM TROMAVILLE!

Population: 12,800 and growing, at least during our more fertile months. When our gun violence, police-brutality numbers, and frequent salmonella outbreaks don't outpace our birthrate.

Well, technically, greetings from St. Roma's Village, but nobody in this county attends mass anymore and the local graffiti artists are tenacious, so the name Tromaville has kind of stuck. I'm told that's called a portmanteau, when you squish a name together like that. Whatever you call it, Tromaville is the name in the popular lexicon. Nobody calls it St. Roma's Village. Nobody but squares and outsiders. And you're not a square, right?

Who am I? Don't worry about that. I've worn a lot of hats, I've made my own damn movies, but for right now I'm your all-seeing, all-knowing narrator. My qualifications? What is this, a job interview? I have to prove my Toxic Avenger bonafides to you? I don't have time for this shit. I attended Yale! No, you can't see my diploma. Why else would I be wearing this sweatshirt if I didn't?

Come on. Never mind that asshole. We've got to start this tour.

There's lots to see. Come, stroll beside our river. While you traverse its rocky shores, take note of the local wildlife, which is rare in both species and mutation. Hey, cool, that bird winked at you! At least, I think it's a bird.

Walk our main street, never minding those needles and vials—there are a lot of diabetics here in Tromaville. See how even the frayed and faded "out of business" signs sizzle with unbound economic possibilities? Times may be tough, in more ways than one, but I'm confident the good people of Tromaville have the small-business acumen and work ethic to turn things around.

Oh, that bumper sticker? Tromaville High, where you'll find some of the most diligent and dedicated honor students in the state. What do you mean, you've "read that's untrue"? Listen, test scores aren't everything! And anyway, we also have one of those tax scams—er, charter schools. We have a charter school, too. New Chemistry High School. So that parents and students can have more choice regarding their child's education. They run a lottery to see who gets in. It's a whole thing; there's been a lot of public debate about it.

Moving on...

Surely you've already noted those smoke stacks on the horizon, but we'd be remiss not to mention that Tromaville is the world headquarters and main manufacturing hub of Body Talk Healthstyle. You know BTH, the chemicals and pharmaceutical conglomerate. They manufacture everything from the pesticides on the food you eat to your baby's favorite brand of diaper-rash lotion to the plastic bump stocks that attach to your uncle's semi-automatic rifles.

Yes, that's the CEO, Bob Garbinger. No, I don't know why his face is on so much of their advertising, but he is handsome, is he not? Yes, I'm sure he whitens them. Look, this really isn't what this tour is about. Please hold your questions and comments until the end.

Where were we? Oh, yes.

Culture, industry, and natural beauty: Tromaville makes and the world takes. That was our local motto until Trenton stole it. Those dickheads.

Yes, northern New Jersey's fourth best kept secret is here, just behind those derelict warehouses. Tromaville has all the folksy charm of Rockwell's America mixed with a modern Euro-Balkan esthetic that helps lend an air of the exotic. You could almost imagine we're in Bulgaria—which we're not, I assure you. We're really not. We're in America.

But we're not here to praise Tromaville. We're here to meet one of its greatest heroes, and he should be waking up any moment now. See him through that apartment window? No, the fire escape doesn't look up to code to me either, but please focus.

Yes, him. Well, okay, not saying you're not allowed to be disappointed, but please, let's not be rude.

Oh. He's stirring. No, that was just him shifting in his sleep, putting his hand down on his late wife's side of the bed, finding it empty.

Yes, I realize there are holes in his socks. They are his sleeping socks, okay?

And he's not a hero yet, but really, just give him a chance. He should be waking up any moment now. He's a single father and it's a school day and... well, let's watch.

Er, read. Let's read. Sorry, force of habit. I've done a lot of DVD intros.

ONE

Winston Gooze nuzzled at a pillow that smelled of corn chips and started awake.

"Oh, shit. I—" he said, his voice cracking with phlegm and sleep. He swallowed, then continued: "I just had the craziest dream. I was in this weird hospital. Everything was white and clean, and there was this giant staircase and I had to..."

With his arm outstretched, the coolness of Shelly's side of the bed seeped in through the back of his hand.

He looked from the stained popcorn-colored ceiling of the bedroom over to the nightstand and the framed photo there. In the picture, Shelly, Wade, and Winston all stood smiling. It was Halloween in the photo and the three of them wore leotards, the scratchy lace of tutus around their waists—two metalhead parents dressed up in pink and fuchsia to support the boy's passion for dance.

How could Shelly have left Winston to do this alone? To raise her son, *their* son, alone?

Maybe if Winston kept talking to Shelly, it could help him stay sane. Maybe it would help him be a good dad, or a good stepdad at least.

So he talked to her.

"But I'm being rude. How did *you* sleep?" he said, trying to keep his eyes on Shelly's picture, resisting the urge to dip them down to the bed and see that she wasn't there.

He waited.

There was no answer, and it was too early and he had too much of a headache to try and imagine one. Anyway, as the pain slithered across the front of his skull, Winston couldn't recall what Shelly's speaking voice sounded like.

That was bad. How could he have forgotten the voice he'd fallen in love with? He could remember what her music sounded like, her singing voice, but not how she spoke.

He sat up and poured a handful of aspirin into his hand. Maybe if he managed the pain, he could remember a little better. He swallowed the pills, and possibly a bug—his bedside water was very old. The painkillers weren't the cheapo store-brand kind, they were a real BTH product that he bought with his employee discount, but sometime last week they'd stopped helping with the pain. The throbbing behind his temples was like a hangover all the time, though of course it was worse when he was actually hungover.

"Okay," *you piece of shit*, "time to start the day."

Winston heard the toilet flush, the muffled slam of a door, then light footsteps. Somewhere in the small apartment, Wade was awake and preparing for school. Winston could guess, just by the rhythm of the footsteps, that the boy was tapping at his chest, trying to get his anxiety under control.

Oh, yeah. Today was tryouts for the *Shoot for the Stars* thing, or whatever New Chemistry High called their talent show. Wade would be performing his dance today—or property movement piece, or whatever—after school. Wade was going to be nervous about tryouts. Winston wondered if the boy had slept at all last night.

Winston showered quickly, only having time to sing/hum half a Motörhead song ("Overkill," obviously) before the water went cold. He didn't have a voice like Shelly had, but he liked to think he brought passion to his performances the same way she did. God, he missed her.

He reached for his towel. It smelled funny and was too mildewed to dry his body effectively, but he hastily rubbed it into his crevices anyway. As he dried, he listened to Wade down the hall, still pacing.

Skin and hair still damp, he ran to the kitchen, pressed two slices of lightly spotted bread into the toaster, and moved to the refrigerator. There were two eggs left in the carton. He and Wade usually split four, which meant Winston would need to go without today. Maybe just a bite. To compensate, Winston added twice the butter to the pan. Eggs were brain food, important to eat before a test, so they'd probably help with a talent show tryout.

As the eggs sizzled, he turned on the TV to hear the traffic report.

"—Village police have released no motive or suspects, saying only that the muckraking reporter's death was, quote, 'quite gruesome,'" the male reporter, Rick Feet, said on the screen, a neutral smile surmounting his cleft chin.

The female anchor, C.J. Doons, swiveled in her chair, eyebrows rising. "And complicated, Rick, from the sound of it," she said. "Harpoon guns are hard to come by, especially in this economy." She paused, shuffling papers and finding her camera. "Switching gears, we have a special exclusive for y'all at home: it's the brand-new video from those far-out shocker rockers you love to hate, Tromaville's hometown anti-heroes the Killer Nutz. And don't forget, the Nutz will be performing this weekend as part of St. Roma's Festival. Me and the morning news crew will see you there. Roll it, Terry."

Winston hadn't heard Wade enter the kitchen, but he could see the boy now in his peripheral vision, sitting at the small table, finger out, tapping his sternum. That was one of the coping mechanisms Wade's therapist had taught him to help him deal with his various neurological and focus issues. There were probably other tricks Wade could use to cope with his anxiety, but at this rate the kid would never learn them—not on Winston's salary. Wade's last therapy session had been over a month ago, before the office canceled all future appointments over non-payment of bills.

On the TV, the Killer Nutz flailed, rapped over each other, and threw hand signals. The one in the straitjacket banged his forehead against the drumkit's cymbals, leaving a bloody gash. The lead singer coated the grille of his microphone in white clown paint. And the big one in the chicken mask… played guitar pretty well, actually. *That one* was talented, at least.

Winston shut off the TV. He must have missed the traffic report. They *were* running pretty late.

He scraped the contents of the skillet onto a twice-used plate, turned to face his stepson, and pointed his chin at the TV.

"Ugh, those dudes. I mean, right?" he said.

Wait, did Wade *like* the Killer Nutz? He couldn't, right? The group was definitely not the boy's style.

Wade shrugged. No opinion, apparently.

The boy was fifteen, but looked younger. He'd applied makeup for school, eyeliner that was clumped on his lashes. If only Shelly were around, she could give her son makeup tips—she'd always looked so awesome on stage. But she wasn't around. And Winston didn't know much about makeup. He'd never had a grungy semi-goth phase himself. When he'd been Wade's age, he'd been more the classic metal-nerd type, using a fake ID to get cheap tattoos he'd regretted even before they'd healed. Buying Jack and Cokes that were mostly Coke because the whiskey made him hurl. Teenaged Winston had thought himself Tromaville's answer to Lemmy, albeit without all the talent or ability to grow cool facial hair. And he still rocked that style, even if it was a little toned down. Puberty had come late, but his handlebar mustache/beard combo was now his pride and joy, even if it was starting to go gray.

But unlike Winston had been, Wade was a good kid, so Winston tried to pay attention to what his stepson was into and keep up with his burgeoning interests. And everything was changing so fast now, at this age, with Wade trying to figure out who he was and who he wanted to become. Testing boundaries.

"I dig that shade," Winston said, pointing at the boy's dark nail polish. It hadn't been there yesterday, but it was already chipped. More nerves, causing Wade to chew at his cuticles, Winston guessed.

"Black Thunder, right?"

Wade shrugged, mumbled something that could have been thanks, could have been a curse word, and reached for a triangle of toast that was as black as his nails.

"I could, uh, try to scrape off the burned part?" Winston suggested.

But it was all burned, just like the butter and the eggs were. Winston pinched the bridge of his nose, the smell of the botched breakfast making his headache worse. Even when he tried, everything seemed to come out burned.

"No," Wade said, his words more than a mumble this time. "It looks great."

He *was* a good kid.

Winston stood and watched his stepson eat a few forkfuls, then looked down at his phone.

"Oh, fuckballs! Quick, eat. We're going to be late."

Winston dumped the plates into the sink, squeezed a few

ropes of dish soap over the grease and yolk, then ran the tap for a little water.

Probably best to let it soak. He'd do the dishes later so they didn't get more roaches. Probably.

Winston ushered Wade to the door, but the boy didn't need much ushering and had already grabbed his backpack and gym bag with his dance outfit, and stood there ready to go.

"Car keys?" Wade asked. "And do you have your ID badge?" The boy was still tapping to self-soothe, but not as much. His anxiety was slowing. Good.

Winston smiled and put his hands in his pockets.

"I mean, who's the adult here, dude? Of course I've..."

He spread his fingers. Both pockets were empty. Retracing last night's footsteps, he found his keys and his ID on the night-stand, grabbed both, and then they were on their way out the door.

The second-floor landing smelled like yellow cake, cream filling, and preservatives—which was a welcome change, because most days it smelled like rat farts.

The bodega must have received a fresh shipment of Krusty Kakes that morning. If Wade was willing to run for the bus, maybe they could stop in and—

"Please! Don't hurt 'im!"

Daisy's voice.

Wade stomped down the rest of the stairs two at a time, and Winston followed after the boy. They pushed out into the street and stepped right into an exchange that was... none of their business.

"C'mon now, I don't *want* to hurt him," the man talking to Daisy said. He was holding the bodega cat, Mr. Treats. "And I know you don't *want* to accept our more-than-reasonable offer for your piece o' property here."

Winston squinted against hazy sunlight, tried to take stock of what was going on.

"But I promise you, ma'am," the goon continued, giving the cat a shake, "one of us is about to do the thing we don't want to do."

Winston had seen the smirking man around here before, but he didn't know his name. He was a member of the Khaki Gang, a name that Winston was only vaguely aware of. He was clad in a khaki jacket and, like his two friends, khaki pants, and was younger than both of his henchmen, dressed in slightly less preppy attire.

The two support goons stood next to their leader, near an expensive-looking sports car idling with its front wheel against the curb. The traffic in the street behind them slowed a little, rubberneckers trying to catch a glimpse of what was going on.

"What are you looking at, tough guy?" the man holding the cat said.

Was he talking to Wade, Winston, or both of them?

Winston put a hand on Wade's arm, then dropped his eyes and pretended to read the headline on the newspapers stacked out front of the bodega.

Oh—BTH's stock was down. Great. He was probably going to be "downsized" or whatever.

"That's what I thought," the man said.

"Yeah, you look away, hoss," added one of the other hoods, wearing a polo and a backward cap.

Mr. Treats began to mewl as the man's grip tightened around the cat's throat. He was beginning to play the poor thing like a furry bagpipe.

A lightning bolt of pain shot through Winston's brain.

He staggered, nearly collapsed.

The thought of it, the stress, was almost too much.

Wade and Winston were about to attend the public execution of Mr. Treats.

Never mind the innocent cat: after witnessing that kind of trauma, Wade wouldn't stop tapping his chest for the next month, at least.

But there was nothing Winston could do. They were three gang members, probably armed, shaking down their nice old landlady who ran the store below them. Sure, sometimes the bodega sold spoiled milk, and Daisy didn't accept returns, but she didn't deserve—

"Okay," Daisy said, stepping further away from her store and onto the sidewalk.

"Okay what?" the man holding Mr. Treats asked.

Winston chanced a look over at Daisy, who lifted her thin arms, the freckled skin creasing.

"Okay," she said, "I'll sell to you. Just don't hurt my cat."

Shit. That would mean they had to move again, Winston thought guiltily.

"Common sense prevails," the man holding the cat said, but he didn't loosen his grip on the animal. "What would you want this old heap of bricks for anyway? Nothing but upkeep. I'll be back with the paperwork tonight. We'll make everything legal."

At least things had de-escalated.

The smirking man whistled and one of the khaki-clad goons moved around to the front of the sports car while the other opened the passenger door for their boss.

"Good one, Spence," the man holding the door said.

So the leader was Spence. Then there was the driver and the yes-man. All three of the gang members got in the car. But Spence still hadn't returned the cat to Daisy. Mr. Treats mewled again. The sound was pathetic.

This wasn't over yet.

Instead of handing the cat back, Spence kept eye contact with Daisy and swung the car door closed.

Daisy began to cry, her sobs muffled by the street's quickening morning traffic. On the sidewalk, a crowd was gathering to watch the show. A delivery man hiked up his shorts, fixing his bulge. A homeless man stopped scratching at the bugs under his skin to see what was about to happen.

Winston felt Wade's muscles tighten under his hand. The boy wanted to help and was about to jump into action. He couldn't let him do that. He could be hurt, or killed.

Whirrrr...

They watched as the car's power window lowered.

Inside, Mr. Treats was hissing and spitting at Spence.

Wade stepped forward, and Winston had to clamp down on his arm quickly. The boy was taller than his stepdad and nearly pulled Winston off his feet.

No, Winston thought. *I'm not letting you get killed over a cat. Even if you're right: somebody in Tromaville needs to do* something.

They watched as Spence dangled Mr. Treats out of the window by the scruff of its neck, beckoning Daisy over.

She took a few steps toward the cat and had almost reached him when—

"Catch," Spence called from inside the car, then threw the cat over the hood of the car and into the middle of the street.

"No!" howled Wade.

"My baby!" screamed Daisy.

"Meow," said Mr. Treats from between the double-yellow line, seemingly oblivious to the tires that rolled by, seemingly happy to be out of Spence's grip.

Winston didn't think. Couldn't think. His headache was too strong, a pulsing blood-rush that whooshed in his ears.

Before he realized what was happening, he was scurrying across the blacktop.

The Khaki goons laughed and the driver revved the sports

car's engine. "Gonna be a double score, cat and loser roadkill."

Brakes squealed and Winston stopped short to avoid the chrome of a bumper. A cyclist swerved.

He reached the cat and looked up to see a 1978 Ford Thunderbird bearing down on them.

"Shit!" he yelled, grabbing for Mr. Treats. The cat scratched and bit him as he scooped it up.

Where was this fight when the bad guy was holding you? Winston thought but didn't have time to say.

Tires screeched. The bus that he and Wade had been rushing to catch whizzed past. Motorists cursed and headlights cracked as Winston navigated—miraculously—back to the sidewalk.

"Wow! You see that? That motherfucker saved a cat," someone in the crowd said.

"My spine!" cried the cyclist who'd gone over his handlebars.

Winston gave Mr. Treats back to Daisy, who started to say something—a thanks, maybe, or maybe an offer of a free slushie—but then the Khaki Gang peeled away from the curb in a cloud of smoke and gutter-gravel.

Winston turned to his stepson.

"Come on," he said, panting. "If we head down to the Strip, we can still catch your bus." His breathing heavy, he directed Wade around the corner.

But by the time they'd made it to the bus stop, they'd missed it from there too.

Winston held his temples, tried to think. He was sweating. He really needed to do more cardio. "I could drive you—"

"It's the wrong direction," Wade said, his voice curt. "You'd be late."

The boy stood quiet for a long while, shoulders slumped and staring forward, as they waited for the next bus.

The adrenaline rush of playing in traffic had temporarily

made Winston's headache abate, but now the pain was back, and worse.

Wade started tapping his chest again.

"Are you in a Yellow, would you say?" Winston asked. "Seems like a Yellow Zone. It's not a Red, is it? If it's Red, maybe you should take the day—"

"Stop with the zones. I'm not ten."

No, Wade certainly wasn't ten. That was a teenager's attitude in his voice. One that hated his parents sometimes.

"Can you do your tapping?" Winston asked, which was a pretty stupid thing to ask, but he was in too much pain right now not to be stupid.

"You see me tapping right now? What does this look like?" Wade made eye contact, a rarity these days, but this didn't feel like any kind of breakthrough. "I'm *doing* my tapping."

"You seem flooded. Why don't we—"

"Why didn't you *do* anything?"

"What?" Winston let the word hang there, but he knew what the boy meant.

"You just stood there while those pricks pushed Daisy around. She's old. She needs to be taken care of. She needs a community she… She needed someone to *do* something. She needed *you* to do something."

This was all going so wrong.

"Do what? I ran out into traffic! The cat's okay. What more could I have done?"

"Anything!"

Winston grabbed for Wade's elbow again, but the boy shook him off.

"Listen to me," Winston said. He could feel his face going red as he struggled to find the words Wade needed to hear right now, grasping for some kind of wisdom. "I know it doesn't seem like it, but listen. As you get older, you'll realize this. Sometimes it's just better to do nothing."

There it was. Father-of-the-year material, that advice. Stepfather of the year, at least, if there were any parenting guilds that gave awards that specific.

Wade just blinked at him.

Ah fuck, what did it matter? Winston's head hurt and he was going to be late for work.

He looked down the Strip, which used to be called Main Street at some hazy point in the past Winston could barely remember. But there were now too many for sale signs on the pawn shops to think of calling it anything other than the Strip. Mesh trashcans overflowed with greasy pizza boxes, energy drink cans, and bloody gauze from the minute clinic on the corner. Winston watched the nearest alley as a woman stretched, scratched her ass, and led a man in a business suit out from behind the buildings by a chain leash, his tongue sticking out like a dog's. A group of Tromaville High kids whistled as the pair walked by.

Beyond that sight, the next bus was coming.

"You got your dance all worked out?" Winston asked, trying to change the subject.

"It's not a dance. It's a property-movement piece."

"Oh, that's, uh, fancy. Property movement."

"It's just a very... specific thing."

The bus was three cars away, already pulling into the shoulder. In the gutter, a squirrel and a rat fought over a dead pigeon. The rat won but was burst under the bus's wheel as the vehicle pulled into the stop.

Winston had to hurry. He had to say something supportive and encouraging to Wade before it was too late.

"Well, whatever it's called, you're going to crush it," he said. "Just get out there and do your thing. People love that shit. Authenticity."

Wade nodded, and his tapping slowed. Winston was reaching him. He was doing it, offering the right kind of encouragement.

The bus's door hissed open and Wade stepped up.

"Your mom would be so proud of you, you know," Winston said.

The bus driver seemed more affected by the words than Wade was.

"I could never do what you do," Winston said.

"Yeah, I know," Wade said.

The doors closed and the bus drove away.

Winston's heart hurt nearly as much as his head did.

TWO

Winston looked through the cracked windshield up at the factory, then at the long, pitted walkway from the end of the employee parking lot to the building.

Above him, in the other direction, over the slime of the river and under the gray sky, was a billboard bearing the image of a green field carpeted with blooming flowers. In the field stood Bob Garbinger, CEO of BTH, and under him was written a single word: *Become.*

Winston had no idea what the tagline was supposed to mean, but he assumed the company had paid an advertising firm a lot of money for the slogan.

He got out of his shitty car and began the long trudge across the parking lot. Oh, well—he may have been a huge disappointment to Wade, but at least he had a long, soul-deadening day of tossing absorbent powder on piles of puke to take his mind off things.

Eh. That was kind of a downer attitude to take.

He should try to do better, get his head straight, or at least as straight as his throbbing headache would allow. Garbinger was right—maybe today Winston could try to *become* something.

Yeah. That was the outlook he should be trying to have.

Zzzzzzzippp.

Winston's work coveralls had one long zipper at the front, two Velcro straps at the wrists, and two more at the ankles.

Safety first. He'd been given a respirator and safety goggles, but the elastic straps on both had stretched out and the company store charged to replace them. But there wasn't really any need for such heavy-duty equipment anyway, not in Winston's assigned sector. Maybe once a week he had to clean corrosive spills, but mostly his job entailed general, non-hazardous maintenance and upkeep. His biggest challenge most days was remembering not to mix up bleach and ammonia when he swapped between floors and windows, which he almost always remembered not to do. Almost.

Today there were no toilets to unclog and the commissary garbage bins wouldn't need to be emptied until after lunch.

He could put one earbud in, zen out, and mop.

It sounded stupid, but mopping was the only duty he enjoyed at work, and he was good at it.

There were newer mops, of course, with sculpted ergonomic handholds and fancy mechanical wringers, but Winston was a fan of the classics: knit cotton, wood handle, sturdy steel joints.

Splash, splush.

He dipped his mop, kept the side of his head sporting the earbud away from the security camera that hummed above him on its motorized joints, and started mopping.

Movement. Rhythm. Soapy water.

When Winston mopped, when he *really* got in the zone with it, he understood what Wade got out of dance.

Splash. Pour. Mix. Sliiiiiiiide.

There was the dull buzz of an alarm, somewhere behind the walls and plexiglass dividers that separated this area of

BTH headquarters from the factory floor, and he side-stepped a running guy in a hazmat suit.

But there were always men and women in hazmat suits running toward those alarms.

You got used to it.

It was probably fine.

Ooops. Winston nearly lost his footing, then pointed out to the stretch of floor in front of him as another man in hazmat protection ran by, his yellow suit squeaking.

"It's wet here. Watch your step."

"Fuck off, Mop Boy," the man said, his voice muffled.

"Okay then," Winston said, smiled, and turned up his music a little louder. In his ear, "Sympathy for the Devil" faded into "Rockaway Beach," the Motörhead covers, because Winston Gooze knew what he liked and was unashamed to embrace it.

After two floors, five hallways each, he reached the check-cashing room. He decided he should take his time mopping here, as it was almost after lunch and that meant hauling several 20-gallon bags of tartar sauce and half-eaten French fries (it was Fish Stick Day) into the commissary trash compactor. That would not be as fun as mopping.

There was a long line to cash checks today. Longer than usual.

Winston mopped the threshold, then entered, making his way down, parallel to the roped-off line. "Wet floor, look out," he said. Nobody thanked him. Nobody even looked up. Nobody cared.

He stepped aside as two burly security guards exited a locked back room. They had a handcart between them and were transporting bags and bricks of cash out of the room.

No matter what the newspapers said, it didn't look to Winston like Body Talk Healthstyle was in financial trouble.

The men and women waiting in line to collect their pay looked haggard. As the cart pushed past them, their sallow faces barely registered the pile of cash as it was pulled out of the door to the room. It would never be theirs, so why dream? Winston's co-workers were more tired than a Saturday of drinking and rest could fix, and that was if any of them could even get a day off. It may have been pay day, but most of them would be clocking in bright and early tomorrow.

Although all the employees looked exhausted, there were clearly some that had it worse than others. The workers from the factory floor had waxy, bloodless gashes crisscrossing their cheeks and necks from the straps of their gas masks cutting into their flesh. Their eye sockets were gaunt and glassy. They bent forward, barely brightening as they stepped forward and were handed their week's pay.

It could be worse, Winston thought. *I could be one of those poor fuckers.*

"Nine percent convenience fee," a man muttered, counting the small envelope of cash he'd been given from the clerk and exiting the room, his boots squeaking on the wet floor.

The line moved. Winston leaned on his mop and realized that the man beside him was wearing a diaper. What department did *he* work in?

"Yer making a mess, Mop Boy," someone said, jostling Winston from behind as they hustled toward the door, counting their money.

Winston stumbled, apologized, and ended up close enough to the other man's diaper to smell that, yes, it was indeed quitting time for this guy. Someone needed a change.

There were probably better places to work, even as a janitor.

And he and Wade were going to have to move anyway, once Daisy sold their apartment out from under them.

Become. Become. Become.

He repeated the mantra. Just a few more hours until he could join this line, get his money, and be out of here. Once he got paid and got home, he could start working on fixing whatever he'd broken with Wade that morning.

Somewhere in the building, another alarm buzzed.

And kept buzzing.

"You gonna get that, Mop Boy?" someone asked.

Oh. That wasn't an alarm; that was the ringer on his phone.

The co-workers around him rolled their eyes as he picked up. Like him taking a call while they waited in line was inconveniencing them that much. *Calm down, people.*

"Hello?"

Someone on the other end of the line cleared their throat and asked him to confirm his name.

"Yes, this is he," Winston said.

The diaper guy shuffled forward to the clerk, handed over his check, and took his envelope in return.

The words spoken on the other end of the phone were muzzy and indistinct, especially with all this background noise and his damn headache.

"I'm sorry, could you repeat that?"

And then Winston wanted to throw up. But if he did, he'd have to clean it up himself, since he was Mop Boy.

He pressed his lips tight and swallowed.

"Uh. What test results?" he asked.

But his headache flared again, and he remembered which test results.

The ones about his headaches. Doctor Walla needed to see him right away.

Maybe the day wasn't going to get any better.

Maybe Winston Gooze would just *become* a corpse.

THREE

Sitting in one of the grandest rooms in Chüdhaven Mansion, the grandest private home in Tromaville, possibly all of New Jersey, Kissy Sturnevan took dictation.

A pair of attendants bowed their heads and glided across the dark room's polished oak floors. Despite the age of the wood, there was not one creak. Their better was speaking and they knew when and how to move silently.

"Chapter Eight, 'On Matters of Humility,'" Mr. Garbinger said, the machine beside him whirring quietly. "Superiority, whether ingrained or striven for, is an obligation."

Kissy nodded and continued to type.

Oak-beamed ceilings rose above them. Antiquities and furniture of nameless value surrounded them, each piece selected by someone with peerless taste. Taxidermy, every last animal shot by the great man himself. This was Robert Garbinger's office, but it was more than that; it was the heart of the house, the inner sanctum. Kissy felt lucky to be sitting here.

"Wait, strike that," Garbinger said, the shadows slanting over his body, seated in the dark. She couldn't see his face, but what she could see was simply exquisite. "...is *yet* an obligation."

"That's much better," Kissy said, adding the word.

"Not too much?" he asked.

Kissy worked for Mr. Garbinger and would never be so bold as to call herself his friend, but she *was* his confidante. And she *did* love him. She had his ear—and sometimes other parts of him—and the great man trusted his executive associate.

"No, just the right much," she assured him.

The transfusion machine behind her boss was beginning to hiss air and gurgle, which meant that he was nearing the end of his session. He was always even more vibrant and magnetic on the days that he sat and took in four pints of gorilla blood. Kissy presumed it was something to do with the animal pheromones.

"Our lessers," Garbinger continued. "Our physical, mental, and, yes, our spiritual lessers, too. They depend upon us as ships in the dark depend on the lighthouse."

"Brilliant," Kissy said, and she meant it. "Bloody brilliant."

As a young girl in Australia, Kissy had loved to hear American accents on TV and in movies, but when she'd gotten here, she'd become disillusioned. To her ear, most American men sounded so vulgar. But not Robert—Bob—Garbinger. He had good breeding, good elocution, good everything.

"We are the light unto the future, a thousand candles unto darkness."

Oh god, she was getting lightheaded. His words! The words coming out of those perfect lips, from that tan, baby-oiled bronze body... A warmth stole all over Kissy, blooming up from her—

A servant moved beside her, setting down Garbinger's post-infusion smoothie and the afternoon edition of today's paper.

She took one look at the headline and her warmth turned cold:

BTH STOCKS PLUMMET!

"Remove that, you absolute donkey," she hissed.

The servant—brainless, really, they'd need to be replaced—nodded an apology, scooped up the paper, and hurried out of her sight.

These doomsaying vultures. They had no idea of the genius of Bob Garbinger. A few financial speedbumps, a few underperforming quarters, and they assumed that the empire her employer had built was in peril. Fools! They didn't understand him the way that Kissy did, his tenacity, his stamina. He had some promising new products in development, and those were just the ones Kissy knew about. Even now, he was busy concocting more innovations in the privacy of his resplendent brain.

Bob would rise again, stronger than ever. Kissy was sure of it.

Oh, dear. She looked down at her dictation. Had she missed something he'd said?

"...and we keep them from the rocks that would destroy them. And those rocks, of course, are..."

Kissy hurried to catch up.

In the shadows, Garbinger grabbed at the IV at the crook of his arm, yanked the tape and needle free, stood, and said the final word for this chapter: "Perfection."

He extended his arms out, his posture Christ-like, and Kissy took in his abdominal muscles. For a man in middle age, who could compete with him? There were movie stars who looked like slovenly losers in comparison.

Two servants, one at each arm, helped Garbinger into a flowing silk robe.

At his hip, the empty transfusion machine continued to pump. The device was starting to sputter.

Garbinger picked up the small remote from the tray beside him and pressed a button.

The machine continued to gurgle.

"This goddamn thing," he said, smacking the back of the remote.

"It's... you press Finish," Kissy said. It was always a tricky thing, trying to help a man who needed no help, but Bob Garbinger wasn't *just* a man. He was a man above men, an Uberm—

"I'm *pressing* Finish," he said, jabbing buttons and shaking the remote.

"It's next to Mode."

"I'm pressing both," he growled. "I'm pressing Mode *and* Finish."

"It can be difficult—"

"Piece of utter shit. Okay, I've got it." The machine powered down, droplets of both his own and gorilla blood speckling the hardwood floor. The servants would clean that up.

Garbinger looked up at Kissy. "Where is Fritz?"

"I'm here, Robert," Fritz said before Kissy could announce him. She shuddered to hear the brother's voice, so sudden, so close.

He was always doing that—hiding in the shadows, startling Kissy with his... his imperfection.

Fritz Garbinger drew himself closer, across the large, dark room.

Step, shuffle, tap, step, shuffle, tap, again and again as he dragged his club foot across the floor, the shoe with its enormous rubber sole leaving scuffs on the hardwood.

"Your brother's been waiting," said Kissy hurriedly. "He—"

"Thank you, Kissy," Fritz said, looking at her. Imploring her to be quiet as he kept moving forward, still not close enough.

"You're welcome," she said, keeping his misshapen and uneven eyes locked with her own.

"*You're* welcome," Fritz said.

There was minimal airflow inside the large room, but still the long wisps of Fritz's thin black hair waved in front of his face like gossamer spiderwebs.

The two attendants who'd helped Garbinger with his robe rolled over a wheeled cart bearing a TV set.

Step, shuffle, tap. Fritz was still walking over, one hand on the silver wolf's-head topper of his cane, the other massaging the muscles in his side.

"He's coming, sir," Kissy said. "It takes him a minute."

It took some practice to read his expressions, as asymmetric as they were, but Fritz looked properly annoyed. Kissy was proud of herself, that she could get under his skin—his pale, sickly skin.

Garbinger wasn't paying attention. He had the television switched on and was watching another news report about the Melvin Ferd incident.

"Not that I'm complaining, necessarily," he said to Fritz. "Or maybe I am, but it didn't exactly look accidental, did it?"

On the screen was an image of a white sheet spotted with blood, tented in the middle from the base of the harpoon.

Fritz cleared his throat and leaned on his cane.

"A harpoon?" Garbinger said. "Really?"

"They had to improvise," Fritz said.

Fritz was such a loathsome, awful thing, always filled with excuses. How could the two men standing before her—one golden and radiant, the other bleached and twisted, one perfect, the other... whatever the opposite of perfect was—how could they have come from the same womb?

"Ah. Improvise. Like jazz," Garbinger said, nodding.

Could it be a fault of the great man, Kissy thought, that he could still love and trust this *thing* he called a brother? Even if Robert Garbinger could be cruel to him, Kissy did still believe, deep down, that he cared for Fritz.

"But what about the traitor?" Garbinger asked Fritz. He pressed another button and the TV set's screen changed to a picture taken from a BTH employee ID file.

J.J. Doherty.

If there were a person alive more hateful than Fritz, it was that dimestore punk witch.

What Kissy wouldn't do to get her hands on that—

"Smoothie," Garbinger said, holding out his empty hand. A servant dutifully swept over and pressed a glass into it.

"I said," Garbinger said, turning his eyes back to Fritz. "What. About. The traitor?"

Fritz sighed and shook his head.

Ah. He and his menagerie of misfits had let the girl get away, Kissy realized. She wanted to react, but it wasn't her place.

There was a quiet moment when Garbinger nodded, letting himself absorb the enormity of his baby brother's failure.

Then he slammed his smoothie glass into the TV screen.

Shards of glass and semi-frozen chunks splattered across the floor. The figures in the room turned kale-green from the light shining through the dripping fluid.

Garbinger walked toward his brother, clenching and unclenching his fists, obviously struggling to maintain his composure.

Fritz winced, and Kissy allowed a slight smile to creep onto the polite expression she'd been trying to maintain. This was going to be good.

"*Maybe* hiring the *pop group* you manage to handle a sensitive corporate *wet works* job was not the best..." Garbinger looked up, either searching for the words or pausing for dramatic effect. Kissy chose to believe it was the latter. "Not the best *operational decision*."

Fritz coughed, then muttered something under his breath.

The audacity of the man, to try and backtalk Bob Garbinger!

"What?" Garbinger demanded. "What was that?"

The warmth was back in Kissy's body. She loved seeing Fritz shamed. It turned her on.

"Monstercore."

"What?!" Bob Garbinger almost screamed.

"Th-they're a monstercore band," Fritz said. "They're crazy and dangerous..."

"*What?!*"

Garbinger turned back to the broken TV set, where a servant was mopping up the spilled smoothie with a rag, leaving only streaks on the glass.

"And this betrayer," Bob Garbinger hissed, pointing at the punk girl's image on the screen. "This viper who was welcomed into the Body Talk Healthstyle heart as family. Who was given employment, community. What does she do? She sinks a knife into not just my back but *all* of Body Talk's back." He paused, catching his breath. "Backs?"

Kissy nodded, even though she wasn't sure what the pluralization rule was, in this instance. English was a funny language.

"Our collective backs. And she's running around with some dumb fucking grievance just when I've got quicksand coming up to my chin."

It was true. It wasn't just the muckraking headlines or unstable stock price; there were other issues at play, other factors conspiring against BTH that the economists couldn't even begin to guess at.

"And now some ginned-up federal inquiry sniffing after their pound of flesh?"

Garbinger pounded at his chest and his robe fell open, revealing a tanned, muscular chest and golden pubic stubble sprinkled like body glitter.

"Do you realize what's at stake right now?"

Fritz opened his misshapen mouth to respond, but his brother didn't let him.

"Everything!"

"I understand," Fritz said.

"Then conduct yourself accordingly." He pointed back at J.J. Doherty's BTH employee picture. "Ruthless execution. Am I clear?"

"As a window," Fritz said.

Garbinger blinked.

"If that's so," he said, "why am I still looking at your fucked-up puss?"

Fritz turned and started to leave, moving faster than he'd limped in but still pretty slow. Kissy winked at him as he went.

Garbinger walked over to the bar and Kissy followed. She watched his brow furrow as he leaned against the brass railing. Where his skin touched, he left steamy smudges on the metal. Now *that* was passion.

She watched his back rise and fall, listened to his breathing, a couple of sniffs that could have been Bob Garbinger swallowing back tears of anger and exasperation.

"Are you okay?" she asked.

He let out a small, choked laugh. "Family is hard, is all."

Fritz was gone now, so it was probably fine for Kissy to be a little more familiar.

She leaned forward and kissed him on the cheek.

"I know what you mean," she said. "When I was growing up, my sister and I never got on."

Was that too much?

"She was the big-boned one," she continued, "so I had no chance in a straight bail-up, but I found that if I hid a roll of coins in my hand and then—"

Garbinger held a well-manicured hand up to stop her.

"I'd like another smoothie," he said, his voice flat.

Oh. She'd overstepped. They were not friends.

"O-of course," she stammered and moved to go get that started for him, her cheeks flushed with the shame of rejection.

“Kissy?” Garbinger asked.

She turned back to where he leaned against the bar. This was it. He’d apologize and sweep her into his arms.

“Just a single scoop of hornet pollen this time,” he said. “It’s quite gritty. And extra cherries.”

She blinked and tried to clear her face of everything but subservience. He was a great man, and it was her job to help enable that greatness, especially now that the jackals were at the door.

“Right away, sir. And I agree, the pollen’s quite chalky.”

Garbinger nodded.

Kissy waited until she was out of the room and halfway to Chüdhaven’s kitchen before she let a single tear fall.

FOUR

Dr. Walla scrutinized Winston's file, narrowing his eyes, then plucked a single sheet of onion-skin-thin paper from it, held it up to one of the exam room's lights, sighed, groaned, then returned it and shuffled through a few more pages, nodding.

Is he going to say something, Winston thought, or...?

"How's Wade?" Dr. Walla finally asked, closing the file.

"Good," Winston said.

"Keeping up with the counseling and whatnot?"

No.

"Basically, yeah," Winston said.

He felt the knot in his chest loosen a little. Dr. Walla wouldn't be spending this much time on small talk if the test results were that bad, right?

"Single parents are heroes. Single step-parents? Double her—"

"Double heroes, yup," Winston interrupted. He'd heard this before. He definitely didn't feel like a hero, and he doubted Wade thought of him that way. "Well, you play the hand you're dealt and all that."

By the way, what kind of hand have I been dealt, Doc? he was about to ask, but then Dr. Walla reopened the folder and began to read again.

"And I hear Wade's going out for *Share Your Gift*?"

"Yeah, tryouts are..." Winston began. Out on the street, in front of Dr. Walla's office, a jackhammer started up. The sound of concrete being pulverized did nothing for his headache.

Dr. Walla didn't seem to notice the noise, continuing their banal small talk without looking up from the file. "Good for him. My Elizabeth's already had her first period. Believe that?"

"Uh." Winston pinched the bridge of his nose. Were there two jackhammers now? "Wow."

Dr. Walla closed the file again and placed it under his arm, apparently finished with it. "It's like, whaaat? Time warp."

"Uh, congratulations?"

"Goes by in a blink."

Between the pain, the stress, and the jackhammers, Winston felt ready to explode. He needed to know why he was here, what was so important that they couldn't tell him on the phone, that the receptionist had urged him to come straight here and not wait until he could get off work. Those hours would be coming out of his pay, with interest.

"Sooo, your office called me..."

Dr. Walla's eyes unfocused for a moment, then he snapped his fingers.

"Right. So. You came to see us about those headaches, and we ran some tests."

"Yes."

I remember that part, you asshole.

He scrunched his eyes closed. He liked Dr. Walla. He didn't know why he'd thought that. He didn't know why any of this was getting to him, causing him to feel a deep, buzzing rage. Wade, the headaches, Shelly's absence, those motherfucking jackhammers...

He opened his eyes and saw that Dr. Walla had turned his back and was doing something to the lightbox behind him.

"Here," the doctor said, and flicked a switch. The X-ray image on the lightbox was suddenly illuminated with a bluish-purple hue.

Wait. Was it an X-ray or a brain scan?

Winston normally wouldn't be able to tell a CT scan from a pap smear, and today, with this thumping headache, he felt even duller. He stepped closer to the lightbox, inspecting the image of the skull and gray matter. Whatever he was looking at, it didn't seem good.

"That," Winston started. "That's me?"

Dr. Walla chuckled and smiled.

"Oh, not at all. This is a healthy scan, so you have some context."

He pulled the film from the lightbox and replaced it with another.

"This is you."

Fuck.

"Oh."

There were clusters of black spots all over the image, but the grouping was especially tight where Winston's headache was currently gnawing at the base of his neck.

"Yeah, take your time. It's, uh, ghastly," Dr. Walla said.

Ghastly? Doctors weren't supposed to say that!

Dr. Walla continued: "What we're seeing here is a very advanced case of..." But then the jackhammers grew louder, drowning him out. Was there a third one out there? Were the construction workers starting a band? Were they taking over? Was it the jackhammer revolution?

He pressed a hand against an ear and felt the room tilt around him.

Dr. Walla was still talking: "...with secondary necrosis of the frontal, sub-frontal, and..."

Winston lost more of the words. Whatever the jackhammers were digging up, the texture of the sound seemed to change. Had they hit a pipe? Winston hadn't heard so much public-works construction in Tromaville in a decade. Were they going to do something about the potholes when they'd finished?

"All of this makes surgery impossible, you see, and..." Dr. Walla looked up from his notes. "Are you okay, Winston?"

Was he okay? He wanted to cry. And die. But actually, no, he didn't want to die, which was why he felt like he was about to cry.

"Fuck. I mean..." Winston sniffed hard, then bit the inside of his cheek to give himself another type of pain to focus on. The pain made him angry, which helped with the sadness and confusion.

"Just tell me. How, uh, how long do I have, Dr. Walla?"

"Best case, six months, a year," Dr. Walla said. Then he made a "silly me" hand gesture and blinked at Winston with a smile. "So, I guess a year is the best case, actually."

A year. Six months. Between those two answers, what did it matter? What was going to happen to Wade? In the best-case scenario, the boy would be sixteen when Winston died and left him alone. Kids couldn't live on their own at sixteen. There was nobody to take Wade. No family. There might be a brother or sister of Shelly's somewhere, but if so they hadn't even come to the funeral. Wade would be effectively an orphan—an orphan who'd need to go into the system. Did Tromaville even have an orphanage? It used to, right? But hadn't it burned down?

"Now," Dr. Walla said, placing a hand on Winston's shoulder. The jackhammers seemed to take five. "There is a drug treatment for this. It's very new and wildly expensive, but it is effective. Very effective. You'll be right as rain after two weeks of treatment, don't worry."

"I..." Winston said. Were those tears on his cheeks? "Fuck, man. I wish you'd said that part first."

Dr. Walla shrugged.

FIVE

Fritz Garbinger huffed and wobbled.

He hated visiting the performance space of Da Underworld. There were too many stairs and his bad leg felt heavy.

The air rising up the stairwell smelled of pipe smoke, cigarette smoke, skunk weed, and an acrid, indeterminate scent that he suspected might be crack.

The band was rehearsing, or at least trying to. While Fritz worked his way down the stairs, pausing to rest occasionally, they started and stopped the same ten-second portion of the bassline to their song "Face to Nutz" four times before he finally made it down to the dingy basement bar.

Fritz thought Da Underworld was a fitting name, because he'd just as likely want to spend time in the actual, biblical Hell.

Here, with one's nose under the clouds of smoke that hugged the ceiling, it was possible to smell the other aromas of the club: stale beer (the cheapest in a can), moshpit blood (blood type: positive for rave drugs), and piss (rat piss, Fritz hoped).

On stage, Venus DeValero still couldn't get that bassline right. And the rest of the band hadn't noticed Fritz enter because they were too busy staring daggers at him.

Their jealousy of the guy wearing a mesh shirt with crusty dreads, a woven beard, and two-day old stage makeup, was palpable. They all wanted to be the hot one.

"From the top, then," Budd Berserk said into his mic.

Why Budd chose to rehearse in full makeup, Fritz would never know. Come to think of it, Fritz had never seen Budd out of his clown makeup. Did he sleep in it?

But they were all in their stage outfits. Nightmare Josh was in his straitjacket, his head wrapped in gauze, pit stains seeping down the long, unbuckled sleeves; Zodiac 3000 had his ski mask up around his nose, the Zodiac Killer's symbol emblazoned on his chest; Him Under The Hood wore his chicken mask; and DJ Cool Cthulhu… well, DJ Cool Cthulhu seemed to be on some kind of party drug, because she was bopping her head to music only she could hear and jamming on a keyboard that wasn't plugged into anything.

Fritz cleared his throat, but none of the band turned to see him, and before he could get their attention, they'd started playing again.

How could Fritz's brother confuse this for pop music? *Clearly* this was monstercore, an aggressive, stupid, poisonous mélange of the worst impulses of nu metal, screamo, and melodic death rap. It was horrific to listen to, of course, but the Killer Nutz did have a certain charisma. How many bands could you say worked better as action figures? They were going to make Fritz a lot of money. They were already a local favorite, and he knew he could break them beyond Tromaville. By this time next year, he could probably even have them on a European tour.

But that was only if they could help him and fulfill their other contractual obligations first.

They reached the same part in the song, and Venus screwed up again. His bandmates threw up their hands.

"What? It's hard!" Venus yelled at them.

Fritz stepped forward, kicking his bad foot against a pyramid of beer cans.

Nightmare Josh clapped his drumsticks together, then pointed to Fritz. Budd replaced his mic onto the stand.

"Yo, Nutz, form up," Budd said.

They all did, climbing down from the stage to form a semicircle around Fritz. For some unfathomable reason, Zodiac crossed the distance via handspring.

Fritz smiled, reached into his pocket, pulled out the printed picture of J.J. Doherty, and held it up so they could all see.

As his brother had said: ruthless execution.

J.J. watched from across the street as the van pulled up to her flop and the Killer Nutz disembarked. With its polished chrome, external speakers, skull badge set into the grille, and obnoxious airbrush mural on the side, it was not an inconspicuous vehicle.

Most of the band was on foot, but one of them was on hands, then feet, then hands again.

She felt the rage inside her grow. These were the bastards who'd killed Melvin. She wanted to make them pay, but she couldn't do that if she was dead too.

Her pocket felt hot from where she gripped Melvin's phone to her thigh. She'd read through his text thread with Sneaky Cheetah, or at least all of it that still existed. At some point he must have gotten nervous and deleted the conversation, or switched phones or sim cards.

She couldn't do much until the Killer Nutz were gone, so she watched the broken, boarded-up facade of the flop, hoped, and waited.

Please don't kill Dennis, she thought.

She watched as the Killer Nutz frightened off a group of teens who'd been sitting on the stoop in front of the building. The teens hadn't been hurting anyone, merely passing around a bottle of malt liquor and spraying over the building's various Nasty Boys graffiti with stuff like "Nazi Punks, Fuck Your Mom."

Typical Tromaville High afterschool stuff.

Now the Nutz were inside. J.J. could hear raised voices, glass breaking, and, for some reason, a chicken clucking.

Please don't kill Dennis.

There was a gunshot, and then laughter.

Although, in fact, Dennis was kind of a sleaze, always asking her if she wanted to "make a movie," so she adjusted her plea: *If you're killing Dennis, please don't do it on the couch. That's mine.*

A few moments later, the band piled back into their van. Obnoxious LED glow lights under the chassis blinked on and the vehicle sped off below the late-afternoon overcast.

J.J. waited until they'd turned out of sight, then counted to sixty before heading inside.

Dennis shivered on the couch. He had a sweating bottle of Herzbach pressed up against his nose, which was oozing blood down into his patchy beard.

"There you are!" he said. "What the fuck? Do you know the Killer Nutz? 'Cause, like, they were literally just here."

There was a large hole in the ceiling over a bowl of half-eaten cereal on the coffee table, now mixed with plaster and wood splinters. That must have been the gunshot she'd heard.

J.J. ignored Dennis. She had to get what she needed and get out. She dropped to her knees.

On the couch, Dennis readjusted the bottle. "They beat the shit out of me! And they were looking for you." Dennis was fine, if he was able to complain this much. As encounters with the Killer Nutz went, he'd come out of it better than Melvin Ferd.

And J.J. didn't like her housemate a tenth as much as she'd liked Melvin.

"Now, I let you stay here off the lease," Dennis continued, "but I said no drama. I feel like I really emphasized that part, and now I'm scared shitless. Look at all this." He waved around him.

The lease. That was rich.

"Look at all this!"

Honestly, looking at the living room, if she hadn't known that the Killer Nutz had just been in here breaking shit, she wouldn't have been able to tell.

J.J. pulled the duffel bag from under the floorboards and stood.

"Don't worry," she said. "They won't be back."

Then she looked at Dennis and saw that his nosebleed had dribbled down, mixing with the pre-existing Cheez Doodles stains on the couch. On *her* couch.

You know what? He could keep it.

"Neither will I," J.J. said, and she let the busted-up door slam behind her on the way out.

SIX

"Speak to an agent."

"If you're a provider, press one."

"Speak to an agent!"

"If you are a patient, press two."

"Agent. Agent. Agent. Agent."

"I had a little trouble hearing that. Did you say you were a provider?"

Somewhere during this screaming match with a robot voice, Winston had popped open his second wine cooler of the night.

Yes, he was a lightweight these days. His days of Jack and Cokes were far behind him.

And the days ahead of him? Those were numbered.

"Agent. Speak to an agent. Speak to—"

"Hi, Mr. Gooze. Yes, I see you in the system." *Finally* a human voice. "I also see that you're an employee of BTH and are enrolled in their Platinum Plus plan."

"Yes, Platinum," Winston said.

Phew.

He took another sip from the bottle. His headache was feeling better already. Thank god he'd taken that pay cut in order to keep their health insurance.

Even if the plan didn't cover Wade's therapy, at least it would—

"The problem is, Mr. Gooze," the voice on the phone said, "the Platinum Plus plan excludes benefits and procedures covered under the Gold plan."

He swallowed, felt the drink's slight carbonation fizz behind his nostrils.

"Wait. Excluded? But I have Platinum!"

"Yes, Platinum Plus. And as I said, sir, only treatments listed on the primary tier are covered. Secondary-tier treatments are covered, but not if you didn't qualify for the Admiral's Plan and unless you selected a co-tier," the voice continued. And it might have kept going for a while longer, but the words had become a drone to Winston.

He looked down at the bottle in his hand. Was it possible that he'd already drunk himself asleep? Was this a fever dream?

Or was he already dead and this was hell? Hell must have Muzak, right?

"But I..." Winston said, growing more hopeless. "Platinum doesn't cover Gold-plan treatment?"

"Sir," the voice said, sounding annoyed, "I'm talking about *tiers*."

Winston let the phone slip through his fingers without hanging up.

He was going to die.

If so, he might as well open up a third wine cooler and settle into the couch.

Wade was up next.

He poked the curtain aside and watched as a girl in a halter-top did a standing backflip and was caught by three guys in identical immaculate white polos.

The dance troupe on stage had perfect rhythm and expensive costumes, and they were popular, so all the students who attended *Share Your Gift* were already going to clap anyway.

Why had Stuart scheduled Wade to perform after this group? Couldn't he have at least put him after the magician? Or the nose ring girl with the hula-hoop and the tiny dog? Or the boy that wore a karate gi while he did competitive eating?

Those were great acts too, but at least Wade wouldn't be following a dance with a dance.

No, he thought, correcting himself.

You're not performing a dance. You're performing a movement.

Stuart, the drama club's stage manager, sidled up to Wade and gave him a "one minute" gesture and then a thumbs up.

Stuart was friendly, or friendly enough that he called Wade by his actual name rather than "poor kid" or "dipshit" or "dead-mom guy," which was one of Wade's least favorite nicknames.

On stage, the music ended, the troupe froze in place under the spotlights, and there was a smattering of applause from the student judges. Wade looked at the three judges. *They* would be deciding his fate? All of those kids cheated their way into New Chemistry, their parents paying the bribes needed to waive the lottery.

But no, he shouldn't worry about class struggle now.

Not a dance. It's a movement, Wade repeated to himself.

Scrunching his eyes closed, he walked out onto the darkened stage, his steps heavy but determined.

He was going to *do* this.

It didn't matter that he was weird, or that he tapped and fidgeted and thought differently and needed extra time on tests.

He would show them who he was and what he could do.

Like Mom would have done.

The first few bars of his music started up and Wade opened his eyes. The spotlight was so bright, he couldn't see. He couldn't hear, either—not his music, at least, but he could hear his own breathing, rasping loudly in his ears.

He stared into the darkness beyond the light, tried to make out the faces of the judges, but he couldn't see them, or their rolling eyes. He couldn't hear the judgmental clicks of their tongues as they waited for him to start.

Why couldn't he just… just…

He looked down at his chest and realized he was tapping. And then, below his tapping hand, he watched his feet running off stage.

Sound returned to the world just in time for him to hear Stuart yelling after him, "Alternate tryouts are next week!"

Winston's mouth was flooded with saliva. He coughed, a glob of wine-scented spit dripping onto the keyboard, seeping into the hole left by the missing Shift key.

"Shit," he said.

Was he slurring? How many had he had. Just the three, right? And at four percent alcohol, he'd better slow down…

Shaking his head to focus his vision, he continued to scroll down the website in front of him.

Plenty of people used Moneyhug.com to get by, and he was in dire need of money, so why not try and crowdsource it?

He read on, trying to make mental notes of what was working for these people.

The top-funded campaigns all had eye-catching titles:

I'm broke & my lung exploded!

Policeman must Relocate to Tokyo ASAP!

Line Dancing For Toddler Dialysis!

How could Winston compete with those? Even with exclamation points?

Why was he even bothering? This was a shitty plan. Even if he could figure out how to make a compelling fundraising page, who would he even share it with? He didn't have any friends. Not even internet friends.

He tabbed over to his bank account, already open in the next browser window.

Next to his balance, a small cartoon trumpet exclaimed, "You are Desti-toot!"

He tried the next window, BTH's insurance portal.

Yes, his claim was still rejected, and the Appeal button had been grayed out. Apparently he'd clicked it too many times.

But then, blinking, he read the banner ad on the top of the BTH website for the first time.

BTH Congratulates You, Mr. Garbinger.

He clicked through. Apparently, tonight Bob Garbinger was receiving the Citizen Shepherd Award for Community Service and Guidance, a banquet event at Mammon Hall. That was walking distance from the apartment!

Winston looked at the glossy photo of Bob Garbinger. That smile. Those abs. BTH may have rejected his claim, but there was no way the guy in that picture wouldn't help. After all, what was a few hundred bucks to Bob Garbinger? He'd help!

Winston burped, remembered how much he'd drunk.

He should go right now. He'd leave a note for Wade explaining that he'd be back late.

Where was a pen?

Before he could find one, he heard the clatter of the apartment's door being unbolted.

Oh, shit. Wade was home.

Winston slammed the laptop shut and laid it on the coffee table, trying to cover the folder labeled "Private Medical Info."

He looked up to see Wade enter the apartment, smiled and hoped he wasn't sweating, hoped he didn't smell too drunk.

The boy looked sullen, eyes downcast.

"Hey, bud," Winston said, trying not to slur.

Then Daisy, their landlord, followed Wade through the doorway. "Saw my man coming home," she said, patting Wade on the shoulder. "Thought he looked kinda low, so..."

Winston looked down at the laptop, scooted a bereavement brochure entitled "So You're Definitely Going to Die, Now What?" back into the folder. If he looked guilty or suspicious, hopefully Wade and Daisy would just think they'd walked in on him looking at porn or something.

Winston stood and crossed to them both. Wade wasn't much of a hugger, but Winston held his arms out anyway. The boy wasn't interested and walked right by him.

"Thanks, Daisy. You okay, bud?"

Wade didn't say anything, just traced the path Winston had just taken over to the couch and flopped down.

Don't look at the computer. Please. I didn't close the tabs. Don't see the folder either, don't look at the—

But Wade didn't do any of that. He just tapped his chest with one hand and stared at a water stain on the wall.

Winston leaned close to Daisy, pitching his voice low. He hoped he was whispering, but who could tell, really, when they were three drinks in? "So, earlier, uh... Are you okay? Buncha hardcases, huh?"

She looked not only upset, but guilty.

"I was gonna tell you," she whispered, wounded pride in her voice.

"I've seen them around. The Khaki Boys. Oo-oooh!" Winston made a fake shiver, as if to say he wasn't afraid of the Khaki Gang, that they weren't tough. But of course Spence and those guys *were* tough and Winston was *very* afraid of them.

"The whole block is gonna be condos or some shit," Daisy said mournfully. "If I don't sell and sign it over, sooner or later there'd be a fire, and then I'd get nothing for it. Or I'd be dead."

"What can you do? I don't blame you. And if there was a fire..." Winston pointed to himself, then to Wade, then wiggled his fingers and did the international sign for "flames licking at my body."

"But where will you two go?" Daisy asked, lowering her voice even further.

Winston blew a raspberry with a little too much spittle. "Wade and I'll get the fuck out of this dump. Don't worry, we..."

He looked over at Wade, remembered how disappointed his stepson had been that morning when Winston hadn't stood up for Daisy and her bodega cat, and sobered a little.

"I'm sorry I couldn't help. Before, with the cat, I—"

Daisy raised a firm hand.

"You got Mr. Treats out of traffic. I owe you."

Winston smiled at her and she smiled back, then left the apartment. Wherever they ended up moving to, he'd miss her.

"What was that about?" Wade asked, still not looking over, his eyes puffy.

"Ah, just adult crap. Don't ever grow up, my man, because it's nonstop when you do." Winston smiled. Wade didn't.

There was no getting around it. Winston might as well just ask.

"So how'd it go?"

Wade turned in his seat to face the wall.

Winston remembered back to the parenting books he'd read,

or at least skimmed through. There were times you were meant to give a kid space and then times you were meant to be there to make sure they didn't stew in their own upset.

He crossed the room and sat next to Wade on the couch, hoping he was guessing correctly what time this was now.

"It couldn't have been that bad," Winston started. "Compared to all those fucking nerds over there at..."

He looked at Wade's expression, and judged that this probably wasn't the tack to be taking.

Winston himself had gone to Tromaville High, but honestly, if New Chemistry had been an option when he was Wade's age, he certainly would have tried entering the lottery. He could have been one of those nerds. Probably was anyway.

The bullying Winston had faced at the public school had been intense.

After a few moments of Wade not responding, just tapping, Winston tried again.

"You wouldn't remember because she stopped playing shows when you were little, but your mom was an absolute killer on stage. Every time, just a bloodbath. Thing is..."

Wade was leaning forward. He'd never heard this before, about his mom, and Winston decided it was time, that knowing this would help Shelly's son.

"Thing is, I loved your mom so much, and this is going to sound bad, but she wouldn't mind me telling you. She couldn't even play that great. She wasn't a *good* guitar player. Just E-E-E-E-E-D! Then E-E..."

Wade winced.

"That's not a bad thing," Winston said. "It sounds like a criticism, but it's not."

Wade glared straight ahead.

"What I'm saying is that her talent was all in her attitude. She commanded the stage, even with all those Es, you know? It was all in the presentation, how she played the couple of chords she knew."

Wade was looking at him attentively now, and he'd stopped tapping, at least for the moment.

He had the boy's attention.

"Here, I'll show you."

He reached behind them both and fiddled with the knobs on the radio.

Wade clamped his hands over his ears as static changed to butt country, then finally to... ah.

It wasn't Motörhead, sadly, or metal at all, but it did have a beat Winston could dance to: funk.

"Wait right here," he said, and ran off to the bedroom he used to share with Shelly.

He'd cheer the kid up if it was the last good thing he did in this world.

Wade didn't know what Winston was doing, but there was an empty wine cooler bottle on the table and, judging by Winston's breath, there would be a few more next to the sink waiting to be rinsed and recycled.

Wade had heard the tapes. He knew his mom's band wasn't great, but he didn't think it was fair to say all her talent was in her attitude.

He stopped tapping then turned in his seat and lowered the volume on the stereo. The small speakers were beginning to distort and Daisy might have been trying to get to sleep in the apartment below.

From down the hallway, he heard a crash followed by the sound of drawers being pulled open and the clatter of a closet door opening.

What was Winston looking for? Had he finally cracked? As much as Winston liked to throw around the label "stepdad," Winston wasn't even that. At least, Wade didn't think he was, because Winston and Wade's mom had never legally been married. Unless there was such a thing as common-law stepdads? Mom had said something about it once, how they didn't think the government needed—

Then Winston was running back down the hallway. "Okay," he said, "let's—" He broke off, panting, to steady himself against the hallway wall, leaving a sweaty handprint on the plaster.

The music was still bumping.

Wade took one look at what his stepdad was wearing and said, "Winston, what the hell? Are you okay?"

Winston Gooze had lost it. And people at school thought Wade was crazy. They should see the forty-something guy he lived with.

The guy who was now, for some reason, wearing a tutu.

"Let's dance," Winston said, holding in his gut to avoid tearing his outfit, his face red, his hips bopping along to the music.

"Phew, yeah," he breathed, and the tights he'd sausaged himself into over his work clothes expanded at the waist and chest, the elastic ready to snap. "See if you can learn this move. You'll really blow them away."

Winston then did a slow-motion somersault over the couch. He didn't have the upper-body strength to vault over, so he just kind of fell down, sliding against the cushions.

But then he was back up on his feet, twitching and gyrating again.

"Come on," he gasped. "Dance with me. Show me a movement piece. Can't... can't match up with this, I bet."

He threw his hands up, then tried to do the splits, stopping halfway to the floor, clearly in pain.

Oh god, this was mortifying! Beyond embarrassing, to see a

grown man acting like this. But still, Wade didn't feel a need to tap right now.

And more than that, he could feel a smile creeping across his face.

Winston kept dancing like no one was watching, but people were listening.

"Hey, Earth, Wind, and Shithead. Turn it down!" Mr. Fleishaker, Daisy's other tenant, yelled from across the hall.

Out on the street, dogs began to howl.

"Come on, do it like me," Winston said, ignoring both their neighbor and the dogs.

"I can't," Wade said. His face was hurting from smiling, and he was laughing now, too.

"Can't is just won't with a doctor's note," Winston said. And he had to have picked that line up from somewhere, but maybe he'd gotten it wrong, because it didn't really make sense.

Winston twirled into a backspin—an exaggerated movement—then stubbed his toe on the coffee table and some papers fell loose from where they'd been wedged under the laptop.

"What's that?" Wade asked, and before he could reach down to help pick up the scattered pages, Winston fell to his knees and began snatching them up.

Wade stopped smiling.

Something was wrong.

Winston stopped dancing and grabbed at the papers and charts, sweating and breathing heavily.

"It's nothing, nothing," he said, jamming the pages back into the folder that had slipped out from under the laptop.

Wade could only see one word: Private.

Once the pages were collected up, Winston stood, clutched the folder to his chest, and began rubbing his lower back, then fanned himself with the folder.

"You know what? I'm... I feel hot. That was a legit backspin. I can... I..." He gulped for air. "I can also do the worm. But I'll show you that later. I'm going to take a little walk. You cool?"

Was Wade cool?

What the hell was Winston talking about?

And a walk? Didn't Winston realize that it was getting late and that they lived—

But there was no stopping him.

Still dressed in the tutu, Winston crossed to the front door and stopped there with his hand on the doorknob.

Wade made eye contact. This felt important, but he didn't know why. Was Winston... was he crying?

"You're," Winston said, louder to be heard over the radio, which was now playing an ad for Body Talk Healthcare's newest line of male enhancement pills. The jingle was gross. "You're such a good kid, Wade. You're... you're gonna be okay."

And then, before Wade could understand what the hell Winston was talking about, he was out of the door and gone into the night.

Drunk and wearing a tutu.

SEVEN

Kissy Sturnevan raised her glass and gave the stem a twirl. A waiter rushed over with a refill.

The waitstaff were all wearing masquerade masks, which was nice. Dehumanizing. As a subordinate herself, Kissy sometimes felt obligated to make small talk with the help, at functions with unmasked waiters. And, worse, sometimes the staff felt emboldened to talk to Garbinger himself, if he could see their faces.

It was better this way. The Commerce Council knew how to throw a party.

But Kissy's feet were beginning to hurt. She'd been standing in heels too long. Nobody in the ballroom dared to take a seat until Garbinger was through holding court.

"Pfffft. 'End of an Era,'" Police Chief Wormer grumbled, continuing his tirade. "Every whistleblower. Oughta boil 'em in molasses. Every journalist. Along with every 'peaceful' protester this country's ever seen. And anyone who says we're not doing enough on the Ferd case."

The chief's approach to law enforcement seemed harsh, but maybe that was the lingering Aussie in her. The police back in Australia didn't make a habit of blasting everything that moved.

But maybe that was why she'd left: she admired American boldness, blasting and all.

"Not that any *sensible* person would," Mayor Togar said, nodding. Next to the mayor, her husband was loading several small plates of hors d'oeuvres onto one big plate. He didn't often contribute anything valuable to conversation, so it was better if he kept himself occupied by building a... was that a shrimp ziggurat?

Mayor Togar leaned forward, putting a reassuring hand on the cuff of Garbinger's jacket. "Surely the corporation's long-term health looks as bullish as ever?"

Kissy didn't like the mayor being so close to Garbinger. Not that Robert had ever given any indication in private that he was attracted to her, but they both knew that if he flirted, it would make it easier to get BTH-friendly legislation passed.

"Oh," Garbinger said, and his smile brightened up Mammon Hall around them, the gold-leaf chandeliers and bleached tablecloths unable to compete with his radiance. "There's always some flux at our level. A company our size—"

"Flux, you see," Kissy said. She hadn't meant to interrupt, but the members of the council—Mayor Togar, Chief Wormer, Cardinal Rooney—all needed to be reassured that, despite the headlines, BTH was as strong as ever. Strong enough, in fact, to crush anyone who implied otherwise.

"Yes," Garbinger said, his eyes narrowed at Kissy. He was a proud man and could fight his own battles.

"Like a change in the weather, a few rain clouds drizzling, a certain fluctuation is expected," he continued. "But be assured, I'm not going anywhere."

"Nowhere except up," Kissy said, then mumbled, "my little balloon." If the rest of the banquet's guests heard her, they gave no sign.

"Ha!" Mayor Togar said. "No! BTH is this township's heart's

blood, and you *are* BTH, Bob. Not to mention that what's good for the goose is, uh, symbiotic and whatnot."

How many glasses of champagne had the mayor had? She was making a fool of herself. *Keep your legs closed, Madam Mayor,* Kissy thought.

"Look upon your good works!" the cardinal said, then crossed himself with a pig in a blanket skewered on a tiny plastic sword.

"Gander!" Mayor Togar said.

They all chuckled politely, the cardinal included, though it was clear to Kissy that he wasn't quite sure at what. The pig in a blanket had disappeared, as had the plastic sword, and the cardinal continued with his mouth full: "The ice rink, the used coat box—"

But then the holy man stopped. He was bleeding out his nose.

"Oop, here we go again," he said in a lower voice.

Kissy handed him a disposable wipe from her purse, told him to tilt his head back.

While the others had been talking, Chief Wormer's expression had been getting redder, like if he didn't let his cop-rage out, his head would explode. "Any fuckstick can write a headline. Here's one for you." He made air quotes. "'Civilian Hypocrites Don't Know What's Good For Them.' See? See how easy that was?" At his side, his wife winced, cooed, and patted his arm. "I'm entitled to my feelings," he whined at her. "It's my right."

"Anyway," Garbinger said, and Kissy was in awe of how easily he could redirect these rejects, these dopes, these... dammit, these elected officials. "When we announce our, uh, next innovation, I think you'll find our intertwined fortunes very much in..." The gathered leaders of St. Roma's Village leaned forward. "...in ascension."

Cardinal Rooney took the blood-streaked towelette away from his nose.

"Can you give us a preview?" Mayor Togar asked. Beside her, her husband made a sound like a neighing horse, trying to quietly clear an airway obstructed by too many bacon-wrapped scallops. "Of what the next innovation might be?"

"Well, it's…" Garbinger said. "Too soon to share any particulars, but…"

He was floundering. He needed Kissy.

"Mayor Togar," Kissy said, leaning in. "Garbinger's hesitant, you can see, because have you ever heard of corporate espionage?" Kissy indicated the nearest masked waiter, then another. Mayor Togar caught her meaning and began looking at every waiter in the hall with a suspicious, angry expression on her face.

"The next innovation is a secret," Kissy continued, "and has to remain a tightly guarded secret. But let's just say… Are you familiar with the term *game-changer*?"

Mayor Togar took a sip of her champagne, then nodded. "I'm not, but… holy shit."

"Exactly," Kissy said.

"It's providence!" Cardinal Rooney interjected, spraying his upper lip, and the rest of them, with tiny droplets of nose blood.

Garbinger must have been disgusted, but he didn't show it. "No, Cardinal," he said. "It's your support from the pulpit." He pointed. "And yours, Chief Wormer, from… elsewhere. Don't think I've forgotten about your help on the union thing."

"Frosted *that* jive!" Chief Wormer said, and his wife patted his arm again, trying to bring his enthusiasm down before he got overexcited. Union busting was one of the chief's greatest pleasures.

"And Miss Mayor," Garbinger said, "Angela—"

"*Mrs.* Mayor," Kissy corrected, looking at the woman's husband.

"Angela," Garbinger continued. "It's you most of all. You're like a, excuse me, but you're like a goddamn human scissor, the way you cut through that red tape."

The mayor blushed into her champagne flute.

"It's true. And you do it because you know that it's good, that when we do well..."

Garbinger reached a bronzed, well-manicured hand toward Kissy. She tried to take it, but he pulled it away. Oh—he hadn't been going in for a hand-hold, merely gesturing to indicate that he meant BTH as a whole.

"When we do well," Garbinger smiled, "we all do well."

"Yummy yummy, in my tummy," Cardinal Rooney said, which was an odd response, because he could have just said "Amen" and that would have fit the situation a lot better.

But Mayor Togar and Chief Wormer nodded in agreement, both smacking their lips, all three of the heads of Tromaville staring at Garbinger and repeating, "Yummy yummy, in my tummy."

"Uh, sure," Garbinger said, then pointed behind him. "Kissy, if you could, ah, keep our friends company, answer any more questions, I've got to..."

She looked over his shoulder. A representative from the Khaki Gang was there. It was the younger Barkabus, in a nice suit, leaning against one of the banquet hall's large bas-relief murals and tapping his foot.

"Sure, I can keep them company," Kissy said, turning back to the three officials, who were still chanting about their tummies.

Braindead misfits, she thought. *But you're useful braindead misfits.*

Winston threw up twice on the short walk to Mammon Hall. The vomiting and the walk made him feel much better despite the haze in his vision and the stomach acid burning in his sinuses.

He sniffed, stood across the street, and stared at the frontage of the building.

"Stay back, VIP only, you fucking animals!" a large man in a nice suit snarled at a small but feisty crowd of onlookers. There were four figures in suits working security, each posted at the four corners of the red carpet that had been rolled out in front of the banquet hall. They were all big, sporting military haircuts and tattoos sneaking out of the cuffs and collars of their suits. One of them grabbed a plywood sign that said "Eat Up While Tromaville Starves" and used it to clobber the protester who'd been holding it.

The rabble were mostly kids not much older than Wade. The punks chanted and jeered. Occasionally one would take a run at the velvet rope and be pushed back.

A limo pulled up to the curb, stopping in front of the red carpet, and the four-person security detail finally lost their patience with the crowd, each producing a billy club from inside their jackets. The back door of the limo opened and the guards ushered the VIP guests inside, cracking heads as they went.

Garbinger was in there, in Mammon Hall, being honored.

And that meant Winston needed to get in there too.

And—

Hurmp!

He swallowed down the puke-burp, spitting out a glob of pink goo that had made it to the back of his throat.

This didn't seem possible. Those guards were serious business. Maybe he should go home, crawl into bed, wait for death.

No. There had to be a way.

Winston scanned the building, looked up to the second floor, where he could see shadows, amber light reflecting off gold-and-cream walls. Then he looked further down the block, where another limo was approaching. Maybe when the guards moved to attend to the next batch of guests, he could—

"Have you tried the steak frites?" a female voice asked.

Winston turned. In the doorway behind him, a man and a woman in eye masks and double-breasted burgundy suit jackets stood and smoked.

"Hell yeah, it rules. Took some fries off Wormer's plate. Replaced them with a couple of ass pubes," the guy said.

"Nice. ACAB."

Wait. Steak frites? Pubes? They each had a silver tray tucked under their elbows. These were...

Winston's ticket inside.

Bob Garbinger sat back in his chair, looking uncomfortable, as if the shadows around them weren't shadowy enough.

Spence had chosen a secluded table, away from the other guests, but he guessed not secluded enough for the little CEO prince.

Oh, well. Tough.

"Look," Garbinger said, "I don't appreciate being buttonholed like this."

Spence chuckled.

Garbinger looked over Dad's shoulder and up at Spence.

"Buttonholed," he said. "Grow up."

Spence wanted to bare his teeth at the man, this rich-boy pretend gangster, but it wouldn't be what Dad—uh, Mr. Barkabus—wanted. This was Garbinger's night. Let him think he was in charge, when everyone in town knew that if you scratched any surface in Tromaville, everything was Khaki underneath.

Dad had many gangs on his payroll working for him, but the Khakis were his favorite. They ought to be—they were Spence's pet project, proof that he had the leadership and organizational skills to take over the whole enterprise one day.

Thad Barkabus, Spence's dad and boss, leaned forward. "What's this now, Bob?" he asked, and that was the voice of a tough guy—gravelly, deep. Spence practiced doing that voice in the mirror all the time. "Are you worried about being seen with disreputable underworld types?"

"It wouldn't help," Garbinger said. "I've already had to clip one loudmouth this week."

Listen to this guy. Clip. It was embarrassing, hearing that kind of... of... cultural appropriation. He should leave the gangster slang to the gangsters. Words like buttonhole were more his speed.

Dad—Mr. Barkabus—reached for the plate in front of him, took hold of the roast chicken on it, and cracked its sternum open with both thumbs before responding.

"Yeah. I heard about that one. The guy you clipped. Harpoon. Subtle." Thad Barkabus had known Garbinger their whole lives, they'd grown up together, but he wasn't going to let the bronzed twerp forget who was boss.

"The harpoon. Everyone's so concerned about this har—" Bob Garbinger started, then did a kind of yoga thing, put a hand across his face, centering himself or some shit. "What do you want, Thad?"

Spence's dad sucked on the end of a drumstick, then swallowed before answering. They had time. Garbinger could wait to make his fancy speeches and play with his coastal elite pals. "What do I want?" Thad Barkabus asked. "I want you to be reminded."

"Reminded?" Garbinger asked.

"Of who bought your slot in this town. Who paid for your seat at the big-boy table over there." He gestured, chicken skin dripping. "Who greased the skids that made your operation go. Growing up, you had manners, Bob. What happened?"

"You..." Garbinger began, then something seemed to register and he tried again, nicer this time, a smile on that tanned face. "You know I'm grateful, Thad."

"Don't tell me that shit." Dad gestured again, and a glob of poultry fat landed on Garbinger's cuff. "Show me."

"It's... look." Spence watched the rich boy squirm. "There's always some flux at our level—"

"Fuck flux. Shit like that might work for those simpletons over there." Thad Barkabus pointed at a small crowd that had gathered to watch the Heimlich maneuver being performed on the mayor's husband. The cardinal was leading a prayer. "But you owe. People ain't buying your snake oil anymore? The FDA getting wise? Too many asthmas 'n' bloody stools?"

"We—"

"Let me finish, Bob. Maybe you squeezed this town too much and too fast. I've driven through Outer Tromaville. I know what it looks like, out there in front of your big house. Maybe you ate your own babies—in a business sense—but I don't give a shit, Bozo."

Garbinger flinched.

Dad continued: "I don't give a shit because you owe. And it would take nothing for me to fuck you and everyone you love in the most sandy and unnatural of ways."

Garbinger put a hand up, changing tack. "Whoa, now."

Spence raised his eyebrows. Some fight in the little one.

"Nobody calls me Bozo anymore," Garbinger said.

Wait. That was the part of the threat he took offense to?

Dad, Mr. Barkabus, set down his chicken bones and picked up a cloth napkin. "Anyway," he said, wiping between his fingers. "You're reminded."

Then he waved the napkin at Garbinger, shooing him away from the table.

The CEO stood. Spence could see that his hands were shaking.

"Buttholed," Spence whispered.

"That's—" Garbinger blurted. Then lower, in a defeated voice as he stepped away into the banquet hall: "That's not what I said..."

Winston couldn't see shit.

One side of his mask had slipped down, obliterating his depth of field. How did the waitstaff even see in these things, never mind pour champagne and line tiny foil doilies with flying fish roe and artichoke dip?

He bumped into the back of someone's chair.

"Watch where you're stepping, pleb," they hissed at him.

Winston nodded that he was sorry, then dug a hand under his coat tails and started scratching.

His tutu was bunched up under the waiter's outfit and itched like crazy. The coat and pants were both too long. He'd rolled the cuffs but had done a bad job and still kept tripping.

He needed to do what he came here to do and get out before anyone realized he didn't belong. He needed to find...

He turned to the stage, where the mayor was speaking, and beside her, just outside the spotlight, Winston could see the man he'd snuck in here to try and meet. Garbinger was wiping at his brow, looking preoccupied.

"A social visionary, thought leader, business builder, not to mention a man of impeccable style." The gathered guests laughed at that, even though it didn't seem very funny to Winston. The mayor shifted behind the dais, holding both hands out to one side. "All of these describe my good friend Robert Garbinger, and it's my honor tonight to present him with the Citizen Shepherd Award!"

There was applause—what felt like too much applause. Winston looked around the room. Women in evening dresses and men in tuxedos were banging on the tables. They were dressed high-class but acting like they were tailgating at a Mad Cowboys game.

He looked back toward the podium to see Garbinger hold his award—a gold statuette in the shape of a lamb—up high.

Had he ever seen Bob Garbinger in person? He didn't think so. During his years of service to BTH, he'd only ever seen him on billboards, or on the news, or on a TV monitor, sending pre-recorded season's greetings during the company lunchbreak holiday party.

"Thank you, Mayor Togar," Garbinger said. "Wow! This means so much. I'm *baa*-side myself." He stepped back from the microphone to admire his award and allow the laughter to subside.

Winston would have been happy to find that the CEO looked less impressive in person, but his golden hair and white teeth were somehow even more convincing in real life, without the possibility of them being photoshopped.

"Seriously, though," Bob Garbinger continued. "I started out, like many of you, pretty low. A real hump."

Hey. He could have been talking to Winston, who was *at this very moment* a real hump.

"But through a steady application of what my father would call bootstraps, I took Body Talk Healthstyle from a dream to a reality, to a way of life."

Winston thought of all the hours he'd put in, mopping, squeegeeing, plunging, to pull Garbinger up by his bootstraps—and still he couldn't find it in his heart to hate the man. There was an authenticity in his voice, a wisdom.

"And why? Because I chose to reject the lie." Garbinger set his award down and used both hands to gesticulate through the next part of his speech. "A friend passes you, asks, 'How are you?' You say, 'I'm great.'"

Then he jabbed a finger out at the audience, and it felt to Winston, a little drunk and blind in one eye, that the man was speaking directly to him.

"That's the lie we all tell ourselves, and we settle for it. We're not great. We're pasty, bloated, lethargic, in some cases morbidly dim. Look at us."

Winston scratched the hair on his chin and looked at his hands. He was indeed some of those things. Most of them, actually.

"I'm speaking generally, of course. But no, seriously, look. Oof." Garbinger pointed back at himself. There was laughter, but less than before. "I want to respond 'I'm great' and have that be the truth. And I want to extend that truth to you. Whether we're talking about cellulasers or our bio-neutral metabolizers everyone loves at Christmastime, or any of our staggeringly successful sexual velocity products—"

A couple seated beside Winston turned and nodded at each other. They knew what he was talking about.

"...it's all a rejection of that same lie. And that is what BTH is about. So, I ask you tonight, esteemed people of St. Roma's Village, leaders and innovators: How are you?"

And with only a second of a pause, the banquet hall began to chant:

"Great! Great! Great!"

Winston looked around at them, these people chanting that they were great. Pearl bracelets swinging from cottage-cheese arms. Nicotine-chew-stained collars. Gold rings from secret university clubs cutting off circulation in fingers. Cosmetic scars dusted with cracker crumbs.

It all reminded him why he was here.

On stage, Garbinger bowed. He was about to leave the podium. Winston had to keep an eye on where he was headed. He couldn't miss his opportunity.

"Great! Great! Great!"

"You getting paid to watch the show?" a voice asked at Winston's ear.

Oh, no! He'd been discovered.

"Move your ass. Table twenty-three needs more wine."

Winston glared at the other waiter.

"Don't look at me like that. Here." The masked figure put a hand on Winston's shoulder, about-faced him, and pushed him toward a table. There were two security guards with earpieces standing sentry behind it, one with a rifle strapped over his shoulder.

There, under the watchful gaze of these guards, sat the mayor, the chief of police, the cardinal in full regalia, and several other important people.

But there was one seat still vacant, and as the crowd still chanted, Garbinger was moving across the hall to fill it.

Winston pulled his mask straight again.

This was it.

Perfection. The man was perfection.

Kissy beamed, feeling so blessed that she was allowed to sit beside him, to take care of him.

"I mean, look, the idea of an award is... That's just not why we do what we do," Bob Garbinger said, a boyish half smile leading to a dimple.

And so humble!

"The process is the reward," she added.

Wormer and Togar were pawing at the statue, getting their oily fingerprints on it.

"But as a focal tool," Garbinger continued, "awards are useful."

"The whole point, really," Kissy agreed, distracted. If these dopes dropped the lamb, they'd break it.

"Well, not the whole point," Garbinger said. Even as he corrected her, it felt nice to have his attention turned her way.

"Of course not, just focally," she said. She was about to ask Wormer to stop making faces at his reflection in the polished gold of the lamb when they were all interrupted.

"Ex—excuse me?"

Kissy looked up to see... a waiter? Talking to them? No, not them; he was looking at Garbinger.

The diminutive man holding the wine bottle looked disheveled and smelled worse.

"I'm in fear for my life," Chief Wormer shouted, opening his jacket to grab a holstered gun.

"No, Chief, it's all right."

Wormer took his hand off the weapon, looking disappointed.

"Yes?" Garbinger said to the waiter.

The short man beside the table removed his mask, set down the bottle of wine, swayed a bit, and looked at his feet, suddenly bashful.

No, this man was no waiter at all, Kissy decided. Mammon Hall would have some standards as to how an employee could dress or smell.

The man pulled out an ID badge from his uniform. He was clearly wearing multiple layers of clothes. The wretched thing was no doubt homeless. He'd probably found a waiter's misplaced mask in the gutter and stumbled in here out of the cold.

"Mr. Garbinger, it's an honor to meet you. My, uh, my name is Winston Gooze. I've worked for you for thirteen years."

Thirteen years. Kissy remembered a presentation she'd attended with Bob. Thirteen years was a much longer tenure than the average employee. Most took advantage of BTH's funerary severance package before then.

"I feel like I do a good job," Gooze continued.

Kissy looked over to Garbinger, who was nodding along listening, showing so much more patience than Kissy herself would have afforded Gooze. The man truly was a saint.

"My reviews are all Meets or Meets-slash-Exceeds, so, you know."

Was there a point to all this?

But Garbinger simply nodded, letting the man go on. Such patience! But this really was unnecessary. One wave of the hand and security could have Gooze street level in less than thirty seconds.

"I'm sick," the man said, and it sounded like he was about to start sniveling. "Dying. And my BTH insurance won't help."

Now the sweaty man waited, looking at Garbinger with wide, imploring eyes, like it was the Great Man's turn to speak.

"Damn. I'm so sorry to hear that," Garbinger said. "What were... What can I do for you?"

Gooze leaned back, wavered again, seemed to think about his answer.

"I thought you could, like, talk to your people about it. On my behalf. I wouldn't ask but... I got a kid."

Expressions softened around the table—all except Wormer's, who still looked like he wanted to shoot someone, preferably Gooze, but really just anyone.

"And I'm fucked, uh, for serious," Winston Gooze said, then added: "Sir."

Well. There was no need for vulgarity.

Garbinger rubbed his chin, looked down at his award,

and then over to Kissy. She wasn't sure what he needed in this moment, and she hated that feeling.

"Can I ask what you do for us?" Kissy asked. It seemed like the right thing to say, because Garbinger nodded.

"Hygiene services, sir. Uh, ma'am."

Kissy clicked her tongue. Then the—janitor?—made a sign with his hands and nervously added: "Mop shop, what-what."

"Hard workers down there," Garbinger said after a moment's consideration. "The white blood cells of our corporate body. Without you, what would we have over at BTH? A bunch of infected mess. Yuck. I have an obligation to you, don't I?"

No, Kissy thought. *You gave this man a job. You gave him a purpose in his pathetic, vomit-smelling, handlebar-mustached life. Obligated? Your obligation is zero.*

But the janitor nodded. The audacity!

"Don't worry," Garbinger said, "Mr…?"

"Gooze."

"Gooze," Garbinger repeated, like he was making a mental note of it.

"Pretty name," Kissy added, unable to hide the disgust from her voice any longer.

"We're going to get this sorted out, rest assured," Garbinger said. And from the tone in his voice, the look in his eyes, Kissy felt she finally knew where he was headed. After a night spent slightly out of sync, they were both back on the same wavelength.

"I… I don't know what to say," the janitor said, squeezing his facemask into a ball.

"You might give 'thank you' a ride around the block," Kissy said.

The janitor started to thank Garbinger profusely, but her boss was through now.

"You can follow my assistant."

Kissy stood. She was an associate, not an assistant, but she didn't mind. Not now.

"Yes, Miss Sturnevan will collect some details from you," Garbinger said. "For insurance purposes or whatever."

"Thank you, sir. You—wow. You rule!" And now the little smelly man was crying.

As he turned from the table, Garbinger raised his glass and winked at Kissy. She ushered him away, trying to touch him as little as possible.

"Really, this means so much," Gooze said to her as they walked together. "I think I have my case number on me, somewhere, and a copy of my insurance card, in this folder that I... Oh, it's bent."

He smelled like chopped garlic and cheap wine. And was that *pink lace* poking out above his waistline?

"That's quite all right," she said. "This way, Mr. Gooze."

"Oh, thank you. Thank you so much. Thank you. Thank you."

He didn't stop thanking Kissy until she'd shoved him out the rear service door and locked him outside along with the dumpsters.

Kissy was back to the table before the raucous laughter had subsided.

"'On my behalf!'" Garbinger said, his face red and wet from laughter—laughter that seemed to be concealing a kind of rage. "See, when I talk about entitlement, this is what I mean."

"Brass neck on that one," Kissy agreed, retaking her seat.

"Brass neck, brass everything," the mayor agreed.

"You should have let me shoot him," Chief Wormer said. "I'm sure my boys could have planted a weapon on him or something. Self-defense." The man was still pent up and nothing his wife could coo in his ear could bring him down.

Garbinger ignored the chief and kept laughing. "'Please give me special treatment because I do what I'm paid to do!'"

"Awful," Kissy agreed.

"And, by the way," Garbinger said, "thirteen years in custodial? That fucking mop boy has got bigger problems than he realizes, sick or not."

Outside in the dark, Winston Gooze dried his tears, listened to the laughter in the hall above him, and came up with another plan.

EIGHT

J.J. Doherty's plan was risky, and it had a lot of moving parts, but she thought she could pull it off. Probably.

She tightened her hood, making sure her face was hidden from any cameras she hadn't spotted, or any whose blind spots she might have misjudged. She wore all dark clothes—black leggings, black sweatshirt—and had applied black makeup to her eyes.

Sometimes it came in handy growing up a Tromaville High hardcore-scene kid. It meant your wardrobe was outfitted for espionage.

The first order of business would be scaling this fence.

She had a small cutter that should be strong enough to snip the razorwire that topped the fence, but it would be tricky doing it with one hand. Did she have the upper-body strength to hold herself up there?

Yes.

She'd been training for this. Not just how to run field loops and other evasion techniques, or the proprietary coding languages she'd needed to hack BTH executive drives; she'd been physically training—crunches, pull-ups, torrented celebrity workouts. She was in the best shape of her life. She was a machine.

She just needed to start.

J.J. put one skate-shoed toe (black) into a hole in the fence, getting a foothold, then reached up, grabbed iron and began to pull herself up.

That was when the lights hit her.

Shit!

She fell away from the fence, ducked into a roll, pulling the duffel up on her shoulder, and hid behind a fallen tree to watch the road.

No, the lights hadn't been spotlights.

They'd been the headlights of a civilian car—a really shitty one with a crumpled fender and a duct-taped side mirror—which was now slowing as it approached the automated gate to the employee parking lot.

This wasn't right. J.J. had made sure she was breaking in during the two hours where there'd be no shift changes. There should be only a skeleton crew of essential personnel and security.

The car stopped at the gate and J.J. could hear the driver cough as he stretched his arm out to scan his employee ID through the card reader.

She watched the figure in the driver's seat struggle.

S—swipe, miss, swipe, miss.

The card finally beeped and the gates began to shudder open.

J.J. looked from the gate over to the razorwire-topped fence, shrugged, and then ran for it, dashing through the gate behind the car before it could close.

She was in.

This wasn't drunk driving. This was barely tipsy driving. He'd vomited up all the wine coolers he'd drunk earlier, and he was *fine*. If Winston was swerving at all, drifting in and out of his lane, it was probably due to exhaustion—that or the black holes eating away at his brain.

God, he hoped that kid on the bike he'd seen on the way out here was okay. How late was it? Would it be dawn soon? Was that kid setting out for school? No, he couldn't have been. He leaned forward and looked up. Sure enough, there were stars poking out from behind the smog.

He yanked the wheel to correct.

A few moments later, he'd arrived. On the horizon, the red lights on the smokestacks blinked in the night, a warning to low-flying planes.

He slowed to a stop at the gate, dug around for his employee ID, then remembered something:

They'll know it's you, idiot.

No they won't, he thought, putting on the waiter's facemask.

He was checking his appearance in the rearview mirror—the lopsided eyeholes on the mask only partly obscured his view, but it was a better disguise than nothing—when he thought he saw a shadow pass by the side of his car. He looked again.

Nothing.

Okay, here we go.

He scanned his ID badge.

Then tried again.

Then again.

Then, finally, the gates to Body Talk Healthstyle creaked open and he drove his car inside.

Fritz Garbinger sat alone in the darkness in the management office he kept above Da Underworld, but it wasn't monstercore music he was in the mood for.

He lifted his pinky finger, slid the pan flute over his pursed lips, and changed the pitch on his mournful melody to... an even more mournful one.

There was nothing wrong with feeling sad, and nothing wrong with a little self-pity, as long as he never let his brother see him indulging in his sadness.

So here, alone in his office, in the middle of the night, he played his flute and thought about all his failures, all that had gone wrong in his life. And as his tears flowed, he thought about ways he could make things right.

The chime of his cell phone sounded strange as it mingled with the notes of his song, and it took him a moment to realize what the noise was.

For a moment the glare of the screen was too harsh for his eyes in the dark, but after wiping away his tears he could see he had a message:

Security breach.

And under it was a surveillance-camera photo of a black-clad figure, their arms and legs a blur as they moved between the pipes and valves of the canning room in Sector C.

It was her—J.J. Doherty.

Fritz kept the phone open, smiling as he typed out a message to Budd:

Summon the Nutz.

Winston Gooze watched from behind the mask as his hands retrieved his mop from where he'd left it this afternoon, and then as he pried off the lid to the metal drum labeled "DANGER: SUPER-CAUSTIC."

They were his hands, but it was like he was watching someone else do these things.

Then he watched those same hands dunk the head of the mop into the fizzy, foamy, emerald-green sludge and twirl the handle around.

But still, this couldn't be him. It didn't seem like something Winston Gooze was capable of doing, ruining a perfectly good mop like that. It didn't line up with reality. This was worse than mixing ammonia and bleached-based cleaners. Way worse.

He pulled out the end of the mop to inspect what the chemicals had done, trying to keep the contents of the drum from splashing on his hands—or his tutu.

The mophead hissed and crackled, giving off a noxious smoke that made his eyes water behind his mask.

Oh god, this was his favorite mop. What had he done?

No. He couldn't think like that. This was the company's mop. The company that had laughed at him. The company that had pushed him out into the garbage when he had the nerve to ask them to help pay his medical bills.

This mop deserved its hissing, smoking, green-glowing fate, just as he deserved help, deserved to live.

He had transformed the mop from a tool of cleanliness into a sizzling knot of deadly chemical evil, and he was glad about it.

He hoped that tonight would end without him using the weapon on anyone, but he was a desperate man.

He *would* use it, if the company chose to push him one more time.

J.J. crept around a corner, walking the path she'd memorized and rehearsed.

Cameras hummed overhead, swinging to and fro as the building around them slept.

Yes, that was the way to think about the factory around her. Devoid of bustling workers mixing synthetic binding agents, or testing cranial stims for maximum bio-load, BTH was a sleeping giant. Yet even as it dozed, the factory floor occasionally made noises, tubes and gas tanks reaching pressure, then failsafes causing that pressure to release. Exhaust and waste pipes flowed and gurgled above J.J.'s head and below her feet. The pipes were filled with liquids and partial solids, and all of them emptied out into the river, and ultimately the ocean, poisoning not only Tromaville but, slowly, the whole world.

And she could stop it, at least for a little while. She wasn't foolish enough to think she could fix the world forever and bring BTH and the dozens of companies like it to their knees—the bastards were too strong for that— but she could at least hurt the giant, give it a bloody nose or a black eye.

She just needed to find the compound listed in the files, the one that Ferd was going to show to Sneaky Cheetah. The one that could throw a wrench into BTH's plans, for the next few financial quarters at least.

The compound was kept somewhere around here, but she wasn't sure exactly where.

It was beyond hazardous, beyond illegal. It was—

Ah, there it was.

The large plexiglass tube, tucked alongside a tangle of similarly sized PVC and iron pipes, swirled and fogged as J.J. approached. The cloudy liquid within seemed to know she was there, curling and responding as she approached and laid her hands on the tube.

She would need to extract it from the top, so she climbed the nearest ladder up onto the service gangway.

She dropped her bag and winced as it clattered on the steel mesh of the walkway beneath her. *Stupid!* Any nearby night-watchman could have heard that. She was so close—she couldn't get sloppy and be picked up by security now.

Quietly, she bent and unzipped the duffel, taking out a pair of plastic goggles. She probably should have brought a respirator too, but it was too late for that. Anyway, what did she care about her own health? Revenge was all she was living for now.

The extractor was an elegant-looking piece of engineering: chrome and glass, with a menacing-looking curled spigot at one end and a textured handhold on the other.

She drew a rubber mallet out of the bag, positioned it over the handle end of the extractor, and got to work, trying to time her whacks with the hisses and burbles coming from the factory floor.

Once the extractor was attached, she began pulling back on the handle and the phosphorescent compound from the tube below slowly began to fill the canister, silky-white runnels in a lime-green goo trickling into the container.

It almost looked appetizing, like something you could order at a malt shop—if that malt shop was located in Chernobyl in 1986.

Come on, fill! Every moment she was up here was another moment she could be discovered.

That was when she heard the rattle at the factory windows and a faint thumping, growing louder.

She looked down at her progress. Almost there. Just a few more seconds. She couldn't leave a single air bubble—who knew what oxygen would do to the volatility of the compound?

The rattle at the windows resolved into a hip-hop baseline.

Oh, god. They were here.

Winston needed to use his employee key ring to enter this wing of the factory. It had taken him a minute to find the right key.

He'd actually gotten lost getting here, taking a wrong turn in the dark.

The factory looked different at night, too, with none of his coworkers around, although maybe that was because he was wearing the mask—or because he was a little drunker than he'd thought he'd been driving in.

After quitting time, the check-cashing office was sealed off by a reinforced metal door with no knob. That meant it had to have been sealed from the inside.

He walked up to the bolted metal outer door and knocked, then waited.

He looked at the mop. The yarn had fused and hardened, the tailband and ends squished outward into several sharp points. The improvised weapon was less drippy and hissing now that it had solidified, but it was no less menacing. Its surface glowed a gentle green and Winston tested it out, hefting it like it was a maul or mace.

When it felt like he'd been waiting long enough, he knocked again, this time with the mophead. The sound was much louder this time, and metal sizzled and paint blistered where the yarn touched the door.

The slot in the door slid open. Eyes peered down.

Winston looked up.

"Uh, trash run?" he said.

The door squeaked open.

Winston couldn't believe that had worked. Did the security crew usually get janitors making trash runs in the middle of the night?

"Hey," the security guard behind the heavy door said. "What's with the robber mask?"

Winston lowered his shoulder and barreled forward, putting all his weight against the door, swinging it open the rest of the way.

"This is a robbery!" he yelled.

His voice squeaked more than he would have liked, but then he was very amped up.

The guard eyed the mop, his wide eyes reflecting the weapon's glow.

Please don't make me use it. Please don't make me use it.

"And I'm very sorry," Winston added. "Like, I'm sorry that this is a robbery. But it is."

The guard seemed to weigh his options, then looked back at the mop. A glob of congealed goo dripped to the linoleum flooring, where it immediately began melting a hole.

The security guard shrugged. No way was he dying for BTH's money.

"Did you, uh, bring a bag or do you need me to give you one?" he asked.

"If you had a bag, that'd be great."

The guard sighed and Winston followed him into the back room, where he began to empty the smaller cash sacks into one large plastic trash bag for him.

"I really had no choice, bro," Winston said to break the silence.

"I don't want to hear it," the guard said, shoveling stacks of bills into the bag.

Winston hoped the guard wasn't going to get fired over this, but then he thought back to his confrontation with Garbinger and the heartless laughter he'd overheard.

Fuck, he probably *was* going to be fired. Winston had pulled this poor sap into the dark, rippling rain cloud of his bad luck.

He was trying to think of a way to make it up to him—maybe

he could leave him with some of the cash?—when the silence stopped being silent and started being… Was that music?

Shit.

It didn't matter. There was probably enough cash in the bag by now to pay for the medication. And even if the meds didn't work, it would be enough that he could leave something behind for Wade. "That's good," he said, snatching the trash bag from the security guard.

He had to get out of here.

J.J. looked down at the canister, which was now completely full—no air bubbles. Good. Now she could run for it. There was no time for stealth.

She hauled ass, arms pumping, the canister in one hand glowing as it shook. How volatile was it? Would it explode if she dropped it? Would it take her hand off, maybe level this whole wing of the building?

It didn't matter, because she wouldn't find out. She wouldn't drop the canister.

But you said that about the hard drive and you definitely dropped that.

No. Too much depended on getting the canister to Sneaky Cheetah.

She slammed through a pair of double doors and then she was off the factory floor, stopping in the decontamination room only long enough to spin the locking mechanism, then headed straight on into the administration and office spaces. Like the positions of the cameras, she'd studied the blueprints to plan the quickest route out of the building.

But you didn't stay out of sight of the cameras. How else do you think they knew you were here?

Outside, the music continued, the beat oscillating in a way that suggested the van was still moving, occasionally accompanied by the squeal of tires. It was that dumb van, that juvenile shaggin' wagon she'd seen parked outside of the squat earlier today. She tried to remember how many of them there were, and counted the instruments she could visualize. Five? No, that wasn't right. There was the dope in the ski mask dressed like the Zodiac Killer. He didn't play an instrument, he just hopped around on stage and danced. So that meant there were six—more than enough for whoever was driving the van to drop off a band member or two at each exit as he circled the building. They could be surrounding J.J. right now, the same way they'd split up to cover the entrances of Melvin's office building.

She'd trained in self-defense, knew her armbars and her chokeholds and how to keep her wrist when she threw a punch. The skinny one in the straitjacket she could probably take, if he didn't have a gun—which he would—but if she ran into the big one in the chicken mask, she'd be dead.

Don't think about that. This isn't your division, but remember the blueprints you've studied. Dead ahead, that's the side door to these offices. They won't be looking there. Probably. *And if they are, you just have to keep running. Keep running and you'll be harder to shoot if they see you. Keep running and—*

J.J. pushed out through the side door and into the cool night air, and kept running into the darkness. The fence was right there. She'd dropped the duffel but had remembered to stash the cutters in one of her pockets. But she was in luck—there was a row of gas tanks along the perimeter fence. She wouldn't even need to scale it, she just needed to climb one of those tanks and she could be over it in—

Headlights, high beams engaged, suddenly flooded the scene with light. She knew she should keep running, but she faltered, momentarily blinded.

The Killer Nutz had turned off their music, left the van idling around the corner, and now it was crawling ever so slowly into view. She could hear the muffler chug, the soft laughter from inside the vehicle. On the running boards, the guy in the chicken mask hung off the side of the van, a road flare burning in his fist.

No. It couldn't be...

They knew where she'd come out. They must have had a way to watch the security footage remotely, must have been patched into the system.

She was trapped. She—

"Oh, shit!" a voice yelled, much closer than the van, and a figure materialized next to her out of the darkness, carrying a long pole behind it. In the half-second before it broke into the glare of the headlights, J.J. had enough time to catch the outline of a flamboyant outfit.

Fuck—another one of the Killer Nutz.

She closed her eyes and waited for the gunshot or knife wound that would kill her.

I'm sorry, Mom, she thought. *I couldn't get them.*

But instead of being executed, she was simply bowled over by the masked figure, the force of the impact knocking the canister out of her hand.

"Oh, shit! Sorry, sorry, sorry," the man said.

Wait. This guy wasn't one of the Killer Nutz.

He looked like a janitor wearing... what was that? A Zorro mask and a tutu?

She shook her head. Who cared who this asshole was? The canister! *Where was the canister?* She staggered to her feet—the janitor tried to help her up, but he was shakier than she was on her feet—and then saw the canister, lying on the soft pillow of a trash bag. Bills—twenties, fifties, a hundred—fluttered in the van's headlights, the wind drawing some more across the pavement.

This guy was robbing the place.

That doesn't matter. Focus.

She reached out for the canister, and that was when she noticed the crack in the glass and heard the pressurized fizz as its pearly-green contents made contact with the open air.

"No!" she screamed just as the canister exploded in a puff of green flame and purple smoke. Simultaneously, the money in the bag below it began to catch fire, sending the flames even higher. The superheated smoke made the air bend and wave in the van's headlights.

The janitor in the tutu had a BTH ID pinned to his chest, and the card came free in her hand as she throttled him. "Do you know what you've *done*?!" she screamed.

"I'm sorry, I'm sorry!" the janitor said again, but his apology was cut off by the hum of an engine.

Oh fuck, the van! The Killer Nutz had been watching them from their van the whole time, but now the show was over and they were going to run them down.

The vehicle was less than a city block away, peeling out against asphalt on its over-inflated tires.

J.J. stood, locked eyes with this man, this *janitor thief* who smelled like a middle-school kegger and had a ring of frilly pink around his waist.

"Fuck," they both said in unison.

Then she pushed away from him and ran for the tanks.

The money was burning—all of it, burning to cinders. And there was a van about to run Winston over.

But the money! Maybe he could just... pat out the flames with his hands. If you had more than half of the bill, it was still legal tender, right? He'd definitely read that under an ice-tea cap or something.

He glanced up. The van's fender was a hungry maw, ready to drink his blood.

No, the money was gone. He should run for it.

He dove out of the way at the last second—actually dove. Forget his dance moves; this was the real ninja shit.

Scrambling up, his knees and back throbbing with pain, he whipped off the mask.

Ahead of him, the woman in black was already at the fence, dragging a small stack of wooden pallets over to one of the gas tanks to make a ramp, evidently intending to climb onto the tanks, then over the fence.

He could follow her.

The van behind him skidded, fishtailing, and the stench of burning rubber hit Winston's nostrils.

As he ran, the mop handle whacked him in the back of the legs. Oh yeah, he'd wedged the weapon behind him to carry the bag. Why had he done that? It was slowing him down, but there was no fixing it now. He'd need to strip off a couple layers of clothing to get rid of it.

The woman was up on top of one of the tanks already, had her hand reaching down.

"Come on!" she yelled.

She didn't know Winston, but still she was ready to help him escape.

That was nice. She seemed nice.

Winston scrabbled up onto the pallets, hissing as he got a splinter, then another. He reached up, but she was still too far away, even when he went onto his tiptoes.

She looked down at him, frowning. Actually, it was more than a frown; it was an anguished, guilty expression.

She didn't want to leave him in danger, but really, Winston was okay with it. He deserved whatever punishment was coming to him. He'd become a criminal tonight.

"I'm sorry," the woman said, then disappeared into the night.

The van braked and skidded to a stop a few feet from Winston. He crawled down from the pallets, his hands in the air.

"You can have the money back," he said.

A figure got out of the van and held a red flare up against his face.

"I mean, it exploded already, but I'll reimburse you. Maybe take it out of my paychecks for a few years or... y'all into crypto? I have a..."

The man holding the flare didn't say anything. Winston couldn't see his face, the chemical flare was too bright, but he heard somewhere behind him the van's side door roll open and more feet touching down on asphalt.

The van, it seemed, wasn't a typical security vehicle.

BTH security mostly scooted around the premises in golf carts, but this van was decked out with way too many speakers, chrome attachments, and airbrushed wizards.

And the man holding the flare was... a chicken?

Winston blinked, not sure what he was seeing.

And the one that was standing beside the chicken was wearing a bulletproof vest and had white makeup smeared over his face.

These were—

"Killeerrrrrr Nuuuuuuuttttzzz!" the man in the white makeup called, a rallying cry for the other figures who'd left the van, who yelled back "Koo-koo-koo!" in unison.

Ah. So these were the Killer Nutz. And the man in the white makeup—that was their lead singer.

And he was pointing a gun at Winston.

"Please," Winston said. What was his name? Buzz? Butt? Budd Berserk! That was it. "Please, I'm a fan, Mr. Berserk. Don't shoot!" Not true, but he'd be their biggest fan if they just let him go.

Budd Berserk stepped forward, tilting his head left and right like a horror movie villain.

But he hadn't fired his pistol yet.

Maybe Winston could talk him out of this.

"I'm a dad. Well, s-stepdad, technically," Winston stammered. "And technically, legally, not even that, but I'm all he has in the world, and I—"

Budd Berserk lifted the pistol, putting the barrel flush against Winston's left eye, and pulled the trigger.

Winston Gooze was dead before he even heard the shot.

Fritz Garbinger sat in the passenger seat of the Nutzmobile and watched Budd shoot the janitor in the face.

"What the *fuck*?!" he yelled, struggling with his seat belt as he tried to get out of the van, trying to get the buckle undone.

He hopped down from the passenger's seat onto the asphalt, nearly tripping over his own club foot, and pulled himself around to lean on the van's bumper.

It took him a moment, but he was moving as fast as he ever had.

The Nutz stood around the corpse, whose brains dripped from the hole in the back of his head. The bullet had bounced around his skull before exiting through the base of his neck.

Fritz looked down at the body, which seemed to be wearing multiple layers of clothing: a dinner jacket over a tutu over coveralls.

"What?" Budd said, looking up at Fritz from where he was crouched, taking a selfie with the body. "You said ruthless execution."

"Yes, but..." Fritz's hands were shaking. His brother was right—these people were morons who could not and should not be trusted with this kind of sensitive work. "This is the one we want," he said, holding up a photograph.

The Nutz all looked at the picture, which showed an athletic, attractive African American woman in her early thirties.

Then they looked down at the body of a white man, in a dinner jacket and a tutu, who must have been pushing fifty.

Venus looked at the photo, then down at the man, then over at Budd, then back down at the man. "I think he's right," he finally said.

"Jesus, fuck! All right, let me think," Fritz said, slamming the heel of his bigger shoe into the asphalt and grinding it down, just to feel something. He took a deep breath, then looked back up at these morons. "Just clean it up. And find the girl."

He climbed back into the Nutzmobile as Him Under The Hood, the big man in the chicken mask, bent, picked up the janitor's body, and stalked off into the night.

How was he going to make this right?

Winston Gooze is dead.

Yes, really.

Really super-dead.

See? The big guy in the chicken mask is carrying his body off somewhere to dump it. We're following them both. The man in the chicken mask, a.k.a. Him Under The Hood, casts long shadows as we find some really cinematic place (budget permitting) to slide Winston's body into the murky, polluted waters that empty out into the river that runs through Tromaville.

They say it's always darkest before dawn, and things are looking pretty dark, eh?

Which means the sun's probably about to—

Yes. I'm serious. Stop interrupting me, will you?

Winston *is* dead.

Why do you think I put in all that description about his brains falling out and how the bullet ricocheted around in his skull?

I guess old Winston won't have to worry about those headaches anymore, amirite?

What's that?

Oh, we've got a wiseass over here.

Yes, I *see* that there's still a bunch more pages left in the book, and yes, okay, I *know* you saw the trailer for the movie. Good for you. You know those things just ruin the best parts.

Let me ask: How do you know it's going to be Winston who turns into Toxie? What if we made J.J. the new Toxic Avenger, taking the franchise in a bold new direction? You don't know shit.

Oh. That was in the trailer too?

Fuck.

And you've seen the movie already—of course you have. You just picked up this book because you thought it'd be fun and kitschy to own the novelization of the remake of a mid-eighties cult classic.

Okay, fine, but can we just have one second where you *pretend* to be shocked? Where you're *surprised* that we killed off the main character in such a brutal and sudden manner? Can you just do us all a favor and pipe down and play along?

Jeez.

Someone's aunt gets them the Syd Field screenplay book for Christmas and suddenly they're the fucking king of story structure.

You must be *real* fun at parties, pal.

Don't look at me like that, Joseph Campbell. I'm 77 years old but I'll kick your ass.

That's what I thought.

Anyway, apologies to the rest of you for your fellow reader spoiling the fun. Don't blame me, blame him.

Of course Winston's only dead in the sense that he's about to be reborn as the title character.

Now, where were we?

NINE

Nobody knows much about Him Under The Hood, the virtuoso lead guitarist and only talented member of the Killer Nutz.

Many people wonder what he must look like under his chicken mask, but no pictures exist and no biographical details have ever been published.

But maybe Him Under The Hood once worked at the Body Talk Healthstyle factory. Or maybe he knew someone who did. Or maybe he just possesses, in some kind of extension of his savant-like understanding of the guitar, a preternatural intuition for how structures are laid out.

Whatever the *why*, Him Under The Hood is able to find the BTH dump site, a site not included on any maps or inspected by any state regulatory offices, in a matter of minutes.

After searching Winston's body to see if there was anything of value besides the chemically mangled mop clenched between the corpse's buttocks, Him Under The Hood hoists Winston's body over the railing and drops him into the drainage pipe with a muffled splash.

He thinks the mop is cool and picks it up, admires it with what looks almost like an infant's wonderment.

Maybe he should keep it.

With the right tools, maybe he could add some pickups and strings to it and transform it into a guitar.

But then, in a moment that might have been more of that preternatural intuition, or perhaps just an attempt to hide evidence, he tosses the mop into the water after the body.

The handle cuts through the water and collides with Winston's right temple, but of course Winston doesn't feel it. He can't feel anything.

Winston Gooze's lifeless body floats. There's enough air still trapped in his lungs to slow his descent, to stop him from sinking.

The head of his mop brushes past his nose. Its green glow pulses once, twice, then goes dark, like it too has decided to die now that its master is gone.

Winston's fingers and hands are still. Scummy water works its way into his empty eye socket, the microscopic particulates in the water bathing the folds of his brain.

The drainage pipe is one of a series of concrete wells that feed into the sewer and the river.

Winston's body floats, but it also hangs in a kind of stasis.

Down here, the normal laws of physics don't apply.

Above Winston's head, tiny streamers of artificial light pierce the gloom of the water. They aren't much, but they allow us to see the expression on Winston's face. It's slackened some in death, but it still looks haunted by shame and regret. Fear and anger are there too, and sadness, because he'd been thinking about Shelly, how badly he'd failed her, and how badly he'd failed her son. The word he was about to yell, right before the end, was *Wade*.

Bubbles leave Winston's body, but no, he's not breathing. It's just gases escaping. There will be more as putrefaction takes hold.

Somewhere in the world above, Him Under The Hood presses

a button and, like the flushing of a giant toilet, the water around Winston's body begins to swirl.

These wells have been engineered so that they can be opened and closed individually. Runoff, rainwater, toxic waste, the never-alive abominations that come out of BTH's secret laboratories—it's all collected here, in these wells, and when room is needed...

Whoosh, flush, gurgle.

...away the waste is carried.

Winston's body is drawn out into a larger waste pipe, on its way to be dumped into Tromaville's water supply.

Think on that the next time you have a tall glass of New Jersey tap water.

During that trip through the sewer nexus, however, something begins to happen.

Remember those microscopic particulates washing over Winston's gray matter? There's more of them now, and they've begun to bind and stretch.

And they've got friends. Zooming in, 100x magnification and more, we see double-stranded DNA reaching out from Winston's dead flesh. These hungry tongues of protein form ropes, and those ropes lash out and ensnare tiny angular granules, each pulsing first neon green, then electric purple, then coal black.

Winston's body is dead, but it's growing somehow, becoming more vital.

Still, his body is a long way from its final resting place, and the sewer pipes he coasts through turn and corkscrew and loop back on themselves. He's tossed around by the current, but his body's new cells are hungry and they try to consume anything they can—his BTH uniform, then the tutu, and even the jacket he convinced that masked busboy to lend him. All fuse with him, become part of him. But the cells are still hungry, gobbling up the algae and waste—commercial, human, and other—that floats past.

The muscle growth that bubbles under Winston's pale flesh is more than a trick of the light, more than a side-effect of the gases working their way up his throat from his guts and voided bowels.

He's becoming stronger.

But it's not enough to improve on what's there, to reinforce bone, to make weak and stringy muscles bulge; the new growth must restore what's been taken.

So the new cells start first with the brain, only to find that not only has it been blown apart but it's been necrotizing for a long time.

No, that won't do. If the host body is to survive, the brain must be improved.

This one may lack in traditional intelligence, but it excels in something lacking in most of the world: moral fortitude. Winston Gooze possesses a will, nearly a compulsion, to do right. That can be repaired, and improved. Drastically improved.

He's always had the will, but he's never had the way.

Let's give him the way.

Next is the eye. The original was small and ineffective. Why not make a bigger one?

Don't be mistaken, these cells aren't actually thinking these things, but they are, as a system, making decisions as they rebuild the dead Winston Gooze into a slightly better version of the dead Winston Gooze.

It takes twenty-five minutes for his body to be spat out into the St. Roma River beneath the Second Street Bridge, but what floats up on the shore is not the same body that went in.

It's stronger, smarter, although still very much dead.

Oh, and look over there—the current has brought the mop this way too. It drifts and bobs among the rest of the flotsam of plastic bags, tangles of fishing wire, and Styrofoam takeout cups currently headed downriver, where it will likely collect along the shores of the Outer Tromaville wastes.

But look, an errant eddy has turned the mop in place, and the head has brushed against the back of Winston's hand. An electrochemical spark jumps from the glowing mophead to Winston's newly toughened flesh.

It's a final goodbye, maybe, a static-zap kiss before the mop continues floating downriver.

But yes, we hold on the hand.

It's still. Dead.

But then it begins to move, and the body heaves, lungs and throat pushing out water and pulling in air. Coughing, spluttering, and grasping for the shore, Winston's body pulls itself out of the river.

It takes a while, with its uncoordinated limbs, but finally the creature formerly known as Winston Gooze is able to stand.

The humanoid creature shivers, then rubs its arms, a thin layer of neonatal slime sloughing off beneath its rough, callused hands. Veins pulse with a faint red-purple bioluminescence. It cracks its knuckles, not like someone waking from a half-hour nap but like something primordial waking from the sleep of eons.

It closes each eye in turn, first its small human eye, then its larger improved eye. An eye that size, as big as a fist, can take in a lot of light and pretty much see in the dark.

The creature looks up, sees the familiar sight of the Second Street Bridge, and realizes that it's close to home.

TEN

"How's Mr. Feets?" Spence Barkabus asked.

"Mr. *Treats* is fine, thank you."

The old bag didn't have to be so rude about Spence misnaming her cat.

The bodega owner applied the final signature and pushed the papers back at Spence. He folded them neatly into quarters, then put them into his inside suit pocket.

"Ah, my pen?" Spence asked.

She handed him the pen.

"And the cap."

She handed him the cap.

"All this traffic out here, you gotta be careful," Spence said, gesturing behind him, though the street was basically empty now except for a few parked cars and some derelicts who'd wandered over from the Strip. It was probably too much, kicking the lady while she was down like this by bringing up the cat, but hey, if you couldn't find joy in your work, it was time to quit, right?

The woman didn't respond.

"I've enjoyed working with you on this transaction. I'd say

we'll rent to you, but..." He smiled. "...the new building probably won't take pets."

No reaction. The broad was giving him nothing to work with.

Oh, well. Now to climb behind the wheel of his badass automobile, parked safely around the corner in that dark alley, and—

Wade was up way too late, but he couldn't sleep. Not only because Winston was gone, stumbling off drunk into the night, but because of the voices coming from down on the street, in front of the bodega.

The man who'd tried to kill Mr. Treats had come back to bother Daisy again.

Wade curled his free hand into a fist.

As you get older, you'll realize sometimes it's just better to do nothing.

Winston was right—there was nothing Wade could do to help Daisy right now. He was just a kid, a twitchy, nervous kid who needed his faux stepdad to come home.

He unclenched his fist and went back to tapping. Tapping and dialing the phone in his other hand, and getting Winston's voicemail, and tapping some more—his sternum, his forehead, his wrist.

But none of the tapping was helping him to self-soothe, and none of his texts to Winston's phone over the last two hours had been marked as read.

True, Winston wasn't really his stepdad, but who else did Wade have? It was late, there was a gangster downstairs shaking down their landlord, and Wade just wanted someone to be here and tell him it was going to be all right. He—

Then he heard another sound—a metallic groan—coming from the fire escape.

"Hello?" Wade said. He looked out the window but couldn't see anything, just the neon glare from the Belgoody Bail Bonds sign across the way and his own reflection in the glass.

He was being silly. They lived on the second floor.

There was nothing out there.

But there it was again, a groan and a clatter this time, like the whole fire escape was about to collapse.

Maybe it was good that Daisy was selling the place. Maybe the whole building was crumbling and dangerous. Maybe it—

Tap tap tap.

There was something out there tapping on the window.

Tap tap tap.

The taps against the glass were timed exactly with Wade's own tapping against his chest.

"Hello?" Wade said again. Then, holding up the phone: "I'm calling the police."

Tap tap tap.

Wade took a step closer and squinted through the glass pane, rippled with time. He thought he could almost see a face out there, but it didn't seem real. It *couldn't* be real—the eyes and mouth were all distorted.

Then the windowpane shuddered as a misshapen hand pressed flat against it, the heat of it fogging the glass.

"Nononono..." Wade whispered.

He was frozen. He should be dialing 911 now, running down the stairs and out onto the street, but he couldn't *move*.

The window was slowly raised in a shower of paint chips. They'd never opened it since they'd moved in. He didn't even think it could be opened, the paint was so thick.

Then a monster pushed its head inside the apartment's living room.

One side of its face was a yawning black hole.

No, not a hole, an *eye*—there was a glowing red pupil floating in all that black—an eye that met Wade's awestruck gaze.

"Hey, buddy," the thing said, then ducked its lumpen, scabrous head forward, trying to squeeze its shoulders through the frame.

Its voice was inhuman, but there was also something familiar about it…

No. No time to think. Wade had to act or he was doomed.

He ran over to the thing, grabbing the first thing he could see—a heavy ceramic ashtray that had been his grandma's.

"Ahhhhhhhhhh!"

It was a scream of pure terror, but also a warcry. This fucking bodybuilding leper wasn't going to home-invade them. Not tonight.

Not after all the shit Wade had been through today.

"Wait!" the creature said, its big eye widening even further.

Wade waited until he was close enough that he couldn't miss, then reeled back and let the ashtray fly.

The monster was already trying to pull its head back out the window before the impact, so as the ashtray connected, squashing its nose, the back of its skull collided with the bottom of the window frame, cracking the wood and shattering the glass.

"Ow!" the creature said, which was a pretty unimpressive thing for a hideously deformed creature crawling out onto a fire escape to say.

Wade watched the monster complete its stumble back through the broken window, flipping over the fire escape railing, and plummeting down to the street below.

There was a crash.

Then Wade called the cops.

Winston's body, which had quadrupled in mass but not size in the last hour, smashed onto the sports car's roof and tore through it as if it was crepe paper.

The windows exploded outward, shards of glass fountaining twenty feet in the air before raining down on his face and into his open mouth.

"God," Winston said, spitting glass. "Ah, shit. Ah, man."

His voice sounded deeper, like a stranger was speaking his own words back to him, right into his ear.

He knew something was different about him, that he'd been in an accident, but Wade had tried to kill him! The look on the boy's face as he'd hurled that ashtray! It was like one of those kids you heard about in true crime shows, the ones that go psycho, boil their pet hamsters into a stew, and kill their parents in their sleep.

Winston needed to have a serious talk with the boy. They needed to get him back in therapy. Maybe some kind of emotional intervention was—

"My car! What the fuck did you do to my car?"

Winston raised his head. The ashtray had smooshed his nose good, but he didn't think he was bleeding.

There was a man yelling at him, upside down. Winston smacked the side of his head and his new eye flipped around in its socket. The man became rightside up.

"Do you know how much that car cost, you dumb motherf—"

Winston stood up, the glass crunching under his feet.

"I'm sorry," he said. "I don't have insurance, but I'm sure we can..."

Then his vision adjusted, seeming to acquire a deeper focus and clearer night vision than he'd ever had, and he realized he recognized the guy now screaming at him from the mouth of the alley.

It was Spence, the Khaki Gang lieutenant who'd tried to kill Mr. Treats.

"You," Spence said now. "You're a..."

While Winston watched, Spence's eyes grew wide. Was he on something? He didn't look so good, sweating, his knees trembling in his khaki pants.

Then his hand dropped to his waistband, produced a pistol, and started firing.

Uh-oh, Winston thought, having the strangest sensation of déjà vu.

Pling, splat, brat brat.

Spence was pretty sure he'd shit his pants, but it was fine—nobody would know. He'd just empty the clip into this... homeless man with mange? ...and then call a tow truck to get home and change into a different pair.

It felt good, to be free to fire his weapon like this. Oh, Spence Barkabus had shot plenty of people before, but there was usually so much buildup to the shooting, and then a faint worry about concealing the crime.

But this—this was refreshing. There was no driving out to the woods to make a guy dig his own grave and then putting two in his skull. No waiting around outside some jabroni's mistress's house for him to leave. Just a guy totaling Spence's car and then the instant, justified gratification of lighting him up.

Only the guy wasn't going down. In fact, he had his scarred junkie arms up in front of his face, like that could protect him.

He'd see about that.

Spence kept firing, taking a couple steps forward to make every shot count.

Bang bang bang click.

From up on the car's collapsed roof, the man, or monster, or monstrous man, dropped his arms from his face.

How could this *be?*

The man looked down at the skin on his hands and forearms in amazement, evidently just as surprised as Spence was.

Had Spence been sold blanks? This was bullshit! But the black market really wasn't what it used to be, with supply-chain shortages and all.

Then the fucked-up-looking guy took two steps off the car's roof, stepping down onto the hood.

Crunch.

Ah, not the engine too!

"I SAID," the guy shouted, loud enough to make Spence's fillings vibrate, "I WAS SORRY!"

Then he screamed, the yell becoming a growl as his larger eye began to glow red and his features contorted in rage.

"Wait, don't—" Spence began, but it was too late. There was a blur of movement and suddenly his hand and pistol were swallowed up in the fist.

The creature yanked. Spence felt a tug, heard the rip of khaki jacket, and...

He looked down and blinked.

His arm had been torn off his body.

He watched as the initial spurt of blood became an oozing drip as his veins and arteries contracted in the chill of the night air.

There was a flash in the alley, then the dull white light of a cell phone.

"Y'all see that shit?" someone said from the entrance to the alley.

"Oh, no!" the creature said, looking back at Spence like this had all been some kind of terrible misunderstanding.

Spence fell backward, the numbness of shock giving way to

the pain of having his fucking arm torn off and then the wooziness of blood loss.

"Oh, shit. Sorry again," the creature said, placing Spence's arm gently down beside him. Then it stomped off down the alley and into the night.

"Hel—" Spence tried, but his voice was too tired.

"Help!" he finally managed.

Above him, behind the fire escape, a face was watching him from an apartment window. Across the way, people called to each other, wondering what was going on.

"It was a fucking bigfoot, I'm telling you! A reptilian bigfoot!" someone screamed from back the way the monster had headed.

There were more footfalls, running down the alley.

"I got it on camera!"

"A demon!"

"A fiend!"

"Those are the same things!"

"Ripped that poor asshole's arm off!"

Spence stared up at the night sky as their shadows ran by, his view obscured by the tangle of cable wires, fire escapes, and chimney smoke, and waited for one of these voices to belong to an onlooker willing to stop and help. But none of them did.

Then, finally, someone came to his side and knelt.

"You," Spence said, looking up as the bodega lady stared down at him. She was holding the fucking cat in one arm.

"Please," he moaned.

She swatted Spence's hand—his *only* hand—away as he reached up for her, then removed the sales agreement from his jacket pocket and pressed it into her housecoat.

"Call my dad," Spence pleaded.

Then, mercifully, he fell unconscious.

NOBODY ANGRY MOBS LIKE TROMAVILLE ANGRY MOBS

Really. No town in America, in the world for that matter, can raise an alarm, pass the torches, and resolve itself into a crowd hungry for street justice fiercer and faster than St. Roma's Village, New Jersey.

It's a major point of civic pride for us.

It's true—we're really good at it.

And to paraphrase Muhammad Ali, it ain't bragging if it's true.

The Que-Capulet Rampage of '86? The Squirrel Day Stampede of '02? I could keep going. All classics.

Oh, you thought "pass the torches" was a euphemism? A bit of hyperbole for comedic effect?

Well, look over there, down where the Strip meets Rochon Way. Only seconds ago those people on the corner watched a video of the monster, saw what it did to Spence's arm, and now one of them's unloading two-by-fours and accelerant-soaked rags from his car.

And that guy in the stained undershirt? Look at the size of the knife he's just produced from his sweatpants. He got out of bed for this!

And that woman has got one of those chains with the spiked ball on the end like in a samurai movie.

And that group of youths all have baseball bats. What are they doing up this late? Where are their parents?!

And that beat cop has his hands outstretched and is telling the crowd to calm down, that it's just one of their neighbors high on angel dust—but look, someone's showing him the video and now he's calling in backup, getting the shotgun from his squad car, and joining the mob as they march down the Strip.

They want justice. They want blood!

They've... they've almost got the bastard cornered! The dogs are barking—they're on his scent!

Don't let him get away! Someone in the crowd just told me he ate a baby! We can't let this happen! THE MONSTER DIES TONIGHT!

Oh, wait.

I forgot that the monster is actually the biohazard-accident-resurrected, gene-spliced, and deformed Winston Gooze.

He's the hero of this story.

This is all wrong. Why are we marching?

We're supposed to be on his side!

Wait, mob, wait up. Please, stop, don't go after him.

Oh, well. They're already gone. And they don't seem in a mood to listen to me anyway.

But yeah, let me use my narrator vision, my omniscience, to check on Winston and see how he's faring.

Okay, patience. Just one sec. Lemme find him.

Ah, there he is.

Yeah, he's got a pretty decent headstart on the mob. And he's fast, too. Even though he's confused, even though he's scared, and even though he's got such a low center of gravity, he's still pretty fast.

Yep, he's reached the outskirts of the township now. And now he's going to have to decide.

He's looking south, toward the stretch of scorched earth that most Tromavillians refer to as the Wastelands or Outer Tromaville. Beyond that, things get even more terrifying as you enter New Brunswick. So hopefully he doesn't turn that way.

Oh no, good job, Winston—he's headed west, into the cover of the trees. Yes, he's decided to take cover in the patch of woodland that borders the village in that direction.

The mob's close behind, beginning to split so its tendrils can explore different cross-streets and alleyways before they reach the woods. It's grown, too—from this high up, the torches look like a clump of tangled Christmas lights—and its chants, becoming more specific and complex, have evolved into full-fledged songs as the hivemind has tried to come up with more words that rhyme with *mutant*.

But at least Winston's ahead of them.

I mean, it's still dark out, and the first wave of the mob has already begun searching the forest, their flashlights and torches thrust under fallen trees and over pine-carpeted clearings, and Winston looks really frightened and alone.

But he'll probably be fine while we change perspectives and check in with some other characters.

Probably.

ELEVEN

There were times, times when they were alone, when Garbinger would show affection. Sometimes he'd even slip and tell Kissy he loved her, call her pet names.

This was not one of those times.

And they were not alone.

"Thank you, Wally," Garbinger said as the faceless servant rolled in a replacement TV cart.

There was no way that one's name was Wally.

Garbinger was handed the new remote and clicked the power on.

The security-camera footage returned, playing from the beginning.

Bob Garbinger breathed in through his mouth, out through his nose, his respiration near-silent. He was calm, too calm, and Kissy, who hadn't even done anything wrong and hated Fritz Garbinger, was suddenly worried for the little brother.

On screen, the three of them watched as J.J. Doherty, the saboteur, fled into the night. They continued to watch as the janitor begged for his life, only to be shot in the face, and then the feed cut to a different camera to show the man in the chicken mask dumping the body down a concrete well.

The footage ended, then looped back to the beginning.

"When," Garbinger, Bob, began, then cleared his throat. "When I have you handle things, my beloved baby brother, my basis of assumption is that you'll not then decide to..."

Big breath.

"...fuck the entire goat!" he exploded, grabbing Fritz by his jacket collar and propelling him toward the screen. "Do you see what you *did*?"

"I... I did what you asked!"

"How *dare* you sass him!" Kissy hissed. She wanted to be a part of this. Yelling at Fritz was something they could do together, to bond as a couple.

But Bob wasn't seeing it that way.

He released Fritz and whirled on Kissy.

"And you!"

"Me?"

"You had one of the anarchists right in your hands and you let him go!"

Kissy was genuinely confused. "I never did!"

But Bob Garbinger was nothing if not prepared. He clicked a button on the remote and the image on screen changed.

It now played a video taken at Mammon Hall the previous night and showed Kissy walking the janitor to the service door moments before she'd locked him out on the street.

"But..."

He clicked again. Now the screen displayed a freeze-frame from the surveillance footage showing the same janitor reaching up, extending his hand to J.J. Doherty, who— No, that couldn't be...

"The betrayer and the janitor are obviously in cahoots!" Garbinger said.

The realization made Kissy's knees weak.

They'd been snowed. Played. That loser may not have even been a loser. Probably wasn't even sick. He was probably some cunning double agent on a mission of corporate espionage, sent to infiltrate the awards dinner. Sure, he hadn't *seemed* like a cunning double agent, but...

Garbinger continued his rant:

"They are out there, possibly more of them than these two, making mayhem against us, working out their fucked-up resentments and anti-capitalist agendas the only way they can: *dirty shenanigans.*"

Kissy held her hand over her mouth. "A conspiracy," she whispered.

"And as if all of that weren't enough, some mighty *freak* made a complete hash out of a dear friend—well, the son of a friend, anyway."

Click. He advanced the screen to the next section of his presentation, which she'd already seen in that morning's status report—a fragment of phone footage, filmed in portrait mode, showing a muscular, bestial man standing over a pleading youth clad in khaki, holding his victim's severed arm in one hand.

The youth, she realized, was Spence Barkabus.

This... this couldn't be good. What was bad for Barkabus was bad for BTH, bad for Robert Garbinger, and, by extension, bad for everyone in the room.

Garbinger's fury seemed spent. He ignored Kissy and Fritz now and focused entirely on the TV footage, pausing it, slowing it, running his hands over the phosphorescent veins ringing the creature's bulging eye.

"So mighty," he said in a soft voice, and she understood. Bob Garbinger was attracted to power—more, she suspected, than he was attracted to Kissy, even on her best days.

"I'm told the young man survived," she said. "Just some stitches, really."

Garbinger shook his head.

"You miss the point," he said, and clicked the remote again. A third and final still image appeared showing two photos side by side, a shot taken at last night's awards ceremony next to a picture from outside the factory.

The tutu.

"The janitor and the freak are one and the same, and somehow..." Garbinger said. He looked over to Fritz, his brother's pale, unappealing mouth hanging agape. "And somehow, because of how you handled things, *we* made it so."

"Made?" Fritz said, pulling a few strands of ratty black hair off his tongue.

"A mutation? An infection? An... evolution?" Garbinger asked, stepping closer to the TV, the light of the grainy images playing across his face. Then, without warning, he shoved the cart over and the TV crashed to the floor.

The servant, "Wally," made a disappointed, exasperated sound.

"Both of you, with me," Garbinger snapped and stalked through his office door, deeper into Chüdhaven.

Both of them? If Fritz was about to be disciplined, surely Kissy wouldn't face nearly the same wrath?

"W-where are we going?" Kissy asked nervously.

"Below," was all Bob Garbinger said, but it was enough.

Kissy knew.

TWELVE

At some point during the night, exhaustion had overwhelmed Winston's fear and sadness.

Wade hadn't recognized him! Had thrown an ashtray at his head! And then suddenly everyone in Tromaville had wanted to kill him!

After the transformation his body had gone through, he'd needed to rest and had fallen asleep in the woods outside Tromaville. But now the sun was up, a gray and yellow dawn sky was visible through the trees, and somehow he was moving…

He blinked, first his small eye, then his wide-angle, take-it-all-in, red-tinted big eye.

From flat on his back, he watched as the treetops above him waved. He was lying on top of something, a sled or travois, and being dragged. But he couldn't bring himself to care who was dragging him or where he was being dragged to.

Maybe the villagers had found him. Maybe he was about to be burned at the stake. Whatever.

In his old life Winston had been someone who frequently hit the Snooze button.

He wanted to go back to sleep, so he did.

He awoke possibly minutes, possibly hours later to the smell of meat being cooked over an open flame.

His stomach gurgled and he turned onto his side.

He'd been tucked in. A dirty blanket that smelled of farts and bleach (at least, he hoped it was bleach) had been pulled up snug around his neck.

"There he is!" a man's voice said.

Winston trained his big eye on a crackling fire, appraising the stringy meat being cooked over the flames, then on the man who was turning the skewers.

"I thought you'd want a breakfast," the man said. He had a white beard, kind eyes, and a few deep sores and pockmarks that looked like they might have been caused by late-stage syphilis.

Winston pulled down the blanket and started to sit up.

The man took a skewer from over the fire and offered it to him.

Its eyes had ruptured in the heat, then shriveled with the smoke, but its long, curved teeth and charred black ears revealed it unmistakably to be a rat.

Winston's stomach rumbled again. The rat smelled good, like hickory-smoked potato chips, but still he hesitated to reach for the stick.

"Ah. An aristocrat, is he?" the old man said, then put three greasy fingers around the rat's head and twisted it from its body, then pushed the now-headless rotisserie rat back at Winston, smiled, and waited.

Winston looked down. The rat still had its tail.

"Thank you," he mumbled, then nibbled a little at its belly, trying to pretend he was eating a chicken leg.

As he ate, he looked around at the man's campsite. There was a rusted-out car, the trunk seemingly used as an armoire; a laundry line; two tents, constructed from different kinds of tarps; and shopping carts used for both storage and furniture.

"Nice, right?"

Winston nodded.

"I found ya in yonder spooky woods, rode hard 'n' put away wet," the old man said.

Winston understood most of those words, but not in that order. He tried some more rat.

"So... what's the issue, chief?"

"I..." Winston recalled the events of the previous day, and oddly enough it wasn't the nighttime events he remembered first. "I'm dying. The doctor says maybe a year."

The man nodded, inspecting Winston's face.

"Dyin'? Dyin', he said? Why didn't you say so, man? Stand by for the parade!"

What?

"This is confetti! This is ticker tape!" The man made jazz hands. "Here comes the big brass marching band, boop-da-doop!" He made a trumpet sound and pretended to play. "We got jugglers and ponies for ya, and ice cream, and them skinny high-kickin' girls." He kicked his feet. "And a miniature train you can ride in circles while eatin' cotton candy until your heart bursts with joy, because, folks..." He smiled, a grin that contained fewer teeth Winston thought it should. "He is dyin'!"

"Uhhh..." Winston had no idea what was going on, why this man was being so mean.

"Well, big whoop. They give you a year? Big ol' can-suck-its-own-dick whoop!"

Winston cleared his throat and set down his rat, which he had been growing a taste for but now didn't want.

Then the old man hit himself with his fist, hard, on the side of his head.

"Apologies, apologies," he said. Then, to himself: "Sarcasm is just anger sneaking in the back door."

He extended his hand.

"Let's start again. I'm Guthrie Stockins."

They shook. Winston still wasn't sure what the hell was happening.

"Winston," he said.

"What I meant, Mr. Winston, is we're all of us dying." He gestured at the camp around them and the woods beyond. "You know this used to be a preserve? Not like a marmalade, like an actual biodome."

Winston looked around them.

"Well, an *outdoors* biodome. It was chock full of critters, before that fart factory showed up. Now there's not one swimming fish left in the river or cricks, air like pancake batter, givin' all the kids assma, and the nervous red warbler is basically extinct."

"Okay," Winston said, unsure of the proper response to that.

"So you dying ain't special, guy."

"Well... *that* doesn't make me feel any better."

"It's not mean ta. But thing is, it's never too late. What's dead sometimes ain't all the way dead." The old man looked Winston up and down, seeming like he knew something that Winston couldn't quite grasp. "Even when it *was* dead."

"You think so, huh?"

"Sure. Look at me. I was a fancy doctor. Big salary, house—important, right? Next thing I know, policemen are holding me down, saying I bit somebody during a budget meeting."

This seemed plausible to Winston.

"While I was in that white room, lonesome as hell, I thought, 'Guthrie, you stepped in it with both feet this time.' But look how things turned out for me!"

Winston looked. Guthrie Stockins had built himself a

girlfriend out of papier-mâché and given her genitalia by turning a rubber kitchen glove inside out.

"See? You never know how the worm will turn. Question is, whatcha going to do with your life in the meantime?"

He stared Winston in the eye—the human one—and waited for an answer.

"Well, what do you want?"

"I want my boy." Winston caught a glimpse of his own reflection in a hubcap. He hadn't really had a chance to look yet, but he knew it was bad. "But he thinks I'm a monster."

"Well, are you a monster?"

It was a good question. Yeah, he seemed a little—he looked down at his arms—veinier than he'd been yesterday, but he was still the same Winston—or at least, mentally he still felt like the same Winston.

"No," he said, looking up at the old man. "No, I'm not a monster."

"Then you go to him. You go to your boy and show him your good heart. Let nothing waylay ya, delay ya, or stand in your path."

Winston got up from the sled and let the dirty blanket pool around him.

He'd expected to be shaky on his feet—his new feet, with their scabby, burned skin and flecks of fused fabric—but there was no soreness, no unsteadiness. In fact, he felt better than he had in years. He didn't have that dry-mouthed, world-was-squeezing-him-to-death feeling he'd woken up with every day since Shelly had died.

Winston Gooze felt... good.

And that was when he saw it, resting atop a pillow of yellowed newspaper and massage-parlor flyers, tucked in like it was a baby.

"Is that yours?" Guthrie asked.

Winston approached and the head of the mop began to pulse with an emerald-green glow, the trash stuck to its head curling black and smoking as it caught fire.

"I found it in yonder crick," Guthrie said. "Must've washed down from the big river."

Winston reached out for the mop, but Guthrie picked it up first, brandishing it like it was some mythical weapon from a forgotten time.

"A formidable item," he said. "Do you know how to use it?"

Did Winston know how to use it? He thought of all the hours, the years he'd spent using it, no spill tricky enough to shake him.

"Uh... for mopping?" he said.

But then he looked at the end of the mop, which had calcified into a heavy, sharp stone that glowed faintly in the morning light.

No, this wasn't his mop anymore, and maybe he didn't know how to use it, but it looked like this wise old man was about to show him.

Guthrie Stockins raised the head of the mop and widened his stance, and Winston took careful note of the old man's movements, was ready to learn from him.

Then Guthrie slid his hands into a new position along the wooden shaft. Winston took note of this as well: proper form.

And then Guthrie just waved the end of the mop around in the air, flailing with no discernible finesse or technique, just a funny-smelling old guy waving a piece of wood around, trying to smash an invisible piñata.

Winston watched him for another minute, nodding, until Guthrie, panting, handed the mop over to him.

He set the pole down his back, where it seemed to fit perfectly along the contours of his shoulder muscles and the swell of his buttocks, held in place by the fabric of his skin-costume.

"Just remember," Guthrie said, holding up a hand to stop

Winston before he could dash off into the morning light. "Those given much will of them have much demanded."

"You mean me, right?" Winston asked.

"Just in general, kinda. But sure, you too."

"Ah."

"With great power, et cetera."

"Say no more."

And with these baffling life lessons and nonsensical words of encouragement, Winston Gooze set off for home.

Guthrie Stockins watched his new pal go and he muttered, "Gosh, he is one ugly bastard though."

THIRTEEN

"How?" Robert Garbinger demanded, the corner of his upper lip trembling.

It was nice, for Fritz at least, to have his older brother's fury turned toward someone else for a change.

The two techs before them trembled. It was kept cold down here, since all the computers and research equipment ran hot, but it wasn't the chill in the air making the two scientists in front of them shake. One of them—either Kupp or Sawser, Fritz could never remember which was which—was sweating through his white coat.

Robert made his question more specific to help them along.

"*How* did this happen?"

"We have..." one of them started.

The other one finished: "A theory."

Fritz, his brother, and his brother's keeper, Kissy, followed as the two scientists led them through a curved stone hallway.

Fritz's bad leg ached, but he kept pumping, trying to keep up with the two of them and stay in formation. It wasn't easy. He wasn't a fast man.

It had been a long elevator ride down to the secret lab

underneath Chüdhaven. Fritz and Kissy had both been reprimanded, up above in Robert's office, but had said nothing to each other on the ride down. This wasn't a "strange bedfellows" situation; Fritz hated the woman and, if asked, he was sure she'd say the same about him. He spit a strand of hair from his face as he walked.

They arrived at the lab some moments later, hair plastered to Fritz's face. The computer monitors all around them showed different angles of the freak in the tutu.

"Freak" was not a word Fritz used lightly. Not when dealing with the Killer Nutz, or massaging his knee and calf after a long day standing, and especially not when looking in the mirror. He'd been called a freak too many times by his brother to ever want to use that word to describe others.

But now, looking at the grainy cell-phone footage of the monster, enlarged and distorted and vector-mapped by computer programs, the word seemed appropriate.

"Waste elements from the new bio-inductor line contain traces of..." Then the nerd on the left, Kupp or Sawser, said a word Fritz couldn't quite grasp. It had too many syllables to even try, and anyway it was too distracting in here with so many clicking, buzzing machines. "Which, among other things, can cause spontaneous cartilaginous growths and certain forms of..." And then the printer next to Kissy spewed out a torrent of data on one unbroken sheaf of paper and Fritz got distracted again.

When he turned back, Robert was nodding. "Obviously, of course. Tell me something I don't know."

"Which is why we, heh, needed to use the, uh, *creative disposal* site," the tech on the right said, making quotes in the air with his fingers. "We believe that the subject," he went on, pointing at the nearest screen, "possesses an extremely rare genetic marker, which in his case triggered some kind of inversion of the typical effects."

"Hypocellular augmentation, muscle accretion, and as you see here," the other tech said, pointing at the zoomed-in outline of a veiny section of the freak's skin.

"Girthening," Robert finished for him, and both geeks nodded. He caressed the nearest monitor and said in a low voice, "You're a very special boy, aren't you?"

Kissy, Fritz, and the two scientists stood awkwardly, unsure if they should continue or if they'd been dismissed, as Robert Garbinger admired the creature on screen.

Then he turned to them.

"Find him and bring him to me."

Robert looked to Kissy first, who opened her mouth, but was clearly at a loss for ideas.

Good, because Fritz had one.

"He has a kid," he said.

Robert looked at him, his expression unreadable, but Fritz had learned long ago that if his brother looked at him with anything other than undisguised disgust, he should keep talking.

"I checked his employee file," he continued. "We can use the boy as bait. We—"

"Your little traps and schemes are amusing," Kissy interrupted, "but this isn't the time for—"

Robert held a finger up, silencing her, and Fritz relished the moment. For him to be chosen over the kangaroo-munching—

"When you were in the crib, brother," Robert started, "Mother would always scold me. She'd say, 'Stop trying to smother the baby with drycleaning plastic!' And many days I've resented her for that." Then he smiled. "But not today! Today I am *proud* of you, Fritz. It's a good plan."

Fritz didn't say anything, only nodded as Robert leaned in and kissed him on the head.

His brother turned back to the techs, who in the meantime

had busied themselves with pretending to read the printout. "If you had the original genetic sample," Robert said, snapping them to attention, "could you recreate the mutation?"

"We... well, there's a risk," one of them said. "Dangerous imperfections, so many variables—it could be lethal to the subject."

"We would need time and—" the other one said.

"Then get it started," Robert said, and turned to leave the chill of the lab.

"Immediately," Kissy added, always wanting the last word.

Fritz smiled.

It was time to gather the Nutz and get the bait.

FOURTEEN

Wade shuddered, twitched, and tapped.

He was sitting cross-legged on the floor in front of the TV, watching the news, his baseball bat lying beside him.

He was ready in case *it* tried to come back.

He'd called the police last night, but they'd never come. The whole force had been busy helping the mob.

"At this time, police have no leads as to the identity of the rampaging maniac," the male anchor, Rick Feet, said.

Then his co-anchor, C.J. Doons, slid into shot to correct him: "*Alleged* maniac. Due process, Rick."

Rick Feet frowned at her, then continued: "Anyone who may have encountered the *beastly* criminal should call the number on the screen."

A number flashed up—again—and this time Wade was ready and scribbled it down on a piece of junk mail. Then he looked over at the landline phone.

He *had* seen the creature. It was possible he'd had a closer look at it than anyone who'd been interviewed on the news, any of the drunks who'd been part of the mob last night and had come home empty-handed.

He stood up, grabbed the handset, and dialed the number. In his ear, the line rang.

On TV, they went back to playing amateur footage of the creature. Wade went over and turned down the volume.

"Aberrant crimes tip line."

"H-hello. I want to rep—"

"Please hold."

Soft jazz music began playing on the other end of the line.

On the TV, the chyron now read "Monster Marauder," with phone and surveillance footage playing.

None of these videos could capture how vile the monster had been, though—how it had dripped, how the red-ringed pupil at the center of its giant black eye had stared into Wade's soul.

How it had stared at him like it knew him.

How it had said, "Hey, buddy."

But then there was a snippet of video footage the news hadn't played yet, or at least one Wade hadn't seen before.

It was a black-and-white, high-angle shot of the monster out behind one of the businesses on the Strip. The quality was poor, but it let Wade get a better look at how the creature was dressed.

"Thank you for holding. How may I—"

Wade hung up and turned the volume back up as the footage looped again.

"It is still unclear what we here in Tromaville are dealing with," Rick Feet was saying. "Could this be a bio-weapon? Could it be MS-13? Might this be some kind of mutated wildlife on its hind legs? It's impossible to say."

But it wasn't impossible for Wade to say, because in the footage he could see that the creature was wearing a tutu.

"Sorry to interrupt your fearmongering, Rick," C.J. Doons broke in, "but there's developing news. Good lord, y'all, we have confirmed reports that several armed individuals have taken hostages at the Miss Meat Lunchatorium on Main and Charles."

Rick Feet slid back into shot, holding his earpiece.

"Formerly Mr. Meat. Thanks, C.J. Let's go there live."

But Wade was having trouble caring about the unfolding hostage situation. They happened all the time.

It wasn't every day that Wade realized he was living with a monster in a tutu.

Fun new bod! Same Great Grub!

Oh, Mr. Meat. What have they done to you?

They'd replaced the fast-food mascot. Unnaturally altered him. They'd put lipstick on the anthropomorphic burger and added a beauty mark. And tits.

That wasn't the anthropomorphic burger Brock Kirkman had grown up with! That wasn't his childhood! That was a woman burger! A gynoburger!

Brock stared up at the sign and fumed. "Fun new bod." What was fun about it? The emasculation of the world was not fun. The feminization of the American nation was not some goddamn *joke.*

To be clear, what Brock and his friends were doing in this fast-food joint wasn't about a culture war.

Yes, their culture was being taken from them, but a culture war wasn't a real war.

Brock Kirkman wanted to start a real war.

He wanted to be heard.

He had a bullhorn in one hand and an Uzi in the other.

Smoke now curled from the weapon, the sharp odor of cordite mixing with the scents of fryer oil, sweat, and perforated bowels.

"Oh god, he shot him!" the cook screamed, crouching over the manager, his boss's blood leaking between his fingers.

Oh, the manager had been shot, all right—gutshot, with a three-round burst from Brock's Uzi.

"Help me! Push down, get pressure. Hold on!" the cashier said, on his knees beside the cook.

Brock ignored the screams of the employees. They wouldn't try anything now. Not in this panic, after they'd seen what happened to would-be heroes. The manager hadn't listened, and now he was going to pay with his life as he bled out on the floor.

Brock now had a moment to speak to his men. To speak to the world, now that the press had started to gather outside.

The bullhorn squawked as he depressed the trigger.

"We are the Mad Lads! We are angry! You will hear our grievances!"

Pugg, Chuck, and Teddy gave the Mad Lads salute, a variation on the Nasty Boys' version but with their own little twist. The four of them were *not* Nasty Boys anymore. They'd needed a group of their own, something more extreme, so they'd splintered off.

"Youse guys don't move a muscle," Pugg said, threatening the four patrons they'd taken hostage, which included a kid in a helmet, two older sluts in polka-dot blouses, and a blind chick in a pantsuit.

"Our once-great western society," Brock continued into the megaphone, "has been enfeebled by estroginal thinking and moral turpitude, but no longer! Today we serve notice! Today we rise!"

"Rise! Rise! Rise!" the rest of the Lads began to chant.

Outside, there was the sound of the pigs getting back on their own megaphone. Normally Brock had tremendous respect for the police, but these cops were in his way, so today they were pigs.

He could see them through the front window—four squad cars, a police line set up, and a plainclothes pig on the handset.

"So, fellas," the pig with the handset said now. "I do understand that you're angry, but what is it you want, exactly? What's your issue with this establishment?"

"He doesn't get it!" Teddy whined. "Let's shoot another one, Brock."

That was why Teddy didn't get a gun, just a dull machete. Brock didn't trust him.

He shook his head—no, he wasn't going to shoot another one. There would be plenty of time for shooting. Right now, they needed to spread their message.

He opened the door and leaned out, trying to keep his body under cover in case they had snipers set up already.

"The change of mascot symbolizes the intellectual dishonesty we abhor!" he yelled into the bullhorn. "It has always been, and should remain, *Mister* Meat!"

"But it's the same great grub!" the detective behind the police line said into his mic.

That was it. Brock couldn't take it.

Even the cops were on the side of this agenda.

He aimed his Uzi out the door, at the line of cop cars, and fired.

Winston heard the gunfire ring out from the next block over, but he didn't stop.

He just pulled the blanket up around his face and kept walking.

He'd found the blanket on his way into town. It didn't smell great, but it was better than the one under which he'd woken up an hour ago, in Guthrie's camp. More importantly, it hid his face from the world. He could blend in and look like every other street person navigating the alleys of Tromaville.

He stopped. He was at a crossroads.

Literally.

The alley to the left would take him home, to Wade, and the alley to the right would bring him to the sound of gunfire, screams, and amplified voices.

He looked left. Nobody on the street, not even in front of the bodega. If he craned his neck, he might even see Wade at the window, pacing, worried about him.

Then he looked right, his big eye zooming in. There was something going on at the Miss Meat Lunchatorium. A crowd was gathered there behind a police line.

Let nothing waylay ya, delay ya, or stand in your path.

Winston shook his head. Should he even be listening to Guthrie's advice? The old man *had* fed him rat.

"Don't shoot! My son is in there!" a woman cried out.

There was another burst of gunfire.

"Somebody please!"

Winston listened to the mother's cries.

Then there were more gunshots.

He remembered how Spence's bullets had tickled last night. How they'd been absorbed into his skin, like ballistic jelly, then been pushed out, his flesh instantly knitting itself back together.

"Someone has to *do something*!" the woman yelled.

He looked left one more time. There was a shadow there, in the apartment window.

What would Wade want him to do?

Winston let the blanket drop away, feeling goosebumps form on his hideously deformed skin in the cool air, and ran off down the alley on the right, toward the sound of danger.

He was going to *do something*.

"Grievance number three," Brock said into the bullhorn. "Anti-Anglo media tyranny! Grievance number four: the fallacy of ethnonomics!"

"We demand to be taken seriously!" Teddy yelled, interrupting Brock's groove.

"Grievance number five: uh… Hold on, my own handwriting, I swear…"

Pugg hooted, pushing the Mad Lads flag against the front window, though the effect was lost somewhat since the glass was covered with advertisements for the new Miss-tery Value Meal.

"Can you idiots shut the fuck up? I'm trying to read here," Brock said, but his men ignored him. They were overexcited now that they had hostages they could terrorize.

Chuck stood by the blind chick and poked her with the end of his scattergun, throwing hand signals the mainstream media had deemed verboten.

"Are you triggered?" he asked.

"I can't see what you're doing," she said. "I'm blind."

He kept waving the "OK" symbol in her face.

"Yeah, but are you triggered?"

This was too much activity. Brock couldn't remember where he was in his list of grievances. Had he read the part about ethics in games journalism yet? He looked down at his list, blinked, and considered starting over, just to make sure all of them were heard.

That was when the blind chick yelled the worst thing you could say to a Nasty Boy or a Mad Lad:

"Why don't you shitheads get a life?"

Brock looked back into the restaurant. Each of the Lads stopped what they were doing and looked back at him. Pugg, Chuck, and Teddy didn't speak, but their eyes all said the same thing—Brock was their leader—and they were right. He had to deal with the blind chick. They couldn't let that kind of insult slide.

They *had* lives. What did she think all these grievances were? All the hours of podcast research and dummy social media accounts? So much of their time dedicated to the cause, and this… this *gyno* had the temerity to tell them to get lives?

Brock laid down the bullhorn and lifted up his Uzi. He would need a free hand for this.

At her table, the blind chick looked around with unseeing eyes, gripping her cane and tilting her head like she was trying to hear what was happening.

"Shitheads?" he said quietly. "Did you just call us shitheads?"

"Leave her alone," one of the broads in polka dots said, but she piped down as Brock waved the Uzi in her direction, looking down at the restaurant's red and white vinyl tiling.

"Whatcha think, boys?" he said, looking over to the rest of the Lads.

"I never cornholed me a—"

The blind woman didn't let him finish. She tossed her drink up in the air, and lime soda and ice pelted Brock Kirkman in the face.

He wiped the soda from his eyes and leveled the Uzi against her left eye.

Never mind. This was no time for cornholing.

"You *never* splash a Lad!" he yelled, then started to squeeze the trigger.

It was a shame her eyes didn't work and she wouldn't see the muzzle flash that would end her life.

Suddenly, there was a tremendous crash at the back of the burger joint. Insulation and fiberglass dust rained down on the Mad Lads and their hostages.

Brock whirled round to face the counter and the kitchen beyond.

"It's gotta be the cops!" Pugg yelled. "They're breaking in the back!" At his feet, the fry cook and the cashier were still crying over the bleeding manager.

How had SWAT gotten here already? It wasn't *fair.* Brock hadn't gotten to read all of his grievances yet.

But no, it couldn't be SWAT. There was no smoke, no *ting-ting-ting* of flashbang grenades being tossed into the dining room, no walkie-talkie chatter or yelled demands to drop their weapons and put their hands on their heads. And Brock would know, he'd been the subject of a raid or two, in his time with the Nasty Boys.

"Watch them," he said to the rest of the Lads. "And no killing. Not yet."

He ducked under the counter, then through the doorway into the kitchen. Outside, he could still hear the chatter of the crowd and the whispered orders of the cops. For some reason, they all sounded confused.

"Whoever's back there, come on out," Brock said, pointing the Uzi at the floor, then turning toward the dark hallway that led out the back of the restaurant.

A shape moved somewhere in front of him.

Then it stepped forward, backlit by the daylight streaming in through the demolished door. Parts of it seemed to be glowing.

Brock stumbled back into the kitchen.

"What the fuck *are you*?" he screamed.

"Just some dude," the shape said. "Dude with a mop."

It was then that Brock realized what he was looking at. The monster. The one from the news that had torn that Khaki guy's arm off.

Well, that wouldn't be happening to Brock Kirkman. He was a Mad Lad, not some Khaki cuck.

He raised the Uzi and pulled the trigger.

Brakabrakabraka—

Hostages screamed and his fellow Lads hooted, but the instant the burst was through and it was time to reload, the monstrous shape ran forward, swinging its weapon—a *mop?*—the second it cleared the doorway.

There was an emerald-green flash in front of Brock's face.

At first, it seemed like the freak had missed, but then he heard the sizzle and smelled the burning fat of his own cheek meat.

There was a cool, wet breeze on his neck, spreading to his chest.

Brock looked into the creature's eyes, one human, one inhuman. Its large brow was furrowed. Then its expression softened as it admired its work. And then it smiled.

Brock stumbled back.

He tried to say something, then tasted the sweat on his neck—and realized he was tasting it with the top of his tongue as it lolled down, his bottom jaw no longer there to support it.

"Oh, fuck!" Pugg yelled, then vomited onto the manager. The cashier and the cook sobbed and dove out of the way.

Brock Kirkman turned to steady himself, then looked down in the fryer basket, where his jaw was floating, turning a nice golden brown.

Same Great Grub!

Before he lost consciousness, Brock heard the rest of the Mad Lads yell, "Get him!"

At least his death would be avenged.

Winston Gooze was not a violent person.

He enjoyed heavy metal music, but he was that guy at shows who would pull kids out of the pit if they were getting hurt, urge them to take a break, drink some water, not throw so many elbows.

Horror movies and video games were okay, but the sight of blood in the real world made Winston feel woozy, even nauseous.

But that had been the old Winston.

The new Winston had just jammed a gun against a man's knees until both his legs broke backwards, and was now burning off his face by rubbing his face back and forth across the textured expanse of a charbroil cooktop.

He stopped shaving off the man's facial features when a machete dug deep into his shoulder.

It barely hurt, but still he turned to face his attacker, a big man wearing war paint.

"Hey. Uh, hey, freak," the man said. "Stop that."

He'd been unable to dig the machete back out of Winston's shoulder, so was now unarmed.

The old, non-violent Winston had never worked a milkshake machine before, but the new Winston found he was quite a natural at making milkshakes, especially once he'd gotten the top of the man's skull off, liquefying his brain and optic nerves into a slurry to make room for all the *really* good mix-ins.

With Milkshake Guy taken care of, Winston turned, his big eye seeking out the last threat in the restaurant.

It was instinctual. Each of the other people—the crying, scared, innocent people—in the Miss Meat seemed to be ringed with a faint aura of light, but the last gang member, the one waving the flag like this was the finale of *Les Mis*, glowed a white-hot red.

It was as if Winston was seeing the hatred and malice inside the man, like his new eye and regrown brain were able to pinpoint and highlight the badness in people.

He felt crazed with bloodlust, capable of doing hideous things to a human body, tying it up in knots and exsanguinating a person to leave it in a shivering, bloody, sharting heap. But he wasn't a monster. He had some level of control. There was some innate force, like a buzzing behind his eyes, telling him when it was okay to avenge.

It was a sensation like a... like a buzzing behind his eyes.

The hostage-taker with the flag banged on the window, trying to alert the police, to yell for help in his final moments.

Winston turned his intestines into an art project, getting at them the quickest way he knew how: through the back door.

When it was all over, the hostages' cries subsiding into sniffles, there was total quiet and the pulsing buzz between Winston's melted ears slowed.

He looked at his wrist. Was that a new bracelet? A scrunchie? When had he...?

Oh. It was an anus and part of a rectum.

"Mr. Monster?" the woman beside him clutching her purse said in a quavering voice.

Winston had a weird double-vision thing going on where he could see the dining room, the floor, and his crotch all at the same time. And then he realized what the woman was trying to tell him: his big eye had popped out sometime during the melee and was now dangling against his cheek.

It popped back in easily, no problem.

He breathed, admiring his work.

Peace reigned once more in the Miss Meat Lunchatorium.

After a few moments of silence, the blind woman asked, "What happened?"

"I've got movement at the door!" a lieutenant beside Detective Lee Swofford said.

"It's the hostages! Hold your fire!" Swofford yelled back.

It *was* the hostages. All of them, all moving out under their own power, except for one, who was holding his stomach while being carried by two employees in hairnets.

The crowd began to cheer. A happy ending, and they didn't get many of those, not these days, not on Chief Wormer's force, where half the time Swofford felt more like private security for BTH than a real cop.

But there was something wrong with this happy ending.

Swofford didn't lower his sidearm and instead kept it trained on the door.

Where were the internet geeks? The guys with the surplus fatigues and too many patches on their jackets? Guys that fanatical didn't just change their minds and give up.

And what about that blur of motion they'd spotted, breaking the police cordon and running around the back of the restaurant?

And all those bloodcurdling screams?

"Oh, shit. It's the monster!" a blue shirt further down the line yelled. Swofford looked.

The figure looked just like the thing they'd seen in their briefing, but it turned out that the shakycam bystander footage and artist's renderings couldn't do the creature justice.

This was one ugly mother.

Swofford drew a bead on the creature. He was one of the best marksmen in his class at the academy, and he'd only gotten better over the years. He squinted, lined up his sights. He was going to put one right between that steroidal little bastard's eyes. But then one of the employees, the guy in the oil-stained apron, dove into the way, waving his hands.

"Don't shoot!" the fry cook yelled. "This little fucking weirdo saved us! He's a hero!"

Lee holstered his weapon, the rest of the hostages running back to join the cook, forming a semicircle human shield around the slimy bodybuilder.

Well, I'll be damned.

A monster hero. In Tromaville. Who'da thunk?

The hero dashed off, arms over his head, pursued by the press and his adoring public.

THE MEDIA LOVES A LOVABLE FREAK

You ever notice that?

A guy like Toxie here can be neck-deep in gore, but if he's got just the right style, says just the right things, and has a look that could be translated to a Saturday-morning cartoon, then he's liable to qualify for Lovable Freak status—which, to media outlets, is a status that exists somewhere between a human-interest story like "Little Franny's hair grows backwards, inside her scalp, please call the children's hospital to donate" and an uplifting, there's-still-some-humanity-left-in-the-world story like a homeless guy jumping onto the subway tracks to save a banker's life and the banker then giving the guy a job at his firm.

Not that I'm taking direct issue with the phenomenon.

Clearly, I love Toxie. We all love Toxie.

A Lovable Freak can be money in the bank.

But I'm trying to encourage you to take the first step toward media literacy here, being aware of what you consume, and it starts with being aware of how these stories are constructed, the lens through which they're told, the biases that frame them, and the soulless multinational corporations that profit because we all, of course, Heart (♥) the Monster Hero.

For instance, the local station in Tromaville—which is an affiliate to a national network, which is in turn owned by a soulless media corporation—has gotten to have it both ways when it comes to Winston Gooze. They get an entire news cycle of a "Look out, a rampaging monster is on the loose!" story, and then, only a few hours later, just as interest is starting to wane, they get to pivot that same story to the Lovable Freak angle.

Both angles equal high engagement. They keep us watching, keep us doomscrolling, keep those advertising dollars flowing so the media company's super-polluting overseas parent company can buy off a few more senators.

They profit from your outrage. They'd foment hatred, rewrite and embellish (or sanitize) every future moment of recorded human history if it would make them one cent more on their quarterly earnings spreadsheet. They'd—

But wait, we're getting away from the story here.

Aaaand one guy just fell asleep. Look at the poor dummy. I start talking about corporate greed and he's out, and now his book's getting all crinkled at the corner.

Sorry, I didn't mean to bring the mood down by getting on my soapbox, honest.

Remember when Toxie wasted those goons in the Miss Meat Lunchatorium?

That was pretty awesome, right?

So now let's see how he's handling his first outing in front of the press, as several reporters and cameramen corner him before he can get away from Miss Meat.

"What's your name, sir?"

"Mm... I'd rather not say?"

"What caused your hideous condition?"

"Uh—"

"Your work shirt, or coveralls, whatever they are—the fabric that seems to be melted into your chest. Can we get a shot of that? That's the Body Talk Healthstyle logo! Are you affiliated with BTH?"

"No comment?"

"Why the rampage last night?"

"That... wasn't me."

Then, just when it seems like poor Winston is about to be overwhelmed, that he might even go red-eyed loco and break a couple of cameras in half and relocate some microphones, the question comes that changes his demeanor:

"How does it feel to be a hero?"

Yes. Here it is. His big moment, when he hits that point in his character arc when he gets to say the thing that defines the carefully constructed hero motif this story's been building toward.

Winston Gooze smiles wide and says, "Sometimes you gotta do something."

As he says it, as the gathered crowd cheers and the mother he heard crying before hugs her son and the cops inside the fast-food joint are puking up their breakfasts because of all the carnage, *that's* the moment—the moment he realizes that he's a hero, that he's not Winston Gooze anymore, that he's...

THE TOXIC AVENGER

FIFTEEN

Spence felt woozy, even though the doc hadn't given him anything yet. Sure, he'd laid out some pills, some needles, a dusty textbook with the title *Limb Reattachment Theory*, but he hadn't administered any drugs.

That couldn't be good.

Oh, wait, there was an IV in his arm.

His *one* arm.

He watched the top of the plastic hose, the dope dripping down from the reservoir, feeling the coolness as it flowed into his bloodstream.

And there was his dad on the couch, knitting and watching the news.

Thad Barkabus had spared no expense. This mob doc, he was the best. The other guy, the one who'd take slugs out for a hundred bucks and some gambling debts—that guy was a podiatrist. This guy? He was a real doctor.

"...and there you have it. Seven people rescued from a violent hostage situation and our exclusive interview with the... the *Monster Hero* has just ended abruptly. He just up, up, and awayed up that storm drain. Guess he's camera shy—as he probably should be."

Spence squinted at the screen as the footage zoomed in to follow a figure as it bounded across the rooftops.

That eye. Those hands. He'd only seen him for a second but that... that...

"Thass him," Spence Barkabus said.

Thad Barkabus finished his row and looked up.

"*Him*? That's him?"

Spence nodded. The motion made him dizzy and he reached out a hand to steady himself, but that hand wasn't there anymore. That hand was on ice in a cooler beside him.

His dad flipped open his business phone and spoke rapidly.

"Yeah, we got this crazy bastard. Yes, I can see him right now. He's headed south on Torgl Avenue. Fan out. I want him dead or alive," Thad Barkabus said, then pushed the receiver to his house coat, and looked over at Spence. "Actually, wait. You still there? Just dead. Yeah. Thanks."

He hung up and Spence started to nod out.

Somewhere in the blackness of the room, the doctor snapped on a rubber glove and asked, "Okay, who's ready to have a learning experience?"

A hero.

They'd dubbed him a hero.

The feeling was indescribable.

It wasn't so much that he felt the need to run away from the reporters than that he just *wanted* to run—and climb, and leap, and bound. With his trusty mop down his back, he felt more than a hero. He felt like a *super*hero.

A few moments ago he'd reached a hand over a gutter, pulled himself up and over the final waist-high brick facade so that he was standing atop the highest apartment building in the whole downtown area, and now he stood there, watching the world below. Up here, the graffiti-covered derelict cars might as well have been classic automobiles, the feral dogs looked like purebreds, and the puddles of antifreeze down on the streets cast dazzling rainbows.

He'd never seen Tromaville like this before.

Though he'd lived here all his life, he'd never felt this kind of ownership of the place. It had never felt like home, the way it did right now.

All these new sensations, his heart so full of pride and love for his hometown... it was making it really hard to pee.

Winston got pee shy, could barely use a public urinal if there was someone else in the room, but he was alone up here.

Come on, get your head in the game, he chided himself.

After all the excitement, and then the interview, he'd been ready to burst, his superhuman bladder unable to hold it. But now that he was able to go, had his dong out and pointed against a tin chimney pipe on this rooftop, he couldn't. He was thinking too much about it.

Clear your mind.

He tried.

No, really *clear it. Stop thinking of how you need to get home, or the difficult conversation you're going to have to have with Wade.*

He squeezed. His pee-shyness could sometimes become semi-permanent if he got this locked up, this self-conscious.

Okay, maybe don't clear your mind. Imagine waterfalls, leaky faucets, firehoses—

Psssssshhhhhh...

It worked! He was going!

God, what a relief.

A hero and the most satisfying piss of his life, all in one day.

Winston sniffed and opened his eyes, his human one watering at the acrid smoke now filling the air.

He pushed against the chimney to steady himself and clear his vision—which promptly groaned and collapsed.

Oh, shit.

His piss was acid!

He looked down, his big eye zooming in, counting the floors that his dangerous urine had already eaten through.

One… two… and it was starting to eat away at the carpet of a third.

"I'm sorry!" Winston yelled down into the hole, then bounded off, horribly embarrassed. He hoped everyone down there was okay and that they could get the roof fixed before the next rainstorm.

SIXTEEN

"Ordinarily, I don't go in for vigilante stuff, but this sonofabitch is okay by me."

The interview cut back to the studio, where C.J. Doons smiled her perfectly nipped and tucked smile.

"Unsure if standards and practices wants us saying *sonofabitch*, but that was Detective Lee Swofford of the Village PD giving his endorsement to the mysterious Monster Hero, who social media has now deemed the Toxic Avenger," she told her audience. "Let's head over to Chet at the Village Action News social media desk to tell us what else the kids—and maladjusted adults—of Tromaville have to say about the hero."

"Thanks, C.J.," Chet said. "He's an 'absolute unit,' seems to be the general consensus—"

There was a knock at the apartment door.

A solid, echoing knock.

Wade fell forward, suffering second-degree rug burns on his elbows as he grabbed for the baseball bat.

"Now the neighborhood association has begun—"

Wade switched off the TV.

Could it be Winston? He'd just been on the news, headed this way, but would his pseudo-stepdad, the Toxic Avenger, use the front door or would he try to use the fire escape again?

There was only one way to find out.

The hairs on the back of Wade's neck were tingling.

Something about this felt wrong.

It wasn't like Winston to knock like that. Even if he'd forgotten his keys, he would have—

"I can see your shadow on the other side of the door," said a voice in the hallway—a woman's voice. "Please open up."

Wade stood on tiptoes to look through the peephole, resting the bat against the doorframe.

There was an attractive, stylishly dressed woman out there. But more important than her look or dress, it seemed like she was alone. There was nobody behind her, Wade could see the stairwell and the door to Mr. Fleishaker's apartment—he angled his eye—and nobody on the stairs.

"Can I help you?" Wade asked.

"I'm looking for Winston," she said.

Wade watched through the fish-eye glass as she shifted impatiently from one foot to the other.

She didn't seem like a cop. Not one Wade had ever seen. The cops around here weren't this hot, and they didn't dress like they'd had a big post-punk phase in high school.

"He's not here," Wade said, his voice cracking a bit. He picked up the bat, then started tapping.

"Listen, I know what happened to him last night. I saw it."

That could mean anything, but it didn't *prove* anything. She was a stranger, and as curious as Wade was to know what the hell had gone on in the last twenty-four hours, he shouldn't open the door for a—

"He was dressed like a ballerina," the woman said, then through the peephole he watched as she held up Winston's work ID.

Wade pulled away from the door. He was beginning to get a charley horse in his left foot from where he'd been standing on his toes. He was a dancer, a *movement artist*, but he was never very good at standing *en pointe* for long periods of time.

He looked at the chain over the door, and considered how easy it'd be to slide it back and let the woman in.

She didn't sound dangerous. She sounded, in fact, like she wanted to help.

"Let me in," she said, "and I'll tell you what went down."

"So that's what went down," J.J. said.

She watched the kid pour himself some more orange juice, then waited as he downed it in one go. She'd just finished telling him how she'd seen his dad get shot in the face and understood that he might need a second to process that.

"Are you, like, a detective or a spy or something?" he finally asked.

"No. I'm not any of those things," she said. "I'm just angry."

She'd told him what had happened, the basic facts, as she saw them, and tried to keep herself and her own motives for being at the BTH plant out of it, but it was time to give him something.

Wade nodded like he understood, then poured himself some more juice and offered her some. She declined, then watched him take a smaller sip. He was getting himself back under control, but he was still doing that thing, tapping his chest with his finger.

"I grew up by the river," she told him. "Floodplain, you know?"

He nodded. Everyone knew Floodplain. It was one of the worst areas of a township that wasn't a great area generally.

"I could see the BTH factory from my yard," J.J. continued. She'd never told anyone this. It certainly hadn't been a monologue she'd given as part of her job interview. "When it rained, you could see that layer of grease over everything, the dewdrops like oily prisms. I never got into the whole bio-booster bullshit—"

"Biohacking?"

"Yeah. But my mom... my mom was a disciple. She looked at Bob Garbinger like he was the Second Coming. She bought everything they put out: serotonin toners, enhancers, and stabilizers, and *re*enhancers."

Wade's eyes went wide, like he knew what was coming next, and she realized she liked him. A lot of teenagers didn't have that kind of empathy.

"But then came the stomachaches," J.J. went on. "By the time insurance would clear her for surgery, the thing they took out of her was as big as a baseball." She gestured toward the baseball bat, now resting against the arm of the couch. "You know what a tumor is, Wade?"

"Uh, we *just* met?"

Okay, maybe he had a little bit of teenage wiseassery in him.

"She was gone in a year, the whole time thinking her cranial stims and positive frequency lamps would save her, when that's the shit—now we know—that killed her in the first place."

She reached across the table, grabbed Wade's OJ, and took a sip.

"My sister died, too," she added.

"Also cancer?" Wade asked.

"Zamboni. She was a great skater, just no situational awareness. It was a rough year."

They sat quietly for a while, the only sounds Wade's tapping and the clock on the kitchen wall, its second hand ticking but not moving from the 6.

"I lost my mom too," Wade finally said.

"Zamboni?"

"Cancer."

"I'm sorry," she said, abashed. "I..." She looked at her cuticles, remembered how frail and wasted her mom had been at the end, how easy it had been to lift her body on and off the john. "There's a lot of that going around, and it's because of..."

She looked at Wade, and he knew. It was in the air they were breathing right now, and probably in the orange juice too—microscopic particulates, invisible rays, unstable compounds with impossibly long half-lives.

Shit. She'd much rather have had the Zamboni take her out than be slowly poisoned by BTH. At least it would be quick.

"Look, I'm trying to expose these monsters," she said. "For both our moms' sakes. Your dad is the key to me doing that."

"Step—Never mind," Wade said. "You got him mixed up in some bad stuff already. You already got him killed too, I guess. Why should he—"

"Mixed up?" J.J. interrupted. She knew she shouldn't be taking this tone with the boy, not after the heavy stuff they'd just shared, but she'd never even seen that asshole before. "He was there already. When I collided with him, he was running out of the building with a bag full of money."

Wade looked suddenly ashamed and glanced over at the messy tabletop, where J.J. saw the bills—overdue, past due, final warning.

Yeah, if she had an anxious kid like Wade, one that maybe needed a little professional help, she'd commit armed robbery too. Whatever it took.

"Look," she said, changing tack. "If I could find where he lives, they will too. You're not safe here, Wade. They're going to come for him. Especially after he's out there giving interviews to the news wearing a BTH uniform."

Wade seemed to think about this for a moment, his eyes darting from side to side nervously.

Then he looked at J.J. and asked, "Can you cure him?"

J.J. paused, thinking. What did she do?

Did she lie to the kid? Say whatever it took to get him out of this apartment and have him lead her to Winston Gooze?

No, that's what *they* would do. She refused to use people like that.

"Not me," she said, frowning. "Maybe someone else can turn him back the way he was, but... I don't know."

Winston's condition seemed pretty permanent from what she'd seen online. But then, she would have thought the bullet in his brain was an irreversible condition too, so...

"Okay," said Wade. Let's—"

"*Shhh!*" J.J. hissed suddenly, holding up her hand.

Something was wrong.

She could hear noises in the apartment building, small stealthy noises under the sounds of car horns and drunks fighting in the street. Whispers.

"We gotta go!" she snapped.

And then the Killer Nutz broke down the door.

Budd Berserk, the front man of Tromaville's biggest band, born Shane "Buddy" Bersinski, wasn't from Tromaville, or even New Jersey.

He was from Long Island, and not even one of the shitty parts of Long Island where things looked kind of like they did in Tromaville—one of the nice parts of Long Island, near a beach!

But while he was still in grade school, his parents had moved him to St. Roma's Village, where he'd made some friends and taken to his new life very quickly.

The evolution of his personal style had started small—wallet chains, dollar-store hair dye, and DVD special editions of movies where the lead actors were very intense, very method, and all lost a lot of weight to play their roles.

But eventually, even before he was in the band, the look he'd cultivated had become a lifestyle—a closet full of surplus Russian police flak jackets he'd bought online; tattoos on the inside of his lower lip that said cool shit like *BROKEN* and, when he got tired of that and it faded, *TWISTED*.

Eventually, that lifestyle once again evolved, becoming a flow, and once he'd figured out how to use the free audio-editing software that came pre-installed on most laptops, he started recording that flow, and the rest was history.

He'd started off by mixing a track with himself saying—

"Koo-koo-koo!" he screamed, stepping through the doorway.

The rest of the Nutz piled into the apartment, all except Nightmare Josh and DJ Cool Cthulhu, who were down in the Nutzmobile, circling the block, looking out for any of their targets.

The apartment was small, so there wasn't much room for Zodiac 3000's acrobatics, but he tried, walking in on his hands, only to crash through the coffee table.

"You heard Budd," Venus said. He was a good hype man—better than he was a bass player, anyway. "Yeah, booooy. Search that shit!"

Him Under The Hood stomped into rooms, flipped beds, tossed furniture, and kicked holes in walls. The big guy's temper was volatile, but he didn't seem to have much in the way of smarts going on under his mask.

Zodiac wasn't helping with the search. He'd dusted himself off from his fall and was now dancing in the small living room, two spent glowsticks in each hand as he rave-twirled. He was useless on stage and useless too, it seemed, as part of a kidnapping.

Budd whistled through his teeth to get his band's attention, but only Venus turned to look.

He pointed out the window: "There."

They both looked down as the woman and the kid scrambled down the fire escape. If they headed for the street, they'd be caught by Nightmare Josh and DJ Cool Cthulhu, but if they ran deeper into the alley there was a chance they'd get away.

How had they missed that? Why weren't Josh or Cool parked waiting under the fire escape instead of out on the street with their thumbs up each other's asses?

"Parkour?" Zodiac asked, head ducked, already prepared to dive out the window in pursuit.

"*No* parkour," Budd Berserk said. He already had the blowgun pulled out from the pouch in his vest and was screwing both halves together, trying to judge if there'd be any wind coming down the alley.

Bands needed representation. There were bands way worse than the Killer Nutz who had reps and were huge. Likewise, there were bands ten times as good as the Nutz who died poor and unknown, never having the luck to find an agent or a manager who believed in them.

Fritz Garbinger was their representation, their meal ticket. He had connections, money. When Fritz had signed the Nutz, they hadn't had a rehearsal space so he'd *bought* them a club to play in, for Christ's sake—a club they headlined at whenever they felt like putting on a show.

And all he wanted in return was a handful of murders and, now, a kidnapping.

That wasn't all that much to ask.

No way they were going to screw this up again.

"They're getting away!" Venus yelled in his ear.

No, they weren't.

Budd aimed at the kid. He'd practiced a shot like this. Once they turned the corner to get deeper into the alley, they'd be in profile and a bigger target.

He put the blowgun to his lips and took his shot.

It was possible he'd missed.

But no, he saw the LED blink of the tracking ball he'd hooked onto the kid's pant leg. Perfect.

"Nutz, we're out!" he yelled. Him Under The Hood was dismantling the kitchen while Zodiac had lifted the neck flap on his mask, sweating from all the dancing.

Venus followed Budd as he calibrated the tracking app, watching the dot on his phone move through the spiderweb of alleys that laced the residential and commercial buildings of downtown Tromaville.

There were a lot of bad things that happened in those alleys, and a lot of bad people inhabited them. You could get lost, hurt, even killed.

"Koo-koo-koo, let's go!" Budd Berserk yelled, and there was no trace of a Long Island accent in his voice.

Downtown wasn't that big, so how was Winston so lost?

He hit a dead end then spun about-face, pausing a moment for his double vision to clear as his big eye caught up with his little one.

Footsteps. Coming from the direction of their apartment and the bodega.

He took a few more steps and hit a three-way intersection, one fork leading to his apartment, one deeper into the alleys, and one to the street, where he could see a little bit of the Strip.

The footsteps were getting closer.

More reporters? Or had the police changed their minds, deciding he wasn't a hero after seeing what he'd done to those internet Nazi fellows?

Winston hid behind a pile of trash, the ring of his tutu now powdered with rancid breadcrumbs and the seat of his pants damp with mineral-slime runoff after pressing up against a weeping brick wall.

No, wait—it wasn't more cameras or the cops. It was Wade!

"Wade!" he yelled, jumping out from his hiding spot, slipping on some kind of drippy balloon animal—oh, gross!

Then the girl from last night, the one who'd blown up his money, rounded the same corner and stepped out of the shadows.

Winston looked over Wade's shoulder, his big eye narrowed in anger. Not a violent anger, he didn't sense evil in the woman, didn't immediately feel the compulsion to tear her to pieces but still... he wouldn't be like this if it weren't for her. He'd still have his normal life, and normal face, and normal urine.

"Wait, what are you doing with *her*?" he demanded.

After the initial surprise faded from his stepson's face, Wade's brow furrowed. "Never mind her." Wade stepped forward, unafraid of what Winston had become. "What is *wrong* with you?!"

"I... I changed," Winston said.

"Not really what I meant, but... does it hurt? Are you hurting?" Wade looked about ready to put a hand on Winston's shoulder, but seemed unsure about touching him.

It was a good question. Was Winston radioactive? Was he making both Wade and the punk cat-burglar woman sterile just by standing this close to them?

"It's not too bad," Winston said. "Sorta like a sunburn."

"She told me what you did," Wade said, jerking a thumb back at the woman, who was panting. So they'd been on the run—but from what? "I didn't ask for all the doctors and therapy and shit," Wade continued, tapping his chest, his face sheened with sweat, "and I didn't ask for you to go out stealing to pay for it! I don't want *any* of this! You had no *right*!"

"I..." Winston began. Not to make this about himself, but

he really didn't think the robbery was going to be the big issue the two of them talked about, once they were reunited. "Wade, the money was for *me*. I'm sick."

Wade paused as he digested this. The woman behind him was looking back the way they'd come, one ear cocked to listen.

"Like I am?" Wade asked, confused.

No, expensive anxiety-management and life-coaching sessions weren't going to fix what Winston had growing in his brain. "Oh, buddy, you're not sick. You're fucking rad, man."

"Uh, I don't think—" the woman started to say impatiently, and Winston growled—a guttural, monstrous sound. The woman mimed zipping her lips.

"So what is it?" Wade asked. "What are you sick with, besides the visible?"

"It's bad," Winston said, choking up. In all the excitement, he'd forgotten about the black spots in his brain. "It's in my head. Not like in an imaginary way, but in a terminal way."

"You're gonna die?"

Winston blinked back tears from his normal eye while his larger eye began to shudder, weeping a thick slime down into his mouth. He couldn't bring himself to tell Wade that yes, he'd be leaving him alone in the world.

"*That* was why you were acting weird last night? You knew and you didn't tell me?" At least Wade wasn't tapping anymore; he needed both hands to gesticulate. "And now you're... you're... you're *this*? And I'm going to have nobody!"

The punk-rock saboteur had stopped trying to get their attention and now seemed fully invested on eavesdropping on their family drama.

"No, Wade. I'm your dad and—"

"You're not my dad. You're not even my stepdad since you and Mom didn't even get married. You're nobody. You're just some guy who never stopped hanging around. And you can—"

No, Wade, stop, enough, Winston thought. He couldn't stand to hear this.

"—just get sick and die if you want to, because I don't give a shit!"

"Listen to me," Winston said, stifling his own sobs, trying to be strong for the boy. "I promise you, I am not going *anywhere*."

Then a shotgun blast tore through Winston's chest, breaking his ribs and rearranging some of his vertebrae. He smashed into the wall of the alley behind him.

Distantly, through half-melted eardrums ringing from the nearby gunshot, he could hear Wade screaming. Then the woman was picking up his stepson and running.

"Run!" Winston said, directing them away from the way he'd come, the dead end. "Get the boy away!" But his voice was so weak and there was so much screaming and yelling, he couldn't tell if they'd heard.

The shot had come from the street, where a vintage tan convertible had driven up on the curb, spilling out four gunmen.

But no, it wasn't a tan car.

It was a *khaki* car.

"Not so tough now, motherfucker," the first of the Khaki Gang goons said, stepping into the alley, smoke curling from the barrel of his combat shotgun.

Ch-klick! The goon advanced a round, the spent shell spinning to the ground to collect with all the other garbage in the alley, and aimed the weapon down at Winston's face.

Well, it *was* too good to be true. Winston wasn't bulletproof. He might have been somewhat bullet resistant, but that shot to the chest? It hurt.

And the next one.

He raised a hand in a feeble attempt to shield his face from the blast.

"No! Don't!" Wade's voice.

No, get him away! Don't let him see!

"Say goodbye, freak."

If Winston could just... There, it was free.

He rolled to the side, yanking his mop from his back, fabric and scabby skin tearing free, and raked the mophead across the gunman's midsection with all his strength.

The gun went off again, booming even louder in the claustrophobic tunnel of the alley.

"Blake, you okay?" one of the other Khaki goons asked as the remaining three of them stepped into the alley.

"Bros... My... my stomach," the first goon said before dropping flat onto his face.

Winston looked over to the alley wall, where the goon's internal organs were clinging to the brickwork like fettuccine. A few strands were still attached to his torso. His mop had done that, unzipping the goon and flinging his guts against the wall with such velocity they'd stuck there.

Winston collapsed to one knee, then stood again, his chest burning from the shotgun blast. He could feel his bones crunching as he moved, hear the splinters of his ribcage moving and changing under his buckshot-perforated muscles.

He braced himself for the bullets that were about to start flying from the other gang members, but the three of them just gawked at their dead buddy and then blinked at Winston in shock.

He couldn't risk dying here. Couldn't risk fleeing in the direction that Wade and the young woman had run. He had to lead these guys away from his son.

So he pushed passed them, running toward the bodega, intending to cut across that street and into the more sparsely populated industrial side of town.

A few moments later, he heard the roar of a souped-up engine.

The Khaki Gang was in pursuit, and Winston's chest was still hurting bad.

J.J. couldn't carry Wade any further. The kid wasn't all that old, or that big for his age, which was probably somewhere between eleven and sixteen—what? She didn't have kids, how was she supposed to tell?—but neither was he so young she could just pop him onto her hip and carry him around.

"We have to go back!" he yelled.

They were out of the alley, standing in a vacant lot behind the Strip, old public works murals on either side of them covered up by gang tags and spray-painted dicks.

Something about being in the open made J.J. feel worse, but she reflected that if she felt bad, the kid had just seen his dad blown away.

The same dad J.J. *had* also seen get shot in the face and survive, so maybe he was okay... but she didn't think so. They'd heard another gunshot once they were around the corner. That was probably the kill shot.

"Wade, we can't go back," she told him. "They're after us. Not just the guys that shot your..." dad? Stepdad? Guardian? "...that shot Winston. The guys that broke into your apartment are after us too."

"But he's hurt! We have to—"

"Shh!" J.J. hissed. "Do you hear that?"

"I don't know. My ears are ringing."

She had that too, but the sound wasn't tinnitus, it was...

Peep-peep-peep.

Wade looked down toward the peeping sound and she followed his gaze.

There was a small blinking diode attached to his pant cuff.

It looked like one of those anti-theft pins they use in clothing stores. How—?

No. It wasn't that.

It was a tracker.

"Run!" she yelled. But she could already feel them there.

J.J. turned.

"Jump scare," Budd Berserk said from where he'd snuck up behind her, and she now found herself face to face with his low-fi clown makeup.

Then the white rapper shot her in the stomach.

She whirled, the shock of the impact spinning her on her toes in a pirouette of violence.

Fritz Garbinger was standing beside Wade.

How had he gotten there so fast, with his bum leg?

She'd never know. She watched as the man in the dark suit put a hand on Wade's shoulder and clamped his hand over the boy's mouth as he started to scream.

No, not like this! She couldn't die so... so anticlimactically.

But that was her last coherent thought as her consciousness and then her life ebbed away on the pitted concrete of the vacant lot.

SEVENTEEN

They weren't getting paid enough for this.

"Quick, you two, get out. He ran in there."

"Yeah, I saw, but what about you?"

"Bro, does it look like I can fit a car in there?"

Shep looked at the dump they'd just watched the "Monster Hero" enter.

There were piles of automotive parts, rusty hulks of cars squashed and cubed, a mountain of broken toilets, refrigerators with no doors, and, beside them, a pile of refrigerator doors.

No. It wouldn't be possible to take the car into the junkyard.

"So leave the car. You saw that thing. We need every gun we can get."

"Leave the car? In this neighborhood? Barkabus'll kill me!"

"Barkabus the elder or Barkabus the younger?"

"Does it matter?"

"Well, it might take the younger one a little longer to kill you. He's not ambidextrous, you know." Shep paused. Maybe he needed to make the joke clearer. "And I hear he's... unarmed."

He smiled. Waited.

"Har har har. Get the fuck in there and go kill this mook, you asshole."

So Shep and Keg-Stand got out of the Khaki Kar, flicked their safeties off, and headed into the junkyard.

There were so many places for the creature to hide in here.

Why hadn't anyone thought to pick up Blake's shotgun? It was the most firepower they had. Shep's and Keg-Stand's heaters were high caliber for handguns, but they knew the shotgun worked against the creature, or at least that it dazed it.

Oh, well. He'd have to aim for the head, pop that big fuckin' eye of his like a zit.

He wondered if they'd run a video of that on the evening news. He—

There was a rattling sound of dirt and pebbles dropping onto sheet metal somewhere ahead.

"You hear that?" Shep asked.

Keg-Stand nodded and pulled the brim of his baseball cap around so it wouldn't interfere with his peripheral vision.

Shep agreed—this was serious. Fashion could wait.

They were in front of a semi-open-air structure, half-covered with tarps where there were missing sections of roof. There was junk piled in front of the entrances so it was hard to tell where the structure ended and the rest of the salvage yard began.

"Flank him?" Shep asked in a whisper.

Keg-Stand nodded reluctantly. "I go this way, you go that, then we meet in the middle?"

Shep nodded.

"Bro, not gonna lie," Keg-Stand said. "I'm scared."

"I'm scared too bro," Shep admitted, "but we can do this."

They both nodded at each other. It was agreed, they'd try and flank him—a solid tactical maneuver, but Shep also hoped it meant that Keg-Stand found the freak first so he himself would at least have a fighting chance of surviving by knowing where the hell the monster guy was.

They separated, each taking one side of the structure, which was smaller than a warehouse but open on both sides like an airplane hangar.

Inside the structure was a maze of stacked tires; mounds of plastic preschool toys, sun-faded and broken; moldering piles of bedlinens that, from the look and smell of them, had to have come from a hospital.

Too many places for—what was it? The Toxic Crusader? No, not that, but close—to hide.

Maybe he should hang back and let Keg-Stand do all the searching, let his companion work his way through this house of horrors while Shep stood at the ready.

Yeah, that sounded good.

He'd just back out of here, slowly and quietly, to avoid giving away his position…

Clatter-clatter-clatter!

He'd knocked into a pile of disused musical instruments—flugelhorns and shit, brass-band stuff.

Fuck! There was something behind him.

Shep jumped, spinning one-eighty and pushing the barrel of his gun into the figure's mouth. But no, it wasn't a person, just a half-inflated blow-up doll, its rubber-reservoir mouth now deep-throating the barrel of Shep's revolver.

"Lol," Shep said, forgetting where he was for a moment. "Sex stuff."

While his attention had been on the doll, he hadn't tracked the hulking shape resolving itself, like a ghost, like a vengeful ghost of the junkyard, out of the wall of refuse behind him.

The Toxic Avenger wrapped two powerful hands around Shep's head and squeezed.

Keg-Stand stepped into a puddle of rainwater that had some *(ugh)* solids in it, and made a face.

He liked to get filthy with the rest of the boys, invite a few girls over, commit some mild, semi-consensual crimes at the Khaki Haus, but this was filthier than he ever wanted to be.

There were, like, turds in here—

A rodent squeaked and ran over his boot. He jumped backward, into the puddle.

—and not just rat turds.

They were supposed to have met in the middle.

He was way beyond the middle, so where was Shep?

What if, in this labyrinth of garage-sale shit, they'd somehow missed each other?

"Shep!" he whispered. "Hey, Shep," he whispered a lot louder, but still with the hush in his voice, so it was okay, it still counted as whispering.

"Hey, buddy," Shep said, appearing from around the next corner, leaning a little.

Thank god!

"Any sign of him?"

"No, but c'mere."

"What?" Keg-Stand whispered.

"Come here a sec," Shep said.

Shep was still leaning. And he didn't sound like himself.

Keg-Stand took a single step closer.

"What for?"

"Because I gotta tell you something."

Keg-Stand took another step.

"But what is it?" he asked. They shouldn't be talking this loudly. The creature might hear them.

"It's important."

Keg-Stand had been wearing the same pair of contacts for like a week longer than he was supposed to, so he didn't notice until he was half a foot from him that Shep's eyes were closed, and Shep's mouth was hanging open, and—Keg-Stand felt the vomit beginning to bubble up into his esophagus—Shep's head had been cracked open at the top, the membranous tissue of his brains pushing through the fissures like the whipped yolk of a deviled egg.

"Oh, *fuck*!" Keg-Stand wailed as the Toxic Avenger dropped Shep's body, stepped forward, and took Keg-Stand's head off his shoulders with a single swing of his mop.

"No, you don't understand. Gutted. Not like he was bummed, man. Blake was *gutted*. Hollowed out like a turkey or deer or, or... a pizza-flavored combo or something."

Winston watched the man behind the wheel of the convertible slide deeper into panic as he yelled into the phone. He wasn't checking his rearview mirror.

"I sent in Shep and Keg-Stand, but they've been in there a while. I'm starting to get worried."

The vibration in Winston's skull, behind his large eye, seemed to get stronger as he crept toward the driver, like something inside of him had become a metal detector, only for evil shitheads. An evil shithead detector.

"Look, sir, I know you said dead, but—"

Winston grabbed onto the man's head with both hands, twisted, and then pulled upward.

The flesh of the man's broken neck stretched like taffy, but eventually his shoulder pulled free from the seatbelt strap and Winston was able to yank out the body and toss it into the ditch beside the car.

As the body cooled, the buzzing behind Winston's eyes seemed to grow fainter, then finally disappeared. So it turned out that brutally dispatching gang members was better than BTH's aspirin. He felt great.

Hey, this was a nice car. Could do without the paintjob and upholstery, but it would be a pleasure to drive something that wasn't riding on two spares, had all its mirrors, and appeared to have a functioning stereo.

But wasn't this stealing? If Winston had slaughtered the people who'd owned it, then took their car, didn't that make him a thief as well as a killer?

He rubbed his chest. His ribs had reset themselves and begun to knit back together, but the point where the shotgun had blown him open was still sore.

Eh, fuck 'em.

He pulled open the driver's-side door, then unsheathed his mop from behind his back and propped it against the passenger-seat headrest.

Now that he'd taken care of the bad guys, he could drive back through Tromaville, pick up Wade and the punk woman, and head back home to have a long chat.

As he settled into the driver's seat, he thought it might be nice to have some tunes, so he started turning knobs and throwing switches on the dash.

The convertible started to bounce on its hydraulics, making the drive back to the Strip much more difficult than it needed to be.

J.J. stared up at the sky above the vacant lot.

A fly buzzed around her face, started to crawl up one nostril, then retreated, and finally landed next to her eye and began to drink her tears.

She didn't have the strength to swat it away, didn't even have the motor control to wriggle her features or blink to get it to fly away.

"Hey! Hey!" a voice called in the distance. Then there was the sound of tires screeching and metal bending and moaning.

"You, hey!"

She couldn't move her head to look. She just stared at the clouds, laden with acid but not quite full enough to rain.

Then the sky was blotted out by a big, ugly face staring down at her. "Where's Wade? Where is he?"

Seriously? This is what's happening? I get a bullet through the spine trying to protect the kid and then get interrogated?

J.J. tried to speak but could barely make a sound.

The Toxic Avenger, formerly Winston Gooze, janitor for BTH, looked down at her stomach, his big eye widening so far she thought it might fall out and bonk her in the face.

"Oh, god, you're really hurt," he said, more to himself than to J.J.

Then he readjusted his vision, put a hand on her cheek, and said, "You need to hold on. I know a doctor."

Winston picked her up and laid her down in the back of the car, but slid an incautious thumb into her exit wound as he was trying to get her buckled in.

The pain was so intense that she blacked out again.

Winston found the cleanest blankets in the camp, then laid the woman atop them, packing her wound with some Miss Meat napkins he'd found in the glovebox. The bleeding had slowed to a weeping drip, but that might not be a good sign. It could mean she didn't have any more blood to give.

He covered the wound back up, then sat beside the woman's head as he watched Guthrie Stockins prep for surgery.

Guthrie moved around camp with purpose. He gathered up a pair of goggles with a snorkel attached, slipped on a ratty surgical mask made from a pair of underwear, and threaded a fish hook with a length of floss to fashion a suture—all unorthodox equipment to scrub in with, sure, but you worked with what you had.

Of course, Winston didn't know the exact specifics of Guthrie's life, but he imagined this was a redemptive moment for the old man. Mentally ill, stripped of his medical license, and reduced to living in a camp in the woods, this was his chance to make a difference, to suit up and start saving lives again.

Who knew? Maybe this would be the moment he rejoined society, resumed practicing medicine once he—

Okay, now he was holding a pickle over a butane torch.

"Uh, what's that for, Guthrie?" Winston asked.

"Gotta sterilize it."

"Are you... No offense, but are you sure you're a doctor?"

Guthrie extinguished the torch.

"Who said I was a doctor?"

"You did!" Winston blurted. He couldn't believe what he was hearing.

"Oh. Well then, in my medical opinion, I think that girl's been dead for a few minutes now."

Guthrie pointed down at the woman.

Winston leaned over J.J.'s face.

"Young lady!" he bawled. Nothing. She wasn't breathing. "Young lady!"

Oh, god. What had he done? He should have driven her to a hospital or something, not into the woods.

No, this couldn't happen. He needed her. She'd know who took Wade, and maybe where they were going.

He looked down at his lumpy, green, misshapen hands, then focused on the purple veins lacing through them. Every chemical imaginable was mixed up in his bloodstream to give him superhuman strength, churning through his mind and driving him to unspeakable—albeit still kind of comical and endearing—violence. His blood was able to heal bullet wounds, knit his broken bones back together…

"Hand me that," Winston said, pointing to the power drill Guthrie had laid out for the surgery. "Now! Come on."

Guthrie lifted it up, checked the battery pack, then handed it over. Winston pulled the trigger and watched the corroded drill bit twirl.

Vreeem-vreeem!

It wouldn't work if he made just a little cut. It would heal right over before he could get any of the blood out.

"Yikes, fella," Guthrie said. "Whatcha doin'?"

But Winston didn't answer. He just pressed the drill down into his palm and pulled the trigger.

Wow. He may have been hard to kill, but this still hurt like a mother.

He wasn't going to try it twice, though, so he kept boring until he was through bone and ligament and he could see the glint of metal pushing through the back of his hand.

The ragged hole in his palm was ringed with purplish blood that glinted in the daylight. He pressed his hand to the woman's stomach, letting their fluids mingle, squeezing up the veins of his forearm like a yogurt pop, trying to keep the blood flowing.

He and Guthrie watched as the hole in his hand bubbled and closed until there was only a greasy streak of slime on the back of Winston's hand to show that anything had happened to it at all.

Winston looked up at Guthrie and the old man nodded, finally seeming to understand what he'd been trying to do.

The moment of truth. Would this work? Had he gotten enough blood out?

They both looked down. Where there had been a hole in the woman's stomach, there was now a glowing purple scab.

As they watched, it feathered out, dried up, and blew away, leaving nothing but new, unbroken skin underneath. And yet she still seemed to be dead, like Winston had healed the wounds of a corpse.

Then, suddenly, she sat up, coughing and hacking, brought back to life, resurrected via a power drill and a few drops of toxic blood.

Winston collapsed with exhaustion.

"Whoa," Guthrie said to Winston. "That was all very biblical. New Testament, though. Which is fine, I guess. Not for me, but fine."

The woman looked at the old man, then around at the camp, her expression veering between disgust and bewilderment.

"I'll send you my bill," Guthrie told her as he began to put away his equipment.

EIGHTEEN

Wade knew about all kinds of different dances. He'd done a lot of research for the piece he'd been rehearsing for *Share Your Gift*.

What the man in the ski mask was currently doing as he drove the van, never more than one hand on the wheel at a time, was known as vogueing.

It was a kind of dance distinguished by its angular movements, specifically hand movements around the face, that developed in the 1960s in—

"What, do you have somewhere to be?" the pale man with the cane and wispy hair asked Budd Berserk, the man in the bulletproof vest and clown makeup.

"Yeah, soundcheck," Budd said. "You're our manager, remember?"

"Oh, the festival," the pale man in the dark suit said, leaning on his cane, polished silver under his grip. The hunchback. He was sitting backwards in the van so he could keep an eye on Wade, who was sandwiched between Budd Berserk and… what was the bass player's name? Aphrodite? Wade didn't know much about the Killer Nutz. They had a couple of catchy songs, but after all this, he really wasn't going to be a fan.

"Gotta sound tight for the community," Budd said, elbowing Wade hard. "A koo-koo-koo!"

The sound hurt Wade's ears. Sweat flowed out from the base of his scalp, wicked up by the cotton of his shirt. He'd calm down if he tapped, but he was focusing with all his might to keep his hands at his sides. He couldn't show he was scared, couldn't show them he was different or they'd find a way to use that against him, mock him, use him to hurt Winston.

They were going to kill him, just like they'd killed J.J. But before they did that, they were going to kill his dad too.

"You'll make soundcheck," the pale man said. "Relax." Then he pushed forward, his cane bowing slightly, and stared at him until Wade met his gaze. "Don't be scared. We just want him."

Wade wanted so badly to raise his hands, tap, chew his nails, something. His pits were wet with sweat. He pushed back further in the seat, hoping he'd stink up this stupid van with its plush upholstery and carpeted walls.

"You're the one who should be scared," he said.

The pale man smiled and nodded, then looked around the van.

"Do you see what he's up against?" He took a hand from his cane to gesture at the band around him. "Me, scared? I think not."

From the passenger seat, the man in the chicken mask leaned over and flexed his bicep so that the leather of his battle vest squeaked against the strain. The keyboardist, who'd been playing a soft synth score, looked up and grinned, revealing teeth filed to points. The man in the bandages, sitting against the door, twirled his drumsticks.

Sure, they looked tough by nineties rap and nu-metal

standards, and they certainly frightened Wade, but the Toxic Avenger could take them.

"Winst—" he began, then stopped himself from giving his stepdad's name. And he wasn't going to call him the Toxic Avenger either. He started again, felt tears well up: "My dad loves me more than anything. What would your family do if someone tried to take you away?"

The pale man seemed taken aback by this question, but then smiled a wormy, yellow smile, and Wade noticed the cluster of sores beginning at one corner of his mouth, and that his eyes were sunken above pink bags. There was something pathetic about the man, something pained. Wade hated that he could almost sympathize.

Instead of continuing their conversation, the pale man turned away.

Maybe Wade had struck a nerve.

Or maybe he'd just sealed his fate.

He wanted to tap so badly, but he didn't for the rest of the drive.

Kissy watched Garbinger watching himself in the mirror.

He was shirtless. Toned. Triumphant.

She corrected her thinking—when they were alone and he was semi-nude like this, she tried to think of him only as Bob.

Fritz had succeeded, and as much as that pained her, he would be here any second, the boy in tow.

No, he hadn't succeeded *yet*, Kissy reminded herself. The boy was just the bait. Fritz still had to draw out the freak.

Bob flexed one pectoral muscle, then the other.

He was like one of the medieval weapons arranged in the display cases behind them: sharp, deadly, honed to a fine point.

He was also, to Kissy, unrelentingly sexually arousing.

The phone rang, shocking them both out of their reverie. Bob pulled himself away from admiring his reflection and Kissy stopped staring at him staring at himself.

He looked at her coldly as the phone rang a third time. "Were you going to get that, or...?"

Kissy picked up. "Executive line of Robert Garbinger. May I ask who—"

"Put him on, Koala-tits."

Thad Barkabus. What a gentleman.

She didn't even announce him, just held out the handset to Garbinger. Bob.

He made her wait a second, arm outstretched, while he covered his muscular chest with a silk robe. As he tied the belt, he admired that statuette of the golden lamb from the awards banquet that now sat on his desk.

"Hello, Thad," Bob said, finally taking the phone, a forced friendliness in his voice. There was a slight difference in timbre when Robert was being genuine, and Kissy liked to think that she could tell the difference.

"Don't you *Thad* me, you cunty jerk."

The speaker on the handset was loud enough that Kissy could hear every conversation her boss had, but for privacy and ego reasons, she frequently pretended she couldn't.

She made an "Is everything okay?" gesture and Bob smiled, gave her a thumbs up, and retreated to the high-backed leather chair behind his desk.

"That Frankenstein asshole just tomahawked half my gang!"

"Well, I'm sorry to hear—"

"Heads crushed, disembowelments, shit that... I don't know. What do my HR people tell their wives and kids?"

"Well—"

"No, I'm not finished," Barkabus continued. "Because then I see on the news that Deformo over here is wearing a BTH patch, that he comes from your backyard, Bob."

"Deformo…?"

"My own name for it. Now, Bob, if it's true you created this thing, you'd better start saying something to convince me not to drive over to that big scary mansion of yours and stick a live rattlesnake up your ass."

"I—"

"Did you know there's undercover feds in town looking to make hay out of exactly this sort of shitshow? Your whole operation is teetering on the brink!"

"Feds? Here?"

"The brink being that you are *suicidally* fucking with my money, Bob."

Bob's brow constricted, wrinkles showing where Kissy had never seen wrinkles before. The cracks in his facade were there for a split second, but then he turned in his chair and saw something that brightened his expression.

Kissy turned to look and saw with a shock that Fritz was looming over her shoulder. The fucking guy had moved so slow! How could he have crept up on her like that?

But he had the boy at his side, one hand clamped on his shoulder, the other on his cane.

"It's handled, Thad," Bob said into the phone, smiling, then stood up.

"You sure?" Thad Barkabus asked.

"You have my word."

"I hope so, Bozo. Okay, you be good. I've gotta go kill this doctor. Fuckin' guy put my kid's arm on backwards," Barkabus said.

"How's that even possible?"

"The inept of the world find a way. My advice to you is to not be one of them."

Then Kissy heard a click. Bob passed her the handset and she placed it back on the receiver.

Bob went to one knee in front of the boy, then touched the side of his face and let his hand linger there for an uncomfortably long time, slipping down to his neck. He was looking at the boy the same way he had moments ago been admiring the golden lamb award.

Both Kissy and Fritz saw the look and, in a rare moment of agreement, both shared a look of unease.

Garbinger didn't congratulate or thank Fritz, Bob merely snapped his fingers at the boy and said, "Put him in the shed."

Dismissed, Fritz limped off with the child.

Then Kissy and Bob were alone again, and Bob looked a little cowed, a little indignant, probably due to the fact that she'd heard him lose face with Barkabus. But she didn't lose respect for him. She knew Barkabus was nothing but a means to an end, a walking underworld charge card who thought he was the real power behind the company. She also knew that he had to think that for their arrangement to work.

"What?" Bob asked her.

For a moment, she wasn't sure what she was going to say. But then she thought about the boy, and about that muscle-bound, glow-in-the-dark freak. She imagined the monster as a sort of cannonball, hurtling his way toward them right now because they had lit his fuse by taking away his son.

"You know how fond I am of Fritz," Kissy started.

"Sure, you love him. But?"

"But I think this is a mistake. Not just taking the boy, but bringing him here, to your home."

"Because?" Bob didn't sound like he was completely

discounting her, but he didn't sound ready to agree with her either.

"You're familiar with Pandora's Box?"

"The exotic revue?"

"The..." Sometimes Bob's lack of frames of reference made it hard to communicate with him. "No. A can of worms is what I mean."

He approached, pointed a finger at her. If he told her to lean over the desk and take a spanking for talking back to him, she would have done it. Gladly.

"The only can I'm interested in," he said, "is *can* I know that you are on my side right now?"

Oh. She'd really misjudged where that was going, and she was hurt by the implication that she could ever *not* be on his side. But he was a great man in a stressful time, and was no doubt starting to feel the press of paranoia.

She needed to reassure him.

"Of course. Where else would I be?"

He cupped her chin in one of his hands.

Yes. This was what they both needed.

He whispered in her ear, his breath moist on her neck, "And I'd like a smoothie. Extra..."

"Extra cherries, yes," she said, trying to make her voice just as breathy and warm. "And no pollen."

What would your family do if someone tried to take you away? What would Fritz Garbinger's family do if someone took him away?

That's what the boy had asked him in the van on the drive to Chüdhaven, and while he waited for Robert to be done with his phone call, Fritz ruminated on the question.

What *would* his family do? Well, it depended whether they

could hire a caterer at short notice for the party.

Robert wanted the boy kept in "the shed." Chüdhaven didn't have a shed—the building and grounds were much too grand to have anything so common—but it did have an outbuilding. It was a recent construction, erected as part of a high-tech extension to Robert's subterranean lair he'd built in the first years of BTH's success, when it had seemed like the company couldn't fail, when those initial product lines were the hottest thing that the pharmaceutical and self-improvement markets had ever seen.

The shed was a generator room for the lab, and it also had a steel escape hatch in the floor giving access to a tunnel in the event of a catastrophic biohazard from which Robert needed to flee.

But the shed was outside Chüdhaven, separated from the main building by nearly an acre of lawn and gardens, and Fritz's leg was much too weak after a long day for him to take the trip.

"Okay now, Wade," Fritz said, stooping (further than normal) to the boy. "These nice, uh, paid mercenaries are going to bring you to your accommodations for the night."

"Accommodations?" Wade asked skeptically. He'd begun tapping his chest, which Fritz supposed was a nervous tic. He had plenty of those himself.

"Yes, your room," Fritz said. He thought of the cold metal floor of the outbuilding, the steel chrome tanks inside and outside containing both accelerants and cryo-freezing materials, the way the hatch took up most of the floor space. "Hopefully one of these helpful mercenaries can find you a pillow and blanket."

He glanced up and one of the mercs gave a soft shake of his gas mask.

No blanket, then.

"Don't worry, I'm sure your dad will get here soon. My

brother will have a talk with him, and all this will be over before you know it." *Sure.*

Wade didn't say anything, just stared up at Fritz like he wanted to kill him.

Fritz didn't blame him.

NINETEEN

Winston Gooze, the Toxic Avenger, sat on a fallen log, on a hill beside Guthrie's camp, and looked out over Tromaville, way off in the distance. Between was the dead, calcified expanse of Outer Tromaville, the old industrial center of town that had been moved upriver when BTH had outgrown that spot, then relocated again when the BTH factory had expanded even further.

The area to the south looked like an atomic blast zone, an endless wasteland punctuated by the skeletal remains of trash and dump trucks, biohazard barrels, and chemical drums.

Winston's big eye zoomed in and spotted a bustle of activity in town.

Of course! Today was St. Roma's Festival. He'd almost forgotten. Since his diagnosis, the days had been running together.

Aw, man. It was already late afternoon. They'd missed it! All the fried food and the cover bands, and the craft show people selling questionable homemade art to out-of-towners at a huge markup. Winston and Wade hadn't missed a TromaFest in years!

He shook his head, his big eye spinning slightly. *Missing TromaFest is the least of your problems, stupid. You can't take Wade anywhere. He's kidnapped, and it's all your fault.*

"Hey," someone said behind him, startling him, his body reacting to the small endorphin rush of surprise by, for a split second, wanting to rip them in half lengthwise, but it was only J.J. It was nice to finally have a name to put to the young woman's face. After she'd regained consciousness, she'd sunk right back into sleep, but in that brief window when she'd been coherent, he'd asked her where his boy had been taken. She hadn't known.

"There's a gentleman down there huffing jenkem who says you saved my life," she said now, taking a seat beside him.

Winston shrugged.

"They took Wade to get to me."

"Yeah."

"And I never really thought about it, but they did all this too, huh?"

He waved a hand over toward Outer Tromaville and the wastelands beyond, taking in the bubbling ponds of noxious sewage and rusted-out barrels leaking their contents into the earth, poisoning the world.

"Folks like Bob Garbinger," J.J. said, "there's no right or wrong for them. There's only winning. He doesn't even think about the harm he's done. He's so self-centered, he can't even *conceive* that he's done harm. If there was a nickel in it, he'd fuck the whole world."

Winston gave a grim nod. "And he has."

"The night we met, I was trying to get hard proof for Sneaky Cheetah."

Who the hell is—?

But she must have seen the expression on his face.

"That's a code name. Sneaky Cheetah's a special agent with a federal corporate crimes task force. He could break them if he had the goods. Not just Garbinger but his company, his connections, the rats in City Hall, that fucking goosestepping police chief, all of them."

Winston said nothing. It sounded like there was more coming.

"So we were trying to help Sneaky Cheetah, my mentor and me. My mentor, he..." By the way she said it, Winston assumed he was more a father figure than a mentor. "His name was Melvin Ferd. He was a good man, a good reporter."

"He sounds like a great guy. A brave man."

"And they killed him with harpoons and shit."

Winston frowned. He didn't want to sound like a goody two shoes but...

"And if you ruin *them* it'll make things okay?" he asked. "Even it out?"

"Nah, look out there," she said, and pointed. "We've already killed the planet. Running BTH into the ground won't change that."

Gosh. He wasn't expecting *that* fatalistic an answer.

"But you don't know that," he said. "Things could change." *It's never too late.* What daytime TV show had he heard that on?

She gave him a look like he couldn't have been that naive, not after what BTH's own chemicals had turned his body into.

"So then why fight if you can't win?" Winston asked.

"The fuck else am I supposed to do?"

"Join me. Help me find him, my boy."

J.J. thought for a moment. "They're dangerous, these Killer Nutz bastards," she said eventually. "We're going to have to go hard."

Winston pointed down at his tutu.

"I am very hard."

Oh, that came out wrong.

"I mean, I'm angry."

"Yeah, no, I get it," she said, eyes down watching at an interesting, sickly-looking bird that had approached to peck at their feet. Well, maybe interesting didn't quite cover it. The bird. It had more eyes than feathers and its scaly, vestigial wings shivered.

Winston looked over at Tromaville, doing his best to squint with his big eye, though his eyelid wasn't quite elastic enough to close. There was a stage set up down there, as part of TromaFest.

He remembered a few days ago—what felt like a lifetime ago—something he'd heard on the morning news, and he knew who would soon be taking that stage.

ST. ROMA'S FESTIVAL IS LIT

Or maybe not lit. Maybe it's chill.

Or who knows? Maybe *lit* or *chill* won't even be in the youth-slang vernacular by the time you read this book. Publishing takes a long time, you know. Oh, you're telling me neither phrase is relevant and hasn't been for years? What do you want from me? I'm old and out of touch, leave me be.

Anyway, the point is, St. Roma's Festival—TromaFest as we call it—is a perfectly pleasant way to spend an afternoon in northern New Jersey.

It's part street fair, part community-wide picnic in the park, and today, because of this year's special musical guest, part monstercore concert.

The Killer Nutz, fresh off their successful kidnapping, are on stage playing the second song of their set, the serviceable if slightly derivative B-side "My Baby is an Ax," which sounds as if Mudvayne had a dubstep era, though not as good.

There's a small crowd of Nutz Headz clumped in front of the stage, trying to get a pit going, but there's too few of them for that. This rarified group is clapping along and mouthing the lyrics as Budd Berserk spits rhymes, but both their lips and the timing of their claps seem to be off, so maybe Budd's freestyling or maybe the Nutz Headz are too drunk and high, or maybe even the most diehard Killer Nutz fans don't really like the band that much.

Set back from the Nutz Headz is a ring of casual fans and curious TromaFest attendees watching the show while they munch hot dogs and walking tacos, Him Under The Hood's guitar virtuosity enough to entertain. Behind them, there's a small sound booth in which a tech is monitoring a row of faders, occasionally making minor adjustments so his boss thinks he's doing something.

This is Tromaville's one nice public park. Yes, really! Look, there's some green grass left, and even a tree or two whose leaves are holding on for dear life despite all the defoliants in the air, soil, and water. There used to be more spaces like this, of course, though most have been reduced to cinders in the blasted lands of Outer Tromaville. But the villagers don't take this space for granted.

There are grills, charcoal and gas; picnic tables set with plastic cutlery and paper plates; and blankets spread over dirt clods so folks can enjoy their meals without staining their slacks.

Yes, *slacks*. Like I said, I'm old. These are the words I use.

During TromaFest, these roads are closed to street traffic, and tents now line the streets on all four sides of the park's square. The good cops of Tromaville help to work security, keeping the peace if any of the Tromaville High kids get too rowdy, while the bad cops take themselves out of the equation—they have their own festival down on the Strip, busting heads. The tents sell everything from street-fair food staples like funnel cakes and Italian sausage sandwiches to DIY crust-punk accessories like those patches you apply with safety pins, never stitch, and boots with pre-gnarled laces.

Yes, it's an oasis of peace and merriment, calm and normalcy, where everyone in Tromaville can recuperate before the break into the third act.

It's almost enough to make us forget that our protagonists were just at their lowest point.

But as pleasant as this gathering is for most Tromavillians, if we look out, scrutinize the faces in the crowd, we notice something. See? Look at their eyes. Even those attendees who are outwardly enjoying the festivities are somewhere, deep behind their eyes, subconsciously aware that life in Tromaville used to be this enjoyable *every day.* They know that something has been taken from their community, then poisoned and irradiated, and that Body Talk Healthstyle is to blame.

But what's this? Someone in a hooded sweatshirt has just paid that sound tech to take a break. (Wow, and he did it for only ten bucks! He must really hate his job.)

Okay. Now, yeah. It looks like the figure in the hooded sweatshirt, she's figuring out which wires she's going to cut, how she's going to splice in that janky old CD player.

And the compact disc *in* that CD player?

Ha.

Who knew they even made karaoke versions of Motörhead songs?

Okay, she's about to cut the cord, and not a moment too soon. On stage, the Killer Nutz are about to start their next song, and I hear Nightmare Josh has a six-minute drum solo in this one.

TWENTY

"Okay, y'all motherfuckers know the words to this next one," Budd Berserk yelled, distorting the mic. "We wantcha loud up in this bitch."

Beside J.J., two women in athleisure wear, their baby strollers parked alongside the sound booth, looked at each other, too confused to be offended at first but getting there. "I—" one of them began. "I thought this was a family event?"

"Sha-lama-wamma, you squeeze my—" Budd Berserk started to scream/sing.

That's enough of this noise, J.J. thought, and closed the wire cutters, snipping the cable carrying the main feed to the stage's speakers. For a moment, there was blissful quiet.

On stage, the bandmates of the Killer Nutz looked around at each other, passing hissed blame. Wah-wah pedals were pressed, cymbals clashed, and Budd stopped rapping when he finally noticed that nobody could hear him. Seemingly unfazed, the guy dressed as the Zodiac Killer kept dancing to music only he could hear.

The crowd looked fifty percent annoyed, fifty percent relieved as J.J. worked to twist the ends of the copper speaker cabling together and get a new song broadcast out on the speakers.

Then she hit Play on the grody CD player Guthrie Stockins had lent them.

Those drums were like magic.

Even in the karaoke version, the entire crowd, and the attendees of TromaFest who had not been paying attention to the music, started to tap their feet and bop their heads.

This song was a classic.

On stage, the drummer, shrugging in his straitjacket, looked at his own drum kit, baffled.

Then the voice dropped in, so powerful and booming that J.J. didn't recognize it at first.

"Only way to feel the noise is when it's good and loud!"

J.J. looked over. The crowd in front of the stage parted.

Winston said he liked to sing in the shower, but J.J. hadn't been expecting this. His voice was great! He sounded just like Lemmy Kilmister, or at least he had a kind of swagger in his voice that convinced you that you were listening to a very good, enthusiastic, and confident Lemmy impersonator.

"So good I can't believe it, screaming with the crowd!"

His superhumanly deformed lungs probably helped with that baritone, to add a whiskey growl quality to his voice.

Elbows jammed into sides. Women (and some men) screamed. The crowd in front of the stage doubled in a matter of seconds as word spread he was here.

You know, him. The guy from TV.

The guy who saved all those people at the Miss Meat.

The Toxic Avenger!

Towering above the crowd like a periscope glowed the smoking head of Winston's mop.

"Don't sweat it, we'll get it back to you!"

J.J.'s head swiveled, worried she was about to be wrestled away from the booth, but all the cops she could see were singing along.

"Overkill! Overkill! Overkill!"

During the chorus, Winston needed both hands to hop on stage, and set the microphone down to climb up, but the crowd picked up the singing.

He nailed the timing, standing just in time to sing, "On your feet you feel the beat, it goes straight to your spine!" right into Budd Berserk's face.

Winston and Budd circled each other warily. It looked like part of the show, like they were about to enter a rap battle, but Budd didn't have a working microphone or the crowd on his side.

However, he did have a handgun tucked into the waistband of his jeans.

Budd drew the pistol and fired.

Nobody in the crowd moved, nobody stopped cheering or singing. Either they thought this too was part of the act or they were too high on the gospel of Motörhead to care.

Winston circled Budd and dodged another shot, holding the mic to his lips with one hand and wielding the mop with the other.

Blam! Another shot. Winston saw his opening and swung the mophead across the top of Budd Berserk's head, searing flesh and cracking his skull like eggshell, yet the front man Budd stayed on his feet, spinning. The crowd cheered as an arc of blood from the mop's follow-through splattered across the bare breasts (and one pair of testicles) that dotted the front row of the pit.

J.J. had never in her life been so happy to see someone be grievously injured.

"My. Brains," Budd yelled as he dropped to his knees.

The fall of the front man served as a kind of starting gun.

The rest of the band swarmed the Toxic Avenger.

The people in the crowd suddenly stopped cheering.

"Look out, Toxie!" a kid on their father's shoulders yelled.

"You can do it!" a girl in front of the booth said. She was

wearing a Killer Nutz tank top. Winston had truly won the crowd over.

"Yeah, fuck 'em up!" the nearest cop yelled.

J.J. couldn't agree more.

Yeah, Winston, she thought. Fuck them up.

They were all coming at him, all except the hulking giant in the chicken mask, who'd pulled the plug from his guitar and fled, jumping off the back of the stage.

Weird. Winston wouldn't have figured that one would be the one to… oh, yeah, Winston remembered. He was chicken.

Winston rolled his big eye back toward J.J. in the sound booth, but she didn't need to be told; she'd seen that the big guy was getting away and she was already in pursuit.

"Gonna skullfuck you," Budd Berserk said, crawling toward Winston—at least, it sounded like "skullfuck"; it could have been anything, really, with all the blood in his mouth and greasy globs of brain sloshing out of the open cup of his skull like the head on a beer.

Winston put the heel of his left foot over the back of the rapper's throat and crushed his larynx. The crowd went wild.

Then the guy in the straitjacket and bandages was on Winston, trying to stab a drumstick into his jugular, but he couldn't push hard enough. Yeah, Winston's skin on that side *was* pretty leathery. He'd have to start a moisturizing regimen.

Winston dropped the mic, flung the man onto the ground, then, with a two-handed golf swing of his mop, knocked off his bandaged head, which sailed into the crowd and was passed around like a beachball until someone finally grabbed onto it, looking ready to keep it as a souvenir.

The two bodies at Winston's feet spasmed and voided.

There was quite a smell.

"Overkill! Overkill! Overkill!" the crowd chanted as the music from the speakers returned to the chorus.

A turntable was smashed across the back of Winston's legs. He faltered but didn't fall. The makeup of the keyboardist/DJ was streaked, which could have been tears shed for her dead bandmates but might just as easily have been how it was originally applied. Winston couldn't remember.

Part of him pitied her, didn't want to hurt her, but as he looked at her, the buzzing behind his eyes intensified. His frontal lobe throbbed as his sixth sense for evil delivered some kind of vision. He was seeing things in split screen: the action on stage in his small eye, and a vision of his attacker in his big eye.

It was afterhours in the Killer Nutz's rehearsal space. He'd passed this place, Da Underworld, but never been inside. Wow, they had a sauna? Cool. The woman, DJ Cthulhu, was dressed only in a beach towel printed with esoteric pagan symbols. She was looking at polaroids of crime scenes, mutilated bodies and vehicular accidents, crimes she might have committed with her bandmates... and she was touching herself.

Ugh. Gross.

On stage, she hissed words he couldn't understand—some kind of dead old-world tongue—then pulled out a silver-tipped baton and circled him.

He whirled to face her, knocking the bassist off the stage with the end of his mop.

That was a happy accident; he hadn't known he'd been sneaking up on him.

The Tromaville High kids in the pit kicked the bearded guy to death when he tried to pull a knife on them.

"Ya!" The man in the ski mask and head-to-toe black sweats did a somersault, then a hand spring, then slipped on a puddle of blood and ended up between Winston and DJ Cthulhu as she swung down with her baton, cracking his neck. He started puking frothy foam through his ski mask.

Winston was getting tired of this.

He threw his mop like a javelin, impaling them both. For a moment he let them struggle there, skewered, then flung them into the nearest speaker stack. Blue electricity arced between the tangle of their limbs, sparks and applause exploding.

"Now, where did the mic go?" he asked. There was nobody left alive on stage to answer him.

Then he caught a metallic glint among all the gore and splayed bodies.

whooshawhoosha

Everyone in the crowd winced as Winston used the scratchy fabric of his tutu to try and clean the blood off the spitguard of the microphone.

"Okay. Testing. Can you hear me?"

"We love you, Toxie!"

"And I love you, but listen up. These dudes suck," he said, gesturing at the bodies stacked around him.

"They clap on the one and three. But more importantly, they're murderers!"

There was a shocked "Oooh!" from the crowd.

"They kill people for BTH! They killed Melvin Ferd!"

There was another "Oooh." He also heard a few people asking "Who?" but they could look it up later.

"Everything Melvin Ferd said, everything he was investigating, turned out to be true. And they killed him for it."

"Fuck BTH!" someone said, trying to start a chant, but Winston held his hands up. A chant would be great, but he was kind of still in the middle of his thing. If they wanted to chant after, awesome.

"You see this?" he said, pointing at himself. "You see me? Look at the river over there." He pointed out, beyond the crowd, beyond the square. "It's full of poison. They're getting rich and we're all of us getting sick! And BTH did it all!"

"Fuck BTH! Fuck BTH!"

Okay, the chant was back—fine, he was done—but now the mob was also turning into the beginnings of an angry mob. Wow, Tromaville really couldn't go a day without one.

He checked pulses—yep, all dead. Nobody he could interrogate.

No, wait—the dude in the chicken mask. He was the last member of the Killer Nutz alive. The last person who could tell him where they'd taken Wade.

Winston had to catch up with him.

J.J. would only get one chance at this.

The guy was really big.

She crouched behind the tree, a length of two-by-four propped up against her shoulder. If she was a hero, she wasn't cut out to be the type of hero the Toxic Avenger was. She was much more comfortable being tech support, doing heroics that involved C++.

She could hear his footsteps, so heavy they were digging up grass clumps and leaving sucking, muddy footprints even though the dirt of the park was pretty solid under her own feet.

His breathing under the mask even sounded like that of a chicken, halting and animal-scared.

She thought of how intimidating he'd been the night Mel had been killed. And now he was on the run, like a coward.

Two more steps.

She tightened her grip and rose from her crouch just as he passed the tree.

Muscles aching, J.J. Doherty swung the length of wood and cracked the guitarist across the neck and upper chest.

He hit the dirt, sent flat on his back.

Wow. That couldn't have gone any better.

She'd clotheslined the big bastard.

He groaned, sounding human but inhuman at the same time, seeming to echo inside his mask, like the mask was much too big for the head it contained. Then he started to rise again.

"Oh fuck," J.J. whispered as the guitarist—the size of a pro-wrestler—pulled himself to his feet with a nearby tree branch, staring down at J.J. as she backed out of his shadow.

She was going to have to hit him again, but where should she aim? Head or balls?

What would bring this monster down?

"Hey, cluckhead," Winston's voice called out.

He sounded winded from running to her from backstage. It was a decent enough quip, though.

"Ur?" the guitarist said, dazed, turning to face the Toxic Avenger.

Winston didn't have the height advantage; he looked up, red pupil of his big eye rolling up up to look at the eyeholes above the guitarist's wattle, and then let out a monstrous growl and dove forward, smashing into the giant at the waist, using his mass like a medicine ball and knocking him back into the dirt.

"Where is my son?!" Winston howled, clawing at the man's mask.

J.J. was unprepared for what was underneath.

The guitarist for the Killer Nutz, the only talented member of the band, was... a baby?

Or at least, he had the head of a baby.

"Oh, jeez," Winston said, and his booming monster voice had dropped a lot closer to its human register. "Oh, god."

The moist, pink baby's head on a giant's shoulders blinked back at him. A thin string of glassy saliva ran down the side of its cheek. It looked up at them both with its big eyes and cooed at them.

Winston swallowed a burp and made a hurking, gagging sound. "I don't know why, it's just so... weird-looking."

J.J. wasn't as grossed out as Winston. Besides, they were in a hurry.

"Where's his kid?" she yelled.

The baby head blinked back at her. It seemed like maybe it couldn't speak, couldn't form words with its tiny brain and dimpled-cheeked mouth.

But then it said a single word:

"Chüd... haven?"

Winston looked up to J.J., his expression asking if that meant anything to her.

Of course. It made perfect sense. Why hadn't she thought to say something before?

If Bob Garbinger was looking to lure the Toxic Avenger into a trap, why wouldn't the CEO of BTH retreat to where he had homefield advantage?

"I know it," she said. "Let's go."

"Cool," Winston replied, then looked down at the baby-headed giant under him.

He picked up the rubber chicken mask and then replaced it atop the thing's head, hiding the uncanny bald pate from view.

"Thanks, I guess," Winston said, getting off the... thing. Maybe he was letting it go because it had helped them, or maybe it was because he didn't want to brutally destroy something that looked like an infant. Or maybe he recognized a kindred spirit, in the guitar savant who hid his baby-head under a chicken mask. After all, they both lived in a world which, even while it adored them and idolized them, saw them as freaks.

"Go on now," Winston said, shooing the guitarist away. "Git."

They watched it stagger off, across a small footbridge, and out of the park.

Winston looked up at J.J.

"Do you remember where we left the car?"

TWENTY-ONE

"No, not like..."

"Sorry."

"You're going to break it! It's motorized. It..."

Ca-runch!

J.J. sighed and shook her head as she drove.

It had taken her a few minutes, but she'd finally found the switch on the Khaki Kar that closed the convertible top. And the one that made the car stop bouncing on its hydraulics.

But Winston had been impatient, didn't know his own strength, and now the roof wouldn't stay closed.

"Sorry," he said. "I can fix it, though. Look."

He held the joint of the car's canvas ceiling to the top of the windshield and crimped the steel together with his bare hands.

It worked, but now there was a large crack in the windshield, spiderwebbing out as she drove.

They stayed quiet for a few blocks after that.

"Roll up your window," J.J. said, breaking the silence. They were about to reach the outskirts of downtown. From that point on, the ride would all be Outer Tromaville, a place where you didn't want to breathe the air.

She was doing the driving, not only because she knew where she was going—vaguely, though she herself had never been to Chüdhaven—but also because Winston seemed spent after what had happened on stage at TromaFest.

He rolled up the window, the glass leaving a half-inch gap where it met the uneven convertible top, and they went back to being quiet.

Eventually, he started to doze.

J.J. looked over at him as she drove. Sure, it had looked like a lot of work, swinging that mop and disemboweling people with it, but she guessed there was more to it than that. She thought of all the secrets that'd been on that hard drive recording all the botched, dangerous experiments that BTH had run and that she'd wanted Melvin Ferd to report on—hell, even the successful experiments if you included all the biological runoff, gene-spliced compounds, and vaccine-resistant biohazards. If a person bathed in all of that, the changes wouldn't just be physical. There was a look that Winston got, when he was in the middle of doing his thing, like he wasn't totally in control.

As she drove them toward Chüdhaven, J.J. thought about the news footage and wondered how much of the "monster hero" sitting next to her was monster, how much of it was hero, and how much control Winston Gooze had over his two halves.

Oh, well. No use worrying about it now.

She drove for what seemed like a dozen more miles, at least. At one point, Winston blew a snot bubble out of one nostril and she turned on the radio to cover the sound of his phlegmy post-nasal drip. Outside, the view barely changed as she guided the sleek, expensive car across miles of chemically pockmarked, unchanging polluted terrain.

There was an expression in business about not shitting where you ate, but it didn't seem like Bob Garbinger had heard of it because his palatial mansion, its maintained grounds and its many topiaries, was bordered on all sides by the shits his company had taken over the last couple of decades. A hellscape wasteland of irradiated land, old BTH development centers, warehouses, and dump sites ringed the hills around Chüdhaven. Bob Garbinger lived far removed from the population center of St. Roma's Village, at the very border of the township's incorporated land, but he'd done nothing to protect the area immediately around where he lived from his own company's waste. On the plus side, all that ruination meant at least there'd be cover for them to hide the car and approach on foot.

"Wake up," J.J. said. "We're here." She pulled up beside a stack of oil drums labeled "EXTREMELY FLAMMABLE" and put the car in park.

There was probably a chance of permanent damage, if Winston kept doing this, but it was kind of fun.

"Seems like two guards," he said.

"Armed?" asked J.J., crouching next to him behind the tree.

"Oh, yeah. Super-armed. Like, with machine guns."

"Fuck. What are they doing?"

"Just talking to each other?"

"Can we sneak in?" she asked.

Winston tilted his big eye, squeezing the base of the orb with his fingertips to see around the edge of the tree while closing his human eye to avoid getting a weird double-vision effect. His vision was getting all red and swimmy and he could feel the eye cooling and shriveling in the breeze as he held it out.

"I don't think so," he said. "There's nothing for us to hide behind. The trees stop on this side of the hill and it's pretty wide open."

"Hmm. Only two guards, though," she said. "I think I have a plan. Just follow my lead."

Winston pulled his hand back behind the tree, then snaked his stretchy optic nerve back into his skull and popped the eye back into place.

He blinked, then held up two fingers in front of him. Then three.

Yup, no damage. He could see just fine.

With both his eyes back in his head, Winston looked over to J.J., who made no effort to hide the disgust on her face. "Ew," she said, then walked out of cover. "Stay here."

He did, watching as she walked down the footpath leading to the mansion. The house was huge with arched windows, gothic filigree, and a heavy-duty iron fence that stretched around its gardens and outbuildings.

As he watched, J.J.'s stride started to change, and she started to swing her hips wide and put more bounce into her steps. It was kind of sexy.

No, he told himself. *Mind on the mission.* He suppressed his rising desire and got ready to "follow her lead" ...whatever that meant.

Winston leaned a little further out of cover, getting ready to run and help her.

The guards hadn't noticed her yet, were still motioning at each other, one hand on the guns slung at their waists, having a friendly argument.

J.J. unzipped her jacket and pushed her chest out. She clearly hadn't expected to get this close to the front gate without the guards noticing her.

Winston stepped out of cover, staying low as he crept forward. This was stupid. He should have been the one trying to break in the front gate. He was the bullet sponge. J.J. had only been shot once, and she hadn't handled it well.

Then she reached up and curled a strand of hair around her fingertip. *Ohhhh.* He understood—this was a honey trap. She'd work her feminine wiles, get the guards to put their guns down, and he'd run up and—

She was within striking distance of the men and they still hadn't noticed her.

"Heyyyy, boyyys," she said, throaty and sexy.

But neither of the guards seemed to think her efforts seductive, they were both startled to see a woman appear beside them.

The guard on the left must have had his finger on the trigger, because as he flinched he blew the top of his friend's head off.

J.J. jumped back.

In his death throes, the headshot guard squeezed off a quick burst of automatic fire, strafing the area in front of him, shooting the other guard in the chest and stomach.

"Whoa!" Winston said, jogging over to the gate. "That plan was insane!"

J.J. turned to him, spitting into the gravel. There was blood on her face and cleavage.

"I... I was just going to distract them."

He patted her on the shoulder as she wiped her chin and zipped herself back up. There was no time. If there were other guards walking the grounds, they would have heard the shots and would be on their way. They'd lost the element of surprise.

"Come on," Winston said. "I've got to find my boy."

They stayed low, putting the garden's hedges between them and the mansion's many windows as they searched for a way in.

They'd stopped in front of a fountain, eventually crouching for cover behind the lip of a fountain featuring an anatomically correct Romanesque statue of Bob Garbinger, standing on a marble column rising out of the center of the pool. The sculptor had gotten the likeness right in the nose and eyes, but there was something about the mouth that seemed off…

Doesn't matter, Winston chided himself. They weren't here to sightsee or judge the art. They had to find where Wade was being held.

"Do we just… break in?" Winston asked.

"No, there's got to be a smarter way. We don't know where they're—"

"Winston! Dad!"

Winston stood. *Wade!*

"Wait, Winston," J.J. hissed, pulling at his tutu, but Winston pulled himself free. He wasn't going to hide anymore.

Stealth wasn't how the Toxic Avenger operated.

Over the next series of hedges, there was a wood-and-steel outbuilding flanked by two large gas tanks. Winston's big eye zoomed in to assess the situation. The door was open a crack, held closed with a chain, and from inside a boy's hand was waving.

"Wade!" Winston called.

"Don't!" J.J. hissed, springing up, still gripping the fabric of his outfit. "It could be a—"

Psssssssttttt.

"—trap."

They both turned toward the sound. The mouth of the statue of Bob Garbinger was now open and belching out a thick yellow cloud of…

…a cloud of…

J.J. collapsed onto the footstones in front of the fountain.

Winston fell harder, splashing face down into the scummy, duck-poop-filled water.

"What did you say?" Garbinger asked, the gas mask muffling his voice but failing to filter out his smugness.

"No, really, when I told you my idea about the knockout-gas statue, what did you say?"

Kissy crossed her arms. Her own mask was beginning to chafe.

"I said I thought it was a waste of—"

"Waste of money. Uh-huh." Garbinger pointed down at J.J., who was lying with her head pillowed under one hand like she was only sleeping. She had very nice skin, Kissy noticed with a pang of jealousy. Then her boss pointed to the creature. It was ghastly to look at. So much uglier than Fritz.

"Money," Garbinger repeated. "Gotta spend it to make it, baby."

She clucked her tongue. Yes. He was a great man, and even in this one hyper-specific area, his impulses had been right. "Well. In retrospect, anyway," she said. It wouldn't do to massage his ego that much.

Below them, bubbles leaked out of the monster's mouth. Winston Gooze. Thirteen years in the janitorial division. Kissy smiled. Well, he'd finally made something of himself.

"Okay, let's get this ugly bastard up and get to work," Garbinger said. "Call the grunts."

Kissy did as she was told.

TWENTY-TWO

J.J.'s eyes fluttered open.

There was a moment, a gauzy half-second of semi-consciousness, when she thought it'd all been a dream. But then she looked over and saw Winston, trussed up and dangling from a support jutting from the wall, his head lolling to the side. At his nostril, the same snot bubble he'd had in the car was expanding and contracting.

Well. He was still breathing, at least.

She looked down and saw manacles on each wrist and more chains around her waist, tethering her midsection to the ground. But maybe there was enough slack in her own restraints that she could reach over and jostle Winston awake, if she could just get her gas-fogged limbs to—

"No no no, that won't work," a voice said.

J.J.'s head jerked round and she fought an urge to puke.

"It has to be positioned here, see? It's going to enter over L3. Then the dermal drill will come in at an angle."

Two guys in lab coats were standing over a piece of machinery, arguing. It was hard to pay attention to what they were saying, partly because she was too busy looking at the contraption and also because what they were saying didn't make much sense.

Parts of the machine were gleaming chrome while others looked like they'd been made out of wrought iron, like it was some medieval torture device that had been updated with space-age alloys and surgical equipment. It had six segmented crablike arms, each tipped with needles, attached to a body that looked like a human spine, each vertebra pincushioned with drill bits.

Beneath the device, on the cart the two research nerds had used to wheel it into the room, was a nest of cables, keyboards, readout screens, and a hard drive, much like the one J.J. had smashed on the asphalt outside Melvin Ferd's office building. Probably filled with just as many damning company secrets.

J.J.'s chains rattled, reminding her that she wasn't in a position to steal anything.

She looked around the room. Three caged lightbulbs. No windows, low ceilings—much lower than you'd expect a room in an eccentric millionaire CEO's mansion to have. Wherever they were, whatever facility this was—if it was even still part of Chüdhaven—they were in deep.

In deep shit, she thought sourly. This was the kind of room you woke up in before being tortured to death.

As if to punctuate this thought, the metal door creaked open and Bob Garbinger entered the torture room wearing a robe and slippers, looking as if he might have just been sipping scotch and reading the paper. So maybe they *were* still in Chüdhaven.

Garbinger ignored J.J., instead crossing to where Winston was chained. He walked a complete circle around the unconscious man, admiring his deformities, playing with the tulle of his tutu.

Both of the nerds stood at attention beside their machine, silent now, watching Garbinger nervously as if their boss was the real danger in the room—which, J.J. reflected, he was.

Garbinger reached out to stroke Winston's cheek, making small circles around a pustule beside his nose, avoiding the snot. Then he smacked him across the face.

He smacked him again, harder.

Winston's big eye, only half-lidded to begin with, opened. The pupil bobbled like the token in a Magic 8 Ball, then focused on Garbinger. The Toxic Avenger's features sharpened. He looked angry. In Winston's throat—a throat that was shackled and bolted to the rest of his chains with heavy eye-bolts—a growl began.

If Garbinger was intimidated, he didn't show it. In fact, he mimed a yawn and waited for the growl to reach a natural endpoint. Then he said, "I feel like you've learned a pretty severe lesson about theft in the workplace."

Behind him, the guys in the lab coats went back to work on their machine.

"The fun thing is, this all started when you tried to rob me," Garbinger continued. "But ultimately, all of this..." He put his hand on the side of Winston's pulsing skull, which seemed to pulse faster the more awake and angrier he got. "All of this is going to make me a fucking barn full of money."

He dropped his hand down to Winston's bicep and squeezed. The veins and tendons there glowed purple and green as Winston struggled.

"I mean, shit, look at those guns, huh? Steroids on steroids! Something like that for the slogan. That'll be how we market—"

"Get away from him, you *pig*!" J.J. hissed. She'd had enough. If Winston still wasn't awake enough or in control enough to speak for himself, she'd do it.

It was almost like Garbinger hadn't heard her, but then he set his jaw in annoyance and turned to her, feigning surprise, like he hadn't even noticed she was chained there until that moment.

"I'm not even talking to *you* right now. *You* make me so goddamn irritated."

She tried to spit in his face, but she didn't have a lot of saliva and her aim was all wrong, so a trail of bubbly spit dribbled down her chin.

He didn't seem to notice that, either.

"Durrr," Garbinger started. "I read an excerpt from Marx in freshman composition and now all I can think is 'businessmen are bad,' durrr."

She… she didn't sound like that.

"Fuck you! I—"

"Be quiet!" Garbinger snapped. His face flashed red for an instant and J.J. recoiled, sure that he was about to hit her, but he just leaned back and added in his normal speaking voice, "The adults are talking. Now, if you don't be quiet, I'll have my mercs skip the interrogation part and simply kill you and bury you in the rose garden. Okay?"

He turned back to Winston, not waiting for her reply.

"Tell me, Mr. Gooze, did it hurt? Your… becoming?"

Winston didn't answer, just stared straight forward, leaning against his chains, probably choking himself in the process.

"That's okay. I'll find out myself if it hurts, then have the boys in the Side-effects Department iron out the wording on whatever warnings we need to disclose before launch. What's a little pain if the rewards are…"

He trailed off, then turned to the two white-coated men and motioned to their machine.

"You may proceed," he said, then started to leave through the room's heavy steel door.

"Garbinger," Winston said, his voice raspy but firm.

He was starting to coming out of his stupor.

Garbinger stopped and turned, smiling at Winston.

"You're going to find out what hurts," Winston said.

There was a beat. The two men, bronzed narcissist and shackled mutant, regarded each other.

"Uh, because," Winston said, "because I'm going to—"

"No, I got it," Garbinger said, "but I just said I was going to find out if it hurt. You're just repeating what I said. So, I don't know, your big dramatic line was kind of a hat on a hat."

"I'll make sure it hurts—"

"No, no. Stop. You're embarrassing yourself. The moment passed," Garbinger said, and walked through the doorway, leaving them alone with the researchers and their device.

Winston frowned and looked over at J.J.

"I'm sorry," he said.

"Well, it wasn't a good line," J.J. said, before she realized that he probably was apologizing for everything else, falling into Garbinger's trap and allowing them to be captured in the first place.

The two techs approached, both looking a little apprehensive about getting within grabbing distance of Winston.

"So, this is pretty bad, right?" one asked the other as they worked.

"Oh, yeah," his colleague answered, uncurling a length of semi-translucent hose and hooking it up to the back of the machine. They pushed the cart and device behind Winston and locked the wheels.

"I mean, like, morally," the other one said. He tightened a crank and the arms of the device reached out and latched onto Winston's back and outstretched arms, the drill bits lining up with his spine.

"Yeah, it's terrible," the second researcher replied, then typed a few quick commands on a keyboard below the monitors.

There was a beep and the drill bits all began to whirl, burrowing into Winston's back. At first it didn't seem like the machinery would be powerful enough to pierce the Toxic

Avenger's tough hide, but then the air filled with the smell of burning flesh and bone as the drill bits cooked the meat around Winston's spinal column.

J.J. wanted to scream at them to stop, but she was sobbing too hard.

Then there was a sound like a vacuum cleaner starting up and the hose now attached to the back of Winston's neck filled with a viscous purple liquid.

Winston began to scream.

It started as the howl of the monster, strong, scary, baritone, but after a few seconds it was the high-pitched human squeal of a very frightened man.

Kissy watched as Sawser—or was that the other one?—let the door swing open behind them.

As it closed, she caught a glimpse of the creature. He didn't look so tough, not as he was at least, dripping bodily fluids, his lifeforce sliding toward the drain in the floor. In fact, he looked kind of pathetic, slumped against his chains, partially asphyxiating himself. Smoke curled from the needles and extraction drills that porcupined the monster's flesh.

"The mutagenics are in range," one of the techs said, "but..."

"But?" Garbinger prompted, snatching the vial from him.

"Some of the sub-sequences are flawed," the man's lab partner answered.

Garbinger paused before responding, holding the vial up to inspect it under the laboratory's clean, white light. The glass vial was filled with a thick purple substance, a few ragged air bubbles clinging to the corners of the container like jelly.

"Then run it again," he said, not taking his eyes off the vial. Kissy wished he'd look at her like that.

"But, sir, the subject will likely not survive another extraction," the first tech said.

Garbinger looked over to his brother, then to Kissy, then back to Sawser and Kupp, and shrugged.

"Let's hope he does, or—" He motioned to Fritz. "—no Christmas bonuses for these two."

Sawser and Kupp shared a look, swallowed hard, and got back to work.

Garbinger, Fritz, and Kissy stood together in the lab for a moment. Fritz looked about ready to break his silence, it was clear he wanted to ask his brother something, the way he was tapping his cane on the floor, but Robert held up a finger.

"I've got to go topside," he said. Then, to Kissy: "I need me-time. It's been a long day. A lot of activity. Keep me updated, but don't disturb me unless it's about this."

"Of course," Kissy said. She was smiling. She loved seeing him happy, and loved seeing Fritz dismissed and disregarded.

Garbinger entered the elevator to head back up to his office, staring down at the purple vial in his hands and repeating, "This, this, *this*" in a whisper.

TWENTY-THREE

Spence Barkabus stood in the shadows behind one end of the room's long, fancy oak table and tried to stay quiet.

His stitches itched, but the doctor—the *second* doctor, the one who'd put the arm back on the right way—had told him he couldn't scratch, and he'd sounded serious, lecturing Spence using technical jargon like *necrosis* and *nerve damage* and *if you keep scratching, your arm'll fall off.*

So even though Spence wanted to scratch sooooooo bad, he let his arm hang motionless in its sling as he waited, looking around the room. Beside the table, a fire raged below a mantelpiece bedecked with various ornaments and awards. There was also a desk, a large rug made out of some kind of animal, gnarly-looking antique weaponry hung on the walls, and a fully functional bar.

Maybe when this was all over, Spence would step behind that bar and pour himself a stiff drink.

Garbinger entered the room, but he didn't notice the four of them, Spence and his two fellow goons, Cooper and Taylor, standing in the shadows while Dad sat at the end of the table. The CEO was too busy looking intently at something he was holding.

Dad cleared his throat, but Garbinger didn't turn; he simply parted a curtain and held the glistening purple object in his hand up to the light.

"I'm assuming," Dad said loudly, "that you heard this?"

Garbinger turned and finally saw Dad sitting there in the shadows, the light from the crackling fire playing across one side of his face. When it came to striking a pose that said "underworld intimidation," Spence's dad was one of the all-time best to ever do it.

Then Garbinger looked over, noticing Spence. And then Cooper. And then Taylor. Three Khaki enforcers, Spence not looking his usually fresh self because of the sling.

The CEO's expression dropped. A rich boy finally having to face a little adversity. Spence loved to see it.

Garbinger was no longer preoccupied with whatever he was holding. Yeah, not the smartest guy they'd ever dealt with, but Garbinger was savvy enough to realize that this was not a social call if Dad had brought this much muscle with him.

"Here, they're playing it again," Dad said. He wheeled the TV cart from behind his chair and unmuted the sound.

"...Village is cutting them off. All municipal cooperation with the Body Talk Healthstyle Corporation is suspended." They all watched as Mayor Togar gave a press conference, her dopey husband standing behind her, nodding and sweating. "This is pending a thorough investigation of the troubling allegations made by the Toxic Avenger at this year's festival."

"And that's not the only hot water, Rick. Let's go over to the—"

Dad muted the news report once more, but on screen the anchor tossed it over to the social media desk and a guy with a tablet showed the public's reaction, scrolling through the hashtags that were currently trending: #fuckthenutz, #Toxie, and, most worrisome, #BTH_Kills.

Then there were clips of the freak addressing the crowd. Just seeing that mofo made Spence's arm itch worse.

"You said it was handled," Thad Barkabus said, leaning forward in his chair. "You gave me your word."

Dad didn't sound angry, which was probably how Garbinger knew he ought to be frightened.

"This... It'll pass," Garbinger said, taking a step toward the table, pulling his silk robe closed like it had suddenly gotten cold in here. "We can wait them out. Tromaville's got a short memory. And I'm not being metaphorical. Like, clinically, there's something in the water that shortens their—"

Spence's dad put up a hand. When a Barkabus did that, people tended to listen.

"Who's this *we* you're talking about?" he asked.

"All of our losses are r-r-recoverable," Garbinger stammered.

On the other side of the table, Taylor undid the zipper on his windbreaker and put his hands in his pants pockets, letting the butts of his pistols hang out. Garbinger looked over at the enforcer.

"That ship has sailed," Dad said, drawing attention back to himself. "This isn't about recovery, it's about survival. You're a target now, which means your whole operation gets pried open and anyone connected to it or you become a target too. Even if they're only surreptitiously connected."

Oh, *surreptitiously*. Good word. Spence would have to remember to look it up later.

"I would..." Garbinger began, moving toward the fireplace, one hand in the pocket of his robe, the other out toward Spence's dad. "I would never tell them anything about you. About us."

"Bob," Spence's dad said, then stood from his chair, crossing to his old friend. "You say that like you'll have any control over what happens."

"But I do! I-I-I will! Moments ago, right here on site, we had the breakthrough of the millennium!" Garbinger blurted. Spence hadn't even been working enforcement and collections that long, but he'd heard that tone of voice before, from people who couldn't pay.

"It's a game-changer! The ultimate bio-booster! We'll call it Champion Sauce."

Spence's dad frowned and placed a hand on Garbinger's shoulder. The CEO continued with his frantic sales pitch, babbling to save his own life.

"Or, if you don't like that name, maybe God Soda. Whatever. The name doesn't matter. We'll have marketing whip up a pitch deck, do some brand testing. Everyone will be eating out of my hand, just like the old days."

"Hush, Bozo. Just hush."

Spence nodded at Taylor, then at Cooper.

It was time. The two enforcers twisted the suppressors onto the barrels of their weapons.

Spence did not, because that would require two working hands, which he did not have because of this asshole's deformed employee.

"Wait!" Garbinger yelled, stepping back from Dad. "Can you just..." He slicked down his hair with one hand, trying to regain that polished coolness Spence had seen him exhibit at product launches and banquet dinners since Spence was a kid. "Do you mind if I have a quick drink?" He waved over to the bar. "Just one for the road, so to speak?"

Cooper and Taylor looked at Spence, their guns drawn.

"Don't look at me," he said, indicating his father.

Dad shrugged. "Why not."

This was fishy. Dad liked Bob Garbinger. They'd been partners for a long time and had made each other very rich, but now Spence could feel that he was letting that closeness cloud his judgment.

They hadn't checked this room, and Dad was standing just a little bit too close to Garbinger, who could have anything stashed behind that bar: a shotgun, a panic button to summon his private mercs, anything.

"We had a good run, huh?" Garbinger asked Thad Barkabus, walking behind the bar, taking his one hand out of his pocket.

"Keep your hands up above the bar," Spence said.

His dad turned back to him and gave him a look.

Spence buttoned it.

"No, really, Thad. You and me, we had a good run," Garbinger said. He had a rocks glass out, was pouring some brown liquor into it. He wasn't drawing a concealed weapon; he really was mixing himself a drink.

"Don't stall, Bozo," Dad said. "It's cheap and undignified."

Bob Garbinger nodded at that and held up his drink. It was bourbon and... what the hell else was in that glass? Some kind of neon liqueur? The kind that tasted like blueberries and was marketed to high-school kids? Disgusting. Spence hated that shit.

Garbinger walked out from behind the bar and over to the other end of the table. Spence started to relax.

Then Garbinger downed the whole cocktail like a shooter and he sat down.

Spence blinked. Were they... were they supposed to shoot him now? While he was sat down?

Dad gave them the nod.

Cooper and Taylor aimed their guns, each taking a few steps away from the fireplace, down the long table. They were making the target smaller—no need to waste bullets.

But there was something going on with Garbinger.

He wasn't begging. He wasn't crying. He was... smiling?

It was hard to see in here. It had been light enough when they'd come in and set up, but now every light in the room seemed dimmer. There was a gust of wind coming from somewhere and the curtains parted, then closed completely, blocking out even more of the light.

"Bozo?" Dad asked.

"Uhhh..." Spence heard himself say.

"Nobody calls me that anymore," Garbinger said, but now his voice was more of a gurgle. The fire popped, flaring, and Spence could see that Robert Garbinger's face had changed too. Was chang*ing*.

His eyebrows had grown out and begun to curl upwards. His nails, usually so manicured, were growing too, not just getting longer but becoming thick and irregularly shaped. His lip peeled back, revealing teeth that were bleeding, reshaping themselves.

But the worst of it was his eyes. The yellow glow of his eyes.

"Fuck this!" Taylor yelled and opened fire.

Pfft! Pfft! Pfft!

Even with the suppressor, the gunfire felt loud, solid, in this grand wood-lined room.

Cooper began firing too, but it was clear by his second muzzle flash that the chair was empty, that Robert Garbinger was no longer a sitting target.

"Where'd he—" Cooper started, but he got no further before the shape rose up behind him and raked its claws down the side of his face.

Cooper's eyeball ruptured, dribbling down his face, and then a second handful of claws dug into his throat and abruptly ended his screams.

Okay, silencer or not, Spence grabbed his pistol from his jacket, his arm and shoulder stinging at the strain on his sutures.

The creature was over the table now, running on all fours like some kind of fucking werewolf as it launched itself at Taylor, who screamed.

Dad was speaking, trying to reason with this fucking manbeast.

"Boz—I mean Bob! Bob, stop this! Let's figure things out."

There was a loud crunch, like a bundle of celery being twisted in half, and Taylor's head was suddenly completely turned around, his nose facing the same direction as his ass. Then the creature brought Taylor's body close and tore off a chunk of flesh from the side of his neck.

It was becoming hard to see.

Somehow the fire had died down in the last few seconds, like all the oxygen had been sucked out of the room.

There were the sounds of wet chewing and thudding footfalls.

"Mister Bark— Dad!" Spence yelled into the darkness. He was supposed to call him Mr. Barkabus on the clock, but now he just wanted his dad.

But he couldn't see him. Couldn't tell where anything was in this big dark room.

Then he could see, but wished he couldn't.

Dad stumbled out of the shadows, collapsing onto his son, who had to drop the gun to hold him up. In the glow of the embers and the light of the small TV, Spence could see his father's *brain* glistening. His dad's mouth worked, but no words came out, just the soft *plop-plop* of shattered teeth and shredded gums dripping onto the hardwood floor from the bite wound that had bisected his head.

And then, out of those same shadows, came Bob Garbinger.

Bozo.

His chin dripping with blood. His new, demonic features hairy and angular on his formerly handsome face. His yellow eyes glowing, narrowing as he approached Spence.

Claws dug into the meat of Spence's injured arm, then yanked.

Spence's twice-reattached limb flew onto the fire. The new kindling caused the flames to lick back to life.

Before unconsciousness claimed him, the last thing Spence Barkabus thought, watching his arm burn, was:

Not again.

THIS STORY'S GOT TWO MONSTERS IN IT?

Oh, hell yeah.

Did you see that thing? I mean, poor Spence only caught it in shadow, and didn't describe it how I would probably have described it. But it seemed like it was pretty cool! That scene—such a bold departure from the original film—will probably have its detractors, especially on Twitter, X, whatever, but I gotta say it here, for the record: I'm a fan!

Seems like even if Toxie and J.J. manage to get out of their chains, they're still going to have to face down Monster Garbinger. And who knows? He looks strong. Our heroes might be six degrees of fucked, if you catch my meaning.

But wait. Kissy's coming back into the room.

She's about to see Garbinger, her boss-stroke-crush—

Oh, gross. He's drinking their blood.

And he's got, like, horns? Or is that his skull pointing upward like that? Wow. And we all thought Winston was ugly. Get a load of this gross troll in a tattered silk robe.

Kissy looks scared.

There's body parts all around Monster Garbinger, where he's huddled on the floor. He seems to eat the soft tissues first. Wow.

That's pretty disturbing, maybe even erotic, watching him chow down on that guy's...

Oh. He sees her. Is Monster Garbinger going to recognize his trusty assist— associate? Or is he too far gone, too much of a monster?

Maybe he'll tear her apart too.

TWENTY-FOUR

Garbinger looked up at Kissy with those bestial eyes.

"Mmmma," he began, trying to speak with his mouth full. A clotted, jellied ball of gore fell out of his mouth. "My love, I feel unwell."

It was such a strange sensation, to go from abject terror to blushing.

My love.

She looked over to the bar, the bulbs there flickering. She saw the bottle and next to it, the vial.

He'd done it.

They'd told him the sample was unstable but he'd taken it anyway.

He was so... *brave.*

Monster Garbinger stared up at Kissy, his yellow eyes softening, silently pleading for her help, for her guidance.

She didn't want him to be like this. She didn't want him to be alone in being like this.

Kissy crossed to the bar, picked up the vial, and before she could even think about it, tried to drink whatever was left.

But there was nothing.

No! There had to be something. She ran her tongue around the inside of the vial. What was left tasted terrible, but there was no way it'd be enough.

An ancient memory surfaced: Kissy in a production of *Romeo and Juliet* as a child, back in the UK, in Year 5. "O churl, drunk all, and left no friendly drop to help me after?"

She turned back to Robert Garbinger, her misshapen Romeo.

"'I will kiss thy lips,'" she quoted. "'Haply some poison yet doth hang on them.'" But then she looked, really *looked* at his freckled, goat-like lips and snaggletoothed fangs, and maybe she wouldn't chance kissing him, not right now.

"Help me, Kissy," Garbinger said, his voice barely recognizable.

She looked around. Thad Barkabus was dead as dead could be, his skull hollowed out, what was left looking like the remains of a meal in a chipped china bowl. Bullet wounds peppered the priceless woodwork of Chüdhaven. And there was so much *blood*. She wouldn't be surprised if it started dripping from the ceiling down in the lab.

The lab!

"Okay," she said, forming a plan. The bad taste in her mouth lingered from where she'd licked the vial. "Never worry. I'll take care of everything."

My love.

Down in the lab, Fritz looked at his brother, slumped in a wheelchair and carted down here by Kissy.

He should feel something—worry for his big brother's welfare. Even if he didn't actually care about Robert, the abusive prick, he should at least be feeling anxiety that the walls were closing in, the feds were at the door, and he himself had been the one to order BTH's most heinous crimes.

And if he couldn't feel those negative feelings, he should at least have a hint of schadenfreude, even joy at Robert's disfigurement—after all, Fritz was now the handsome Garbinger brother.

But he couldn't make himself feel anything.

"I don't want explanations!" Kissy yelled at Kupp and Sawser. "I want results!"

She looked bad. Haggard. Much less kempt than usual. Her skin was sallow, her makeup was streaked, and her teeth had a yellowish tinge.

"His body is rejecting the serum," Kupp said.

Kissy looked to the mercenary by the door, eyeing his rifle.

"There's—" Sawser started to add, but Kissy cut him off.

"Get it to unreject the serum. Can't you see the..." She pointed to Robert. "...the mental state he's clearly in?"

Robert was monologuing:

"Take dictation, my dear. Superiority... whether striven for or ingrained, is an obligation..." His voice trailed off and he leaned onto one arm of his wheelchair and farted loudly. He nodded, like he was agreeing with the fart. "That's even better."

"We warned him it wasn't perfected," Kupp said, gagging as the stink of Robert's monstrous gas reached him. Fritz held his breath.

"So fucking perfect it!" Kissy screamed. She put a hand on Robert's shoulder, but he didn't seem to notice her, kept dictating to her even though nobody could understand what he was saying.

"We'll... we'll try," the lab tech said.

"My god, you two are tedious. Who signs your checks?"

Those orders given, she turned to the armed guards.

Fritz had always wondered, in case of an emergency, if something happened to Robert, how he would handle running things. It turned out he didn't have to worry: Kissy was second in command.

He hated her, and it was good to feel something after the numbness he'd experienced at seeing his brother brought low, turned into a monstrous shell of his former self.

She whirled to the pair of armed guards flanking the doorway. "You two," she barked. "The mess upstairs. It needs to be taken care of. No traces."

"And the hostage?" one of the guards asked.

He meant the boy.

"No witnesses either," Kissy said, dismissing them.

"Wait, what?" Fritz asked, and the two guards stopped and looked at each other doubtfully, unclear who their boss was at this moment. The chain of command.

Fritz leaned forward on his cane, feeling some blood return to his limbs. He'd kept still too long.

"You didn't think we were going to just let the boy go?" Kissy said. "After this?"

She indicated the lab, then the door to the holding cell containing the boy's father and the spy.

Fritz had to agree she had a point, but he looked down at Robert, who was licking the drying blood from his long fingernails, like a cat grooming its paws. His eyes were unfocused, the new hair on his chin curling like a billy goat's beard.

"But he's a child," he said.

"And it was your sterling idea to bring that child here in the first place," Kissy said. And she was smiling. There was something wrong with her. She looked almost demonic—maybe not as full blown a transformation as what Robert had undergone, but she'd done something to herself.

She turned to the mercs, snapped her longer-than-normal fingers together, and said, "Take care of it."

Fritz took two steps toward the elevator, nearly falling over on the second.

"No!" he shouted.

They all looked at him. Even Robert seemed to pay attention for a moment.

"We're not going to do that," Fritz said. "Not going to kill the boy."

Kissy walked over to him, her heels clicking, a slight smile quirking the side of her mouth, and Fritz was unnerved to notice she had a few new wispy hairs growing on her upper lip.

"You disloyal gimp," she said in a whisper just for the two of them. Her breath was putrid. "That is your brother I'm trying to protect."

Fritz leaned on his cane, looking past her toward the transformed Robert. The creature was shivering, at once horrifying and pitiful to look upon.

"No it's not," he said. And now he was sad, to have lost Robert like this, a vibrant man no longer able to put a sentence together.

Kissy didn't rage. Instead, her smile widened until he could see pointed yellowed teeth. In one swift movement, she snatched his cane, and before gravity could pull him too far forward, she brought a knee up to smash into his crotch. The pain was truly blinding, the white flash of the fluorescent lights above them becoming absolute for a moment.

Then she started to beat him with his own cane. It was a lightweight model—it needed to be, for him to haul it around, he was such a frail man—but still the blows stung. It was almost exactly the same sensation as a mother beating her lame child with a hickory switch, which was a sensation with which Fritz Garbinger was very familiar.

He screamed, but the blows kept coming. He crawled forward, reaching out for his brother, for Robert's help, but the thing that had been Robert Garbinger just stared forward blankly, one clawed hand scratching at the horn-lumps atop his head.

Eventually, the *thwack-thwack* of the cane stopped and Kissy threw it down beside Fritz.

"What are you all looking at?" she snapped at the four other men. "You two." She indicated Kupp and Sawser. "Fix him. And you two." She nodded at the men with guns. "No witnesses."

TWENTY-FIVE

J.J. couldn't hear everything happening on the other side of the torture-room door, and she couldn't understand half of what she did hear, but what she could hear and understand wasn't good.

"Hey, come on," she said, struggling against her own chains, trying to reach Winston to jostle him awake. She was able to reach out, put a hand on his shoulder, send him rocking in his own restraints like a baby in a doorway jumper.

He swung, leaking streaks of viscous goo on the floor. Whatever they were extracting out of the Toxic Avenger with that machine, it was leaving him depleted. He'd be dead soon.

"Winston, get up!" she hissed, then decided to tell him the bad news, if it was going to make a difference:

"Winston," she said. "You *have* to wake up. They're going to kill Wade!"

His eyes opened, but only for a moment, and J.J. couldn't tell whether he was lapsing back into unconsciousness or he'd just given up.

What did she do? Was there even a way out of this? Certainly not if she didn't have the Toxic Avenger's help, and right now the hero had no mop, no blood, and no will to live.

"Mel would be so pissed at me," she said to herself.

Sometimes talking to herself made her think better.

"Pishhed," Winston slurred, drooling down his front.

"Huh?" J.J. asked.

He opened his eyes, his big eye rolling over to look at her, the pupil contracting to an alert pinpoint.

"Pissed," he repeated.

Uh… okay. Maybe whatever the scientists had done to him had caused him to have a stroke. Maybe he was already brain dead.

"I…" he said. "I gotta get my dick out."

And then he began to buck against his restraints, thrusting into the air with his groin.

J.J. watched him flounder there. It may have been the lowest point of her day, which was definitely saying something.

"Get it *out*?" she asked, repeating his words back to him. Seeing if he really wanted to continue down this path, if this really were their last hours on Earth. If there was any sense to what he was saying and doing at all.

"*Take* it out, sorry." He kept thrusting but he wasn't getting anywhere, just making himself dizzy as he spun.

"Your *dick*?"

"My wiener. I'm sorry, I don't know the right words."

"I told you they're going to kill your boy," J.J. said, trying to speak slowly and clearly. "Just so I understand: What do you think this moment is, exactly?"

"Please," Winston said. "There's no time. You have to trust me."

She looked him in his one human eye as best she could as he twisted back and forth in his chains.

He wasn't crazy. He was sincerely asking her to help take his dick out. He thought it would help somehow.

"I swear to god," she said, "if you're being perverted right now…"

She reached out. Oh lord, she was doing this. Would she even make it? Would her own chains have enough slack to let her reach?

He needed to stop moving or she wouldn't be able to—

She closed her hand.

Got it. She eventually managed to grab onto the crotch of his pants, the leotard stretched over them, and held on, making eye contact.

Was he absolutely sure about this?

Winston nodded.

"I promise you, I am not a pervert," he said. And then, with his Toxic cock out, he added, "Okay, watch out. Don't let it splash you."

"Wait, what?"

"I'm going to piss in my face."

Okay, Winston.

This is it. This is the big game.

Pee shyness is one hundred percent a mental obstacle.

He closed his eyes, then tried to pull himself up. He was so weak. His muscles felt like taffy.

"You're not looking, right?" he asked.

"Believe me, my eyes are closed and I am turned away."

Why had he asked her that? Hearing her voice so close, in the same room, clenched his urethra and froze his bladder.

Relax. It's all in the mind.

Your boy needs you.

He tried again. It wasn't enough to just piss. He needed to get it...

He could feel the tendons in his shoulders and arms howl as he pushed against his restraints like they were a pair of still rings in a gymnastics routine. But this wasn't just any gymnastics routine.

This was the goddamn Olympics.

He crunched his stomach muscles, trying to get his feet above his head… and it worked! Gravity caused his penis to flop forward so it was pointed in the right direction. Now he just needed to…

Ugh. Why was this so hard? Why was pee shyness the one aspect of his old body that continued to haunt him in his new one?

Focus! You just need to…

Do something! Wade's voice yelled in his head.

Yes.

He was a hero, and heroes didn't get piss shy.

Drip-drip-pat-drip…

It started as a spritz, but soon it became a warm, splashy stream.

He crunched his abs, wiggling to redirect his member and make sure he got good enough coverage to really give the thick shackles around his neck a good dousing.

Psssssssstttttt.

It was working! It was warm and kind of salty, and it was working! His corrosive piss was eating away at the chains! The ring around his neck popped open, his left wrist snapped free, and then… then he fell to the tile floor, dripping. He shook himself like a wet dog, making sure not to burn J.J.

"Okay," he said. He still had a little bit left in the tank. "Don't worry. I'll have much better aim now."

Once J.J. was free, she took a moment to gag and rub at her wrists.

Winston looked around the room, his eyes falling onto the machine with its tubes and drills. That thing had hurt him so bad. He was feeling better now, but they'd tortured him with it, taken something from him.

He raised his fists above his head, ready to smash the device to pieces.

"Wait!" J.J. yelled.

He paused at the last second and she dove in front of him, pulling wires out of the base of the machine.

"Evidence," she said, holding up a hard drive. "Maybe even a cure."

Winston nodded, tucked himself in, and zipped up. She was right. And besides, smashing the machine would make a lot of noise and attract unwanted attention. She was trying to think several moves ahead. He needed to get his head in the same state.

"Okay, you get to the car," he said. "I'll get Wade."

She nodded. He punched the steel door off its hinges and they entered the lab.

His mop was there, in a glass cylinder in the center of the room. It had all kinds of diodes, meters, and Geiger counters attached to its handle and head.

Science would have to wait to study it. He needed it right now.

Wade peered through a half-centimeter gap in the doorway, but there was nothing new out there, just the same gardens, the same dumb statue, and the same big, ugly house.

He pulled his head back from the door, rubbed at his nose where he'd left a bloodless divot by pressing his face to the slit to look out.

He shivered.

He was cold, nearly too cold to tap.

There were plastic tarps in the outbuilding, bungee cords, and car batteries, but there was nothing soft and warm, nothing he could use as a blanket as the night approached and the air got colder, never mind anything he could use to escape.

How long had he been in here? An hour? Two? Five?

He'd tried tugging at the hatch in the floor, but it had been sealed shut from the other side.

Worse than the cold, worse than the uncertainty, Wade was lonely, more than he'd ever been. Of course he wanted his dad, wanted to make sure Winston was okay, but even a guard or anyone else to talk to would have made things more bearable, would have made him feel like he wasn't so alone. Even the dapper hunchback, Fritz. They'd probably have stuff in common, something to talk about, both of them being weird and all.

There was a sound outside, the *bleep-bloop* of a walkie-talkie, and Wade pressed his eye back to the door.

"Take care of it, she says. Do you believe that shit? Isn't she Garbinger's assistant? Why are we taking orders from the chick whose main job is working the calendar app?"

There were two guards approaching from around the corner, the front of their tactical vests smeared with gore.

"Real tough talk," said the second guard. "You saw how scary she is. You *yes ma'am*'d her just like I did, and just as fast. But yeah, I know what you mean. Stuffing chewed-up body parts into garbage bags? Not why I joined Blackstar Security after the war."

"You want that, call a cleaning service," the first guard agreed. "We're supposed to *make* the bodies, not bag 'em up."

"Speaking of which," said the second guard, unslinging his rifle from behind his back and racking the slide, "who's going to shoot the kid?"

"Doesn't matter to me."

"Nah, I can hear it in your voice. You want to do it."

"It's okay. Really. You can do it."

"No, man. I insist. We can do it together."

"Ah, thanks, pal."

Wade backed away from the door, tapping furiously at his chest.

Oh, shit.

The holes in Winston's back had nearly healed, but he was still light-headed. He needed electrolytes, or the caffeine-and-sugar jolt of a soda or something. Anything that would help replace all the purple goo they'd sucked out of him with that machine.

They'd found their way out of the lab fairly easily, but how big was this fucking house? He was so lost. But it felt good to have his mop back, at least.

On top of the wooziness of blood loss, his brain had begun to buzz again, the same way it always did now when he was in a fight and there was some evil bastard nearby.

He closed his eyes, tried to listen to the buzzing. He leaned forward on the balls of his feet, then backwards on his heels.

It was subtle, but the buzzing was leading him. He just had to listen to it, follow it.

He swayed some more.

Yeah, that way. There were some real evil bastards that way.

He let out a roar and pulverized another wall. He didn't have time for doors now. "This way," he said, pointing at the next room's far wall.

J.J. crouched through the hole he'd made, cradling the hard drive with two hands.

"How do you know?"

"I know. My kid's in trouble. I don't know how I know, but I know."

One more swing of his mop, creating a cascade of rubble and powdered sheetrock, and they were outside, near the fountain and the sculpted marble ass of Robert Garbinger.

"Be careful," Winston said.

J.J. took one hand off the hard drive long enough to give him a thumbs up, then ran off the way they'd entered the grounds, headed back to the car, giving the fountain a wide berth.

Alone now, Winston slowed his breathing, tried to listen

to the buzz, but he found that he didn't need it—he could hear them.

And then he heard the rattle of a rifle being racked.

"Who's going to shoot the kid?"

Wade!

Winston started to run in that direction, too angry to make sense of the rest of what was said.

He rounded the corner and saw the guards with their rifles out, standing beside the shack they'd seen earlier.

The one with Wade inside!

A guard fiddled at the padlock chaining the door closed. "Can't never remember the combo to this thing."

"Winston! Winston, help me!" Wade yelled.

The guards turned to look at whoever the boy was yelling to.

There was a few dozen yards separating them. Would Winston make it to them in time?

The guards both raised their rifles and he growled his frustration.

Fuck.

Winston ducked low, pried a half-brick out of the footpath below him, and lobbed it.

It caught the first guard right below the lip of his helmet, caving his face inward. His body slumped against the door, the outbuilding wall shaking behind him, head cleaved in half.

Wow.

For someone who'd never played sports, that was a hell of a throw.

"Nooo!" the second guard yelled.

Winston had just killed his friend, so it made sense he'd be upset. Winston hefted his mop up and started running toward the shed as the man kept screaming.

Well, you're about to join your buddy, buddy, because I—

The guard opened fire—*blamblamblamblam.*

And then not a *blam* but a *ting* and the hiss of released pressure.

No!

The gas tanks on either side of the shed exploded, causing all four walls of the building to collapse and blowing off the roof.

Wade! was Winston's last thought as the blast knocked him to the ground and the flames engulfed him.

Winston Gooze woke to the beep of a heart monitor and looked up at the unfamiliar white ceiling of a hospital room.

Then he looked down.

His sheets were white too. Everything in the room, in fact, was white.

"Wade?" he heard himself ask.

"He's fine," a voice beside him said.

He turned his face to see… Shelly. His wife. Oh god, she was beautiful.

"Wh-what happened?" he asked.

"You had an accident at work," she said, leaning over, slipping her hand under the sheets and squeezing his fingers.

"But the doctors say everything's going to be okay." The monitor registered his heart beating a bit faster.

"Holy shit," Winston said. "I had some crazy dreams."

"I bet."

He reached a hand out from under the covers to wipe some of the sleep cracklings out of his eyes.

His eyes. His two normal-sized eyes.

Winston pulled away from Shelly, put both hands in front of him, and looked at them. No green skin or glowing veins. He'd lost some muscle tone, but he was healed.

"I want to get out of bed," he said. Whatever accident had

landed him here, he'd recovered from it. He felt great, not sore at all, and wanted to walk.

Shelly offered him her arm and he was on his feet. They left the very white hospital room and entered the very white hospital hallway.

Over the PA, music played. It was a soft doo-wop, the kind of music you'd hear in a gangster movie, when they flashed back to the protagonist's life in the '50s.

It wasn't *their* kind of music, but it was nice. He could get used to it.

They walked and talked.

"I think Wade hates me," Winston said.

"He doesn't hate *you*," Shelly said. "He misses *me*."

"He wishes I'd died instead."

"He doesn't wish anybody'd died. He just wishes things were different."

He peered into one of the other hospital rooms, but there was nothing there. All the doorways opened onto inky black voids.

Oh. This is the dream, he understood in that hazy way that dreams still seem real, even once you realize that one wasn't.

"But things aren't different," Winston said, looking over at his angelic wife. His dead wife.

"No, they're sure not," Shelly agreed.

"Can I stay here?" Winston asked.

He knew what that meant, and so did she.

"Yeah, you can if you want."

They passed through an archway, and suddenly they weren't in the hospital anymore.

Below them was a grand staircase.

They walked to the top step and Winston looked down. The stairs were polished marble that stretched as far as he could see.

That was... a lot of walking.

He looked over at Shelly. She looked sad, but no less beautiful. And then he remembered the ravings of a homeless, paint-huffing malpractitioner.

"I can't be waylaid or delayed, or..."

There was a wisdom to the words now that he hadn't recognized before.

"Will I see you again?" he asked Shelly.

"Probably not," she said sadly.

He took the first step down the stairs that led back to Earth. Back to Tromaville.

Then he stopped for a moment and looked back up at her.

"I fucking miss you, dude," he said softly. There were tears in his eyes. Must have been the altitude.

"I know, baby," she said.

He turned and started climbing back down.

He didn't look back again.

TWENTY-SIX

There was smoke in the air, and Winston's big eye felt like it had been parboiled.

He must have been out for only a second or two, because there was still debris raining down on the garden from where the shed had exploded.

He should search for Wade and recover the body, but would he be able to stand the sight of that? Wade's little hands, with the black nail polish? His head? The shoes he wore to dance practice?

All that Winston had been through—the physical and mental transformation, being chased through the streets, becoming a hero people cheered—and his quest had been ended by a stray bullet from an unnamed goon.

It wasn't fair.

But life wasn't fair, and nobody knew that better than Winston Gooze, widower, janitor, and loser.

The rubble behind him shifted, and for a moment he thought Wade might have survived the blast. But it wasn't Wade standing there.

"You," Winston said.

Robert Garbinger, the *new* Robert Garbinger, stood there in the smoke. The CEO of Body Talk Healthstyle brandished an oversized battle axe. The thing looked like an antique, but Winston could see the blade was sharp.

"If we're being honest," Monster-Garbinger said, "I'm happy to be here with you. Things were touch and go for a moment there while my men got the formula perfected, but I'm happy now."

"I'll be happy when it's over," Winston said.

Yes, they had to fight to the death—of course they did—but Winston *would* be happy when it was over, when this monstrous bastard had buried that axe in his neck and put him out of his misery. Maybe they'd die together. Maybe they wouldn't. Who fucking cared?

"It was over the moment you crossed me. Everything else is just... mopping up." Monster Garbinger smiled, the skin of his forehead stretching tight over his horned skull. He eyed Winston's weapon. A mop wasn't much of a match for honed steel.

Winston didn't react. Not verbally, not physically. That seemed to annoy Garbinger.

"Was it worth it, janitor?" he said. "Did you get what you wanted?"

"I... lost... *everything!*" Winston pulled both arms out as he screamed. He flexed his muscles, which felt about ready to burst out of his skin.

"Then we're not so different, you and I," Monster Garbinger said, pointing at him with a long nail. Winston flipped him off in return. "I like to scream *everything!* too."

With that they were running, crossing the distance to each other.

They met, weapons clashing, petrified wood against leather-wrapped hilt. It took all of Winston's strength to keep the axe blade off his neck.

Human Garbinger had been taller than Winston, but Monster Garbinger was possibly twice Winston's size.

Well, that just meant it was a longer fall to the ground.

Winston kicked, and Garbinger needed to pick up his foot to dodge, giving up his leverage.

But Garbinger wasn't just tall; he was lithe and *fast*. He disengaged and was swinging back down with the axe before Winston's big eye had even tracked him moving.

"Fuck!" Winston yelled, bringing the mophead up at the last second—and not only did the calcified, glowing yarn of the mop stop the blade, but the axe started to sizzle.

"Shit!" Garbinger said through gritted, pointed teeth, bearing down, melting his own weapon but pushing the blade closer to Winston's big eye.

The mop cut through flesh pretty easily when swung, but this was a new scenario to figure out.

Winston turned his head, trying not to die. The stench of vaporizing metal was truly awful. Red-hot molten droplets singed Winston's clothes, burning into the meat of his leg, but it was the *smell* that was still the worst part. His lungs felt as if they were filled with mercury as the thick gray smoke poured into them.

Garbinger sniffed, his eyes watering. He couldn't take it either. Garbinger pulled with both hands, freeing his axe before the mophead could melt it down to the hilt.

The damaged weapon was still usable, and in fact looked even grizzlier now that Winston's mop had melted a big crescent into one side of it, giving it several more stabby points.

Garbinger stepped back, pausing for a moment to admire the modifications to his weapon.

Over his shoulder, the statue of his former self loomed.

"Thanks, Mop Boy," he said, standing above Winston.

Garbinger bent his knees, then pushed off the ground,

jumping high into the air.

Winston tried to block, but Garbinger knocked the mop aside and Winston had to let go of it so he could grab onto the hilt of the axe.

The crescent divot in the axe, the metal there still warm, fit perfectly over Winston's neck like a collar. Or like a guillotine.

Stone and brick ground against metal as Garbinger pushed down. Flat on his back, Winston was trapped. If Garbinger was able to push the axe half an inch more, it'd be over. Winston's elbows pushed against footstones of the garden. He tried to free himself but couldn't get the leverage.

"I was hoping this'd take longer," Garbinger said, drool from his asymmetrical maw unspooling into Winston's face.

Winston let go of the axe, and Garbinger's weight pushed the weapon further into the ground. Winston's Adam's apple bent against the metal.

He stretched out behind him, searching the footpath for his mop. Moss and grit dirtied his fingernails as he clawed. He felt blood trickling down his neck, felt the suffocating pressure of the axe. But then his searching hand found what it was looking for.

He didn't have the range of motion to swing, but he didn't need it. The head of the mop flared green, Garbinger's eyes flashed yellow in response, burnt hair vaporizing. Winston's gorge rose at the smell as Garbinger tried to get away. But he couldn't get away, not now. Winston pushed the glowing mophead against the side of Monster Garbinger's face.

The creature howled as its skin blistered, then popped, the pus boiling as it touched the head of the mop, causing its skin to melt even faster.

The monster in the classy evening robe reared back, clutching at its melted face, its nose now a crater, strands of cooked, gooey flesh webbing its fingers together.

The burning flesh smelled a lot better than the molten metal had, or the burning hair.

It smelled like barbecue.

But there was no time for Winston to wonder when he'd last eaten. The axe was still pinning his neck to the ground.

He got a hand under the blade, cutting and burning himself as he did, and pushed the weapon away, then stood up.

Garbinger, now blind in one eye, seemed like he was regaining control after all the pain and panic. Winston looked down at the medieval weapon. The axe was almost... almost shaped like a Frisbee.

Yeah.

"Hey, Bob," he said, and Garbinger looked up, one yellow eye furious, the rest of his face a ruin.

Winston threw the axe, getting a good spin on the blade.

But he shouldn't have gotten cocky and warned the monster that there was a projectile incoming.

With his newfound monster-speed, Garbinger ducked out of the way. The axe sailed by, embedding itself into the marble statue's crotch.

They both looked at the statue. A small puff of yellow knockout gas belched up from statue-Garbinger's mouth.

Shit!

Then Garbinger was scrambling backward, sloshing into the fountain and grabbing the axe handle, but the blade was wedged deep into the marble, though, and Garbinger seemed unable to get it loose. He shook the handle, trying to free it, but succeeding only in looking like he was jerking off his former, human self.

Winston flexed his shoulders, stepped high to get into the fountain, and readied his mop. It was time to end this.

J.J. felt bad about leaving Winston to rescue Wade on his own, especially since the boy had been kidnapped on her watch, kind of. But the universe had entrusted her with another important purpose: getting the hard drive to safety.

That night outside Melvin's office, she'd dropped the first hard drive. Then outside the BTH factory, she'd dropped the canister that would have allowed Sneaky Cheetah to make some arrests.

This time, her butterfingers would *not* strike again.

She just had to make it back over the wooded hill to the irradiated trash heap where they'd parked the car.

Her legs burned as she ran until the manicured grounds of Chüdhaven turned to dusty red soil under her feet.

She crested the hill, looked down, and, yes, the car was still there. It hadn't been found by security, and hadn't been towed because no traffic cops patrolled Outer Tromaville.

She was almost there.

Descending the hill was easier than climbing up it had been, but she couldn't get cocky or she might slip on a discarded length of PVC pipe, or a nonbiodegradable grocery bag, or a toilet-seat lid—for some reason, there were a startling number of toilet-seat lids, and whole toilets, in the Outer Tromaville wasteland. So she chose her footing carefully, and kept both hands on the hard drive as she navigated between the sparse tree line.

Eventually she reached the car, climbed in, and made sure she was sitting safely before placing—not throwing—the hard drive into the compartment in the car's central console.

She'd done it! She made it back to the car without dropping it.

Looking out the windshield she smiled, but she couldn't celebrate yet. Now she had to wait for Winston and Wade to crest the top of the hill and then—

Suddenly, the driver's side window imploded. A chain snaked

in and looped around J.J.'s neck, and before she could register what was happening, she was yanked out of her seat.

She hit the ground, coughing and spluttering as dirt flew up into her eyes and nose, then gagged as the chain pulled tight and the world began to constrict to a dark pinpoint in her vision.

Kissy Sturnevan, Executive Associate, stood over her, then knelt on J.J.'s chest and pulled the chain tighter. Blackness crowded around the edges of J.J.'s vision.

"You *dare* fuck with perfection?" Kissy yelled down at her, easing off the chokehold just enough for J.J. to sip a tiny pocket of air.

Kissy was looking... pretty far from perfection, with her blackened eyes, jagged smile, and suppurating skin. The lady was all fucked up.

Kissy gave one final tug, then let go of the chain. The back of J.J.'s head conked down into the earth. She was alive, for now, but so weak.

Kissy spit on her, then yanked open the car door.

J.J. tried to raise a hand to stop her, but couldn't.

"Where did you put it?" she asked.

After a few seconds of searching, she ducked back out, triumphantly holding the hard drive, and shook it in J.J.'s face.

No, J.J. thought. That was what she'd been fighting for. What a bunch of people had died for.

"Did you think you could—" she started to ask, shaking the device in J.J.'s face. But then she looked up, having seen something coming down the hill at them.

J.J., with no small effort, rolled over onto her side to follow her gaze up the hill.

"Robert!" Kissy wailed. "Your face!"

Winston Gooze, the Toxic Avenger, was fighting some kind of monster. The pair of them were tumbling end over end. They slashed at each other with their weapons, bouncing off every tree stump and old truck tire on the way down like a pinball machine.

Then J.J. recognized the robe and realized it wasn't a monster Winston was fighting.

"Robert! Oh god, your beautiful face!" Kissy moaned, her eyes glued to the fight, and J.J. noticed that her worried expression made her look more human, less feral.

But she didn't care how human Kissy was—now was her chance.

She looked around, then crawled to the nearest toilet-tank lid, pulled herself to her feet, and brought the heavy ceramic lid down on the back of Kissy's head. The hard drive flew from the executive assistant's hands and came down in the dirt.

"Don't be broken, don't be broken!" J.J. pleaded.

But the drive couldn't be her priority right now.

She had to help Winston.

Trash.

Waste.

Garbage.

Junk.

Winston couldn't remember a time when Tromaville didn't look like this, or even if he'd ever once thought of the city by its proper name: St. Roma's Village.

It used to bother him, the town being one step removed from a landfill, but now that he himself had been dumped and reborn anew, the trash felt like home.

The one good thing in his trash pile of a life had been his family. But with first Shelly and now Wade gone, the whole world might as well have been the litter-blasted ruins of Outer Tromaville. What did he care?

His brain buzzed behind his eyes.

All he cared about was killing this motherf—

Garbinger got in a good lick with the dull part of the axe head and Winston staggered back, rubbing his lower back. He swung the mop, the blood from his smashed nose dripping into his mouth, and then Garbinger was raking his claws across his chest and all his confidence crumpled.

He felt the fetid air of Outer Tromaville enter his wounds.

Garbinger swiped again, missing not because his aim was off but because Winston's body was falling back, his hand holding his torn abdomen.

Shunk! Garbinger's claws sunk into an oil drum, the thick liquid splashing the ground as he pulled his hand away, recentering his aim for the killing blow.

"No!" a voice yelled, and J.J. appeared behind Garbinger. She hefted something rectangular and white, a red bloody splotch already in its center, and struck Garbinger's head with it. There was a porcelain crunch as it smashed to pieces, the tip of one of the monster's horns also breaking off.

Ah. A toilet-tank lid.

Garbinger dropped forward, rolling over Winston, and a moment later J.J. collapsed to the dirt right beside them.

"Where's Wade?" she asked.

Winston couldn't answer. He sat up and put the end of his mop into the ground, using it like a crutch to pull himself up.

"W-where's Wade?" J.J. asked again.

Winston was crying.

"Oh," she said, laying her head down in the dirt to cry herself.

Winston looked over at Garbinger—still breathing—and the woman in the skirt suit, who was starting to stir.

His brain buzzed when he looked at both of them. Maybe when he was finished with Garbinger he'd snuff her evil out too, if only to stop the buzzing behind his eyeball.

"You should have..." he began as he lifted Garbinger up, swatting away the axe as the barely conscious troll-man tried to raise it, then stamping on it for good measure, shattering the head and handle to shards and splinters.

He sheathed his mop behind his back.

He'd need two hands for this.

"You should have just..." he tried again, trying to get the words out while he held Garbinger still with one arm and punched him viciously with the other. When the muscles in his punching arm got sore, he alternated. And when it felt like every one of Garbinger's ribs were broken, he started on his balls. And when that felt like too much, he switched to the goat-man's face again.

"You should have just *helped me!*" Winston screamed. "It wouldn't have cost you *anything* to help me!"

Amazingly, Garbinger was still able to speak through his swollen face and broken teeth. "But... I'm... a monster," he said. And then he pulled those broken teeth into a demented smile.

Something inside Winston broke then. He reached behind his back for the mop, ready to jam it down this monster's throat, burning away every organ on its trip down his esophagus to his toes. But then he heard a familiar voice.

"Dad!"

He looked up, being sure to keep his grip tight on the lapel of Garbinger's robe.

"Dad! Please don't. Please don't kill him!"

Not a ghost. Not another hallucination.

Wade was *alive.*

The boy was a few yards away, and he was accompanied by... some kind of hunchback goth?

IT'S IMPORTANT THAT WE PAUSE HERE AND BACK UP FOR A SECOND

I know, I know. We're at the best part in any action story. We just did that bit where there's not one but two climactic battles going on, overlapping—one fight between the male protagonist and the male antagonist, and then a separate (not as flashy) fight between the two female leads—a "cat fight," as we used to call it. And, well, I don't know whether society is still clamoring for that particular trope, but here we are.

Anyway.

Wade appearing here isn't another one of those frou-frou dream sequences. Like when Winston got to talk with his dead wife in heaven or whatever. Scenes that further character arc and theme but not plot.

And it's *not* a deus ex machina. Not really. Promise.

No.

Wade *really is* standing there.

Remember the hatch at the bottom of the shed, which we established existed as an escape route for Garbinger out of Chüdhaven's subterranean lab, should he ever need it?

And remember how we also established that Fritz Garbinger had serious moral reservations about killing a kid?

Well, it turns out that, in the seconds before the shed blew up, good old Fritz hobbled to the rescue, opening the hatch and calling, "Hurry, we have to go!"

And go they did.

So there you are. Now you're all caught up.

Now Toxie has the mutant Garbinger on the ropes, is ready to deliver the killing blow, and Wade's just appeared to try and stop him.

Wait. This isn't going to be one of those stories where the protagonist kills a hundred anonymous goons but it becomes some kind of dark night of the soul for him when it comes time to kill the *real* bad guy is it? One of those hollowly moralistic "Don't kill him! It'll mean you're no better than he is!" pleas?

Those are always lame.

Oh, well. I guess I shouldn't judge the scene before I see how the screenwriter and this novelization schmuck have handled it.

Let's hear what Wade has to say.

TWENTY-SEVEN

Winston stared at Wade across a chasm of dead grass and rusted waste barrels, and the boy stared back.

They'd been like this for twenty seconds, maybe less, but the bruises and cuts on Winston's knuckles were already healing.

"Wade?" he said.

"Please," Wade said, taking a step closer. "Don't kill him."

Winston looked down at Garbinger's pulped and broken body. The troll-man might already be dead, so it was possible that that ship had sailed.

"It's not who you are," Wade went on.

Winston looked at him, the angel on his left shoulder.

There were tears in the boy's eyes.

Then he looked back to the busted-up goat guy, the *actual* horned devil on his right shoulder. Garbinger was still breathing, faintly. If he had the same goo that Winston had in him, maybe he'd heal and survive.

The buzzing behind Winston's eye flared, getting louder.

No! Wade was right. Winston could fight the buzzing, the craving and compulsion to kill. He could choose *not* to obliterate every murderous asshole he came into contact with.

He opened his fist and let Garbinger's body drop to the ground beside the pierced oil drum. Garbinger twitched, falling into a puddle of spilled oil.

And the buzzing in Winston's brain stopped.

There was still quite a distance of old sheet metal and broken bathroom fixtures between Winston and Wade, so the boy needed to raise his voice to be heard:

"I knew you could do it, Dad. You're not a killer."

Dad. Winston wasn't used to that word, used in that way—directed at him.

Wait. Not a killer?

"I mean, I kind of already..." Winston mimed throwing a brick. Wade had been there for that one. However he'd managed to survive the shed explosion, he'd probably seen what had happened outside it just before it blew.

"Oh, that guy," Wade said. "That was self-defense! You were protecting me."

"Yes." Yes. "I was!" He was.

"You're *not* a killer," Wade repeated.

"No. I'm not."

The guy behind Wade, leaning on the cane, stared down at his shoes. J.J. was pretending to be unconscious, but Winston was sure that her eyes were half open.

It was awkward. They all knew except Wade.

"Right?" Wade asked.

"Right. Yes," Winston said. *No.* "I'm not a killer." *Yes, you goddam are.*

He didn't know how to break it to the boy. He couldn't remember how many it'd been since he popped off that preppy guy's arm, but even just the incident on the stage at TromaFest—that was a *lot* of manslaughter.

Maybe Winston could keep Wade from watching the news

for a couple of days…

"You didn't kill anyone else, did you?" Wade asked doubtfully.

Winston really didn't want to have this conversation here, in front of all these strangers, standing in this dusty, polluted wasteland.

"It's just, when you say self-defense, I—"

"Look out!" J.J. yelled suddenly.

So she had been awake!

Winston turned just in time to see Garbinger, mid-pounce, wielding the shattered axe as a makeshift spear, aimed at Winston's chest.

"Three, two, *one!*" the monster growled.

Reflexes—and the buzz—took over, and Winston swung up the head of his mop. It was a clumsy hit, since he didn't have much time to aim, but sometimes clumsy hits became happy accidents.

The mophead glowed and smoked, burning a hole into Garbinger's chest and stomach, while the shaft of the mop swept Garbinger's body through the air.

The hairy robed body tumbled once, then twice—a full somersault—and landed on top of the Khaki Kar.

No. Not on top of the car. *Into* the car. Garbinger had so much mass, and Winston's hit had so much velocity (not that he was any kind of physics expert), that the monster had torn through the hood and buried itself in the engine block, where he groaned and wiggled but couldn't free himself.

Before anyone else could react, J.J. was on her feet and dashing to the car. She dove into the driver's seat.

Winston saw where this was going and yelled, "Ignition!" At least it wouldn't be him doing the killing this time.

J.J. nodded. "Now *that's* a good line."

She turned the key, revved the engine, and the convertible's souped-up pistons went to work.

Winston had seen and done a lot of violence in the last couple of days, but this was… excessive.

Garbinger screamed, the sound something between a human man begging for his life and a goat caught in a thresher.

First it was just blood rushing out of the sides of the engine like a Las Vegas fountain, but then all the blood was spent and Winston was pelted with high-speed flecks of bone and gobbets of flesh. It was like being caught in a grisly hailstorm.

J.J. was saved from the worst of it, being behind the car's windshield.

When it was over, his face dripping, Winston looked over at Wade.

"This is Fritz," Wade said, indicating the dandy-goth. "He saved my life."

Winston nodded at the man, who was pretty gross-looking—not the type of person he wanted hanging around his kid, but who was Winston to judge a book by its cover?

Wade was tapping, but with all the blood on his shirt, the sound it made was kind of spongy.

"You called me Dad," Winston said.

"I know," Wade said.

"I…" Winston started to say, but then choked up. When then the words came, he said, "I love you whhhaaaaaaaaa—"

There was a tickle in his throat. More than a tickle, in fact—like a sharp displacement of his vocal cords.

Ropes of purple blood spritzed Wade's face and the boy began to scream, tapping so hard he was leaving an indentation in his chest.

Winston tried to reassure Wade, but he couldn't speak.

His eyes crossed, the big one rolling around in its socket like it'd been knocked loose.

Oh. Well, would you look at that?

Winston's been stabbed in the throat.

Kissy had loved Robert Garbinger.

He'd been perfect, even with the weird horn thing and the extra hair.

And this fuckwit, this colossal pimply *prick*, had killed him.

Kissy twisted the shard of wood, working it from side to side, trying to widen the gap in the Toxic Avenger's neck.

Ha. Avenger, my ass. What did this *loser* ever avenge? The Broom Closet Crusader. The Detergent Defender. The Protein Spill Protector.

Pathetic.

Next she'd use her bare hands to slash open the kid's chest, claw his heart out, maybe even take a bite out of it. Hopefully the janitor would be alive long enough to watch her do it.

Then she'd get that bitch in the car.

Then she'd break every bone in Fritz's body. And then...

Then she'd take a vacation. Somewhere warm.

But first...

Kissy pulled the splinter out. The hole in Winston's neck was wide enough now. She should stab something else. Maybe that dumb fucking eye.

A black streak moved through the air as she readjusted her grip and stabbed down.

"That's enough!" Fritz said, parrying her strike with his cane, wobbling to stay upright without its support.

Great. He was the slowest person she'd ever known, but it seemed he could be fast enough when he wanted to be, though, when it was convenient.

The soft-hearted gimp had saved the boy when she'd *explicitly* ordered him not to.

Well, Robert was dead, and he wouldn't want his brother to be the face of BTH...

Kissy slid the point of the axe handle up the length of the cane, flicked the end, and slashed Fritz's throat wide open.

Ga-huck!

Fritz made a choking noise, then bloody froth bubbled up on his lips as he grabbed his neck, trying to hold his blood in.

And now there was another smell, more than blood, shit, and dustbowl terrain: an astringent stink of turpentine. She'd have to hurry up taking her revenge or the smell would settle into her clothes.

She turned to the boy and the woman, J.J. Doherty, formerly an employee of Body Talk Healthstyle and soon to be formerly alive.

"Keep away!" J.J. cried, huddled over the boy, shielding him with her body.

Well, if she *really* wanted to go first...

Kissy stabbed down, aiming at the top of the traitor's head, wondering how far she could shove the axe handle in J.J. Doherty's skull—and then Winston barreled into her and tackled her to the ground, the hole in his throat still bleeding toxic gunk all down himself and, now, all over her.

Fuck! What would it take to kill him?

She tried stabbing at him again, but as she raised her hands, she realized that she was soaked in more than just blood.

The drum they'd landed next to. It had been poked full of holes and now it was leaking all over. *That* was the source of the turpentine stench.

The Toxic Avenger sat on her chest, pinning her under him, his fucking tutu tickling her chin, his mop raised above him. It was glowing and smoking, as it did normally, but now it was emitting green sparks too.

Kissy's eyes went wide as she saw the warning label on the drum.

Kissy read, a last moment where she could read, could render letters into words:

EXTREMELY FLAMMABLE

Then the freak pushed the mophead into the puddle and a green flame took them both to hell.

TWENTY-EIGHT

Winston Gooze awoke to the sounds of a beeping heart monitor.

Somewhere in the room, there was also the chatter of a TV turned down low.

But unlike last time he woke up in a bed like this, the hospital ceiling above him was a streaky beige color and the room smelled like boiled potatoes.

So this was definitely the real world, then. Not heaven.

"Are you awake?" a voice asked.

Winston turned, seeing the room through the familiar red tinge of his big eye. He was still his toxic self—the hospital hadn't "cured" that—and beside his bed there was a woman in a smart pantsuit and dark glasses. She looked like a cop.

Oh, yeah—all the bloody murders he'd done.

She shifted in her seat and Winston studied her glasses, her body language, and realized she was blind.

"Yes. I'm awake," he said.

"Good," the woman said, patting down a crease in her suit. There was something familiar about her. "Your son went to the snack machine. Neat kid."

Winston wasn't sure what to say.

"He is. Uh..."

He looked down. No handcuffs, and his wounds from the fight had all healed. How long had it been? Had he been asleep for more than a few hours?

"Am I under arrest?" he asked.

She gave a soft chuckle. "No, not at all. I'm not even sure..." She cocked her head toward the TV. "Turn that up," she said, and pointed.

Winston found the remote control wrapped up in his sheets and turned up the volume.

"...data hack. The anonymous information, leaked to a federal task force that had already been in town investigating BTH, revealed a massive conspiracy of fraud, bribery, illegal toxic dumping, and even murder for hire. Several city officials, including the mayor and chief of police, were taken into custody. CEO Robert Garbinger remains at large, as does the Toxic Avenger, the mysterious vigilante whose appearance precipitated this investigation, an investigation that has seemingly shattered the once ubiquitous company, along with instigating a series of class-action lawsuits."

C.J. Doons, the female anchor, was smiling as she delivered this news.

Rick Feet, her co-anchor, was not.

"Splendid. One of our greatest business minds is pilloried. Cancel culture. Just because—"

"Shut the fuck up, Rick," C.J. Doons said, still smiling. "Chet, what's going on at the Village Action News social media—"

Winston clicked off the TV. The Toxic Avenger wasn't at large; he was right here, in the hospital. Then he realized what must have been going on: he was being hidden from the media and any possible criminal prosecution.

"Sneaky Cheetah," he said, turning to the blind woman.

She nodded. "I don't pick the code names," she said, nodding that he was correct. "But you can call me Sarah."

"Sarah," he repeated.

"We're going to sweep you under the rug, Toxie," she said. Then: "Wait, do you prefer Toxie or Winston?"

He shrugged. "Either's good."

"Well, without you and your friends, none of this would stick. Indictments of this kind, these people... they can be slippery."

He thought of all the little chunks of Garbinger raining down. There wasn't much left of him to indict.

"But you know what I did," he said.

"I know you saved a lot of lives," she replied. "I was in Miss Meat, under cover, in the wrong place at the wrong time." Ah, yes, *that* was where he knew her from. It felt like a lifetime ago. "You were a hero that day. Whatever else, you'll always have that."

He frowned.

"Maybe not always. For a year, maybe, best case."

It was something he hadn't wanted to think about, during his adventure, but even if he'd saved Tromaville, he still had all those black holes in his brain. That headache that had become a buzzing behind his eyes once he'd transformed.

"Actually—"

"Fuck!" Winston yelled, startled by the sudden appearance of Dr. Walla at his bedside. "You scared the *shit* out of me!"

"I thought you saw me here," said Dr. Walla. "I've been here the whole time, eating my lunch." He was holding a large sandwich with a couple of bites taken out of it.

Winston blinked. How had he not noticed the man?

Dr. Walla took another small bite of his sandwich and swallowed. "Well, anyway, I was waiting over here because I wanted to tell you the good news as soon as you woke."

He put his sandwich down on the side of Winston's bed, getting crumbs all over.

"What is it?" Winston asked.

"Lebanese bologna and cream cheese. Take a bite. It sounds weird, but I promise—"

"No." Winston liked the guy, but there was also a part of him that thought pulling his arms and legs off would be fun too. *"What did you want to tell me?"*

"Oh, yes."

Dr. Walla picked up an X-ray film from the chair beside him and placed it in the room's lightbox.

The dark spots were still there, but they were much smaller.

Winston felt his heart soar, but then he pumped the brakes on his enthusiasm.

"Wait, is this just more context?"

"No, that's *you*," Dr. Walla said. He retrieved his sandwich, talking while he chewed. "You've been out for almost two weeks. Your medical directive allowed for life-saving measures, and I figured this qualified, putting you on the very expensive treatment. But honestly, I dunno. I'm not a lawyer."

Wait, two weeks? Very expensive treatment?

"Yes, you're in recovery—except for your hideous condition, obviously," Dr. Walla continued.

"But I can't pay for it!" wailed Winston.

Had Dr. Walla just saved his life but ruined his finances?

The doctor smiled, chewed his last bite of crust, then looked at Sarah, who was smiling too.

Each taking an arm, between them they got Winston into a wheelchair, piled a few blankets on top of him, wrapped one around his head, and the doctor rolled him down the hall to the hospital entrance.

Fritz Garbinger watched from his own hospital bed as the Toxic Avenger, covered in a few blankets that didn't do much to disguise his form, was wheeled past his door.

Was it really necessary for him to be still cuffed to his bed's handrail? It had been two weeks! And he was cooperating! And he'd saved the boy!

A few moments later, the sound of applause floated through the open window.

"Some kinda party out there," Officer Snow said, not looking up from his magazine.

Officer Snow. Well. At least he was a little kinder than Officer Nagai had been.

Fritz reached his free hand over to his bedside table and found his electrolarynx.

"Can – I – Have..." He paused, took a breath, and repositioned the voice box. "...some – More – Apple – Juice?"

"Shut up," Officer Snow said, turning a page.

Next to him, Fritz Garbinger's roommate bucked against her restraints, laughed an evil, annoying laugh, and stared at him with those sickly black eyes.

"Nothing at all!" she cackled.

She did that now. It was practically all she said.

God, he hated this town.

Outside the hospital, a group of twenty or thirty people had gathered.

They were the Good People of Tromaville.

Winston recognized most of them, even if he didn't know their names.

"They all chipped in to pay for your treatment," Dr. Walla said, rubbing Winston's shoulder, leaving crumbs.

First to approach his wheelchair was Daisy. She had Mr. Treats under one arm. Cats don't usually like to travel far from home, or crowds, so he understandably looked a little stressed.

"Thank you," Daisy said. "From both of us."

The hostages from the Miss Meat were there—the boy with the helmet, his mother, the two women, the gutshot manager, who was also in a wheelchair but alive.

All of them were alive because of Winston.

The fry cook removed his hairnet and clapped Winston on the shoulder. "You saved us so we fixed your brain, my man!"

Guthrie Stockins was here too, but he stood apart. Not because of agoraphobia, but because nobody seemed to want to stand next to him. Winston toasted him with an invisible glass, and Guthrie returned it by taking some model glue from his coat pocket and inhaling deeply.

Tromaville High kids with tattoos and piercings pushed in, crouching beside Winston's chair to get selfies.

"Stay off hard drugs," Winston said, unsure what he was supposed to be saying to the youth of America.

"Hell yeah, Toxie! Great job!" a dirtbag-looking guy with a beard said, then pressed down on an air horn.

Several of the older folks in the crowd scowled at this, but the guy just shrugged. "Pardon me. I'm excited, okay?"

Winston's big eye scanned the crowd, and he spotted a familiar head making its way through the press.

Neat kid. He remembered Sarah's words.

"Excuse me, can you make way?" he said, waving people aside.

There was someone out here he wanted to see more than all these random well-wishers, as much as he appreciated them.

Wade, not tapping, just smiling, held his arms out for a hug, nearly tipping Winston out of his chair. With his arms around his stepson, Winston also caught sight of J.J. at the back of the crowd, not being part of it, her sweatshirt hood up and her duffel bag on her shoulder.

Wade gave him one more hug, then stood beside Winston as more Tromavillians approached for more selfies and autographs.

J.J. was laughing, looking like she was about to go catch a bus.

He flashed her a peace sign, not really knowing what to do in this situation, and she flashed one back, also looking embarrassed.

He raised a clenched fist, but she shook her head. *Don't do that.*

Yeah, that was probably too much. That was...

Overkill.

He curled out two fingers and made his fist into metal horns.

She nodded and returned them.

Yeah, that was exactly right.

HOW MANY ENDINGS DOES THIS BOOK HAVE?!

I mean finding out Kissy and Fritz were still alive was cool and all, but it seems like every character is getting a curtain call. What about that sex worker who was walking a guy on a leash in Chapter 1? What's she up to these days? The fans want to know!

When we made the original *Toxic Avenger*, we sure didn't have the time or money for any of this shit, but back then we also didn't have terms like *IP* or *cinematic universe* or *post-credits sequence*, so I guess it's just good to roll with it when times change. Especially when some giant multimedia conglomerate is picking up the tab. Spend your money how you want, guys!

Speaking of, when we're done here I'm on my way to the check-cashing place next to the corner store.

Oh, I'm being told it's just this one last scene.

They promise.

EPILOGUE

Dance Number
Property Movement Piece

These nerds at New Chemistry High put on a pretty good show, Winston had to admit.

He hoped that golden retriever would be okay though.

Actually, it probably wasn't okay for him to call high-school kids nerds, not now he had the eyes of the community on him.

Not now that he was the Toxic Avenger.

Probably best to call them high achievers or something.

But if the little high-achieving rich kids down there at the judges' table somehow gave Wade bad marks, or made him cry, or in any way triggered a need to tap...

The buzzing rose up behind Winston's eyes, just a little, and he pushed it back down.

It turned out that it wasn't connected to the black holes in his brain after all. It was completely unrelated, a kind of superpower that he could tap into whenever he was faced with evil or injustice.

And he was getting better about living with it.

Well, somewhat better. He had stopped an assault on the way over here and turned the perp inside out, but one day at a time.

Oh, he knew that tune.

It was about to begin.

Stuart gave the thumbs up and Wade leaned out from the wings and looked out at the audience.

There were a *lot* of people out there, more than there had been at tryouts and way more than there had been at alternate tryouts.

The lighting tech tried to find him with the spotlight as his music started.

This isn't a dance, Wade told himself.

It's a movement.

He adjusted his top hat, picked the wedgie out of his leotard, and stepped out onto the stage.

The audience wasn't feeling it at first, and Winston was worried he was going to have to go down there and lecture them.

But the school had been nice enough to let him sit in the balcony alone. This was Wade's night, not Toxie's, and as soon as Wade started the prop-comedy segment of his piece, the whole auditorium was cheering and clapping along with the music.

Wade was incredible. He moonwalked. He ribbon-danced. He sent live doves flying out over the audience—from where, even Winston couldn't figure out. Then he produced an oversized hammer and started smashing squashes. The first two rows ended up covered in pumpkin pulp, but still the crowd cheered, demanding more.

Winston Gooze was so proud of his son, and he knew that somewhere else, somewhere cleaner and with more stairs than Tromaville, Shelly was proud of him too.

She was proud of them both.

ACKNOWLEDGMENTS

First and foremost, thank you to Lloyd Kaufman and Michael Herz, for giving the world Toxie. If you couldn't tell by looking at this book, or any of the other stuff I've written, there'd be no Adam Cesare without Troma. And if there were an Adam Cesare, then, sure, maybe he'd be more respectable, dress better, have a real, steady job with health benefits, but he wouldn't be interesting.

And there'd be no novelization without Macon Blair, the only filmmaker crazy enough to remake *The Toxic Avenger*, and the only one skilled enough to have it turn out good and worthwhile! Macon actually read an early draft of this book and gave expansive notes, helping it be better, tighter, funnier, and goopier. Can't name many writer/directors who'd do something like that, but Macon cares! Big thanks go to all the folks at Legendary who brought us this new version of *The Toxic Avenger*: nothing would have happened without them. Thanks also to Davi Lancett and Fenton Coulthurst, the editors who helped nurture this twisted mutant of a book into its true malformed self, and the rest of the Titan team who supported them every step of the way.

Thanks also to my agent, Alec Shane, and my coterie of (here unnamed) professional, personal, and financial advisers who started their phone calls "You want to write WHAT?!" and then listened as I calmly explained "No, you don't understand. I have to do this. I love the Toxic Avenger."

And I do. I ♥ the Monster Hero.

ABOUT THE AUTHOR

Adam Cesare is the *USA Today* bestselling author of the Bram Stoker Award–winning Clown in a Cornfield series, the basis for the hit film, the graphic novel *Dead Mall*, and several other novels and novellas, including the cult hit *Video Night* and the YA psychothriller *Influencer*. An avid fan of horror cinema, you can watch him talk about movies on YouTube, TikTok, Instagram, and the rest of his socials.